NEST OF
THORNES

Eva Thorne Book 5

Lorel Clayton

Lorel and Clayton Colgin
author@lorelclayton.com
www.lorelclayton.com

Publisher's Note: This is a work of fiction. Names, characters, places, and incidents are a product of the author's imagination. Locales and public names are sometimes used for atmospheric purposes. Any resemblance to actual people, living or dead, or to businesses, companies, events, institutions, or locales is completely coincidental.

Book Layout ©2013 BookDesignTemplates.com
Cover Art: Clayton Colgin

Nest of Thornes/ Lorel Clayton.
ISBN 978-0-6486760-6-5

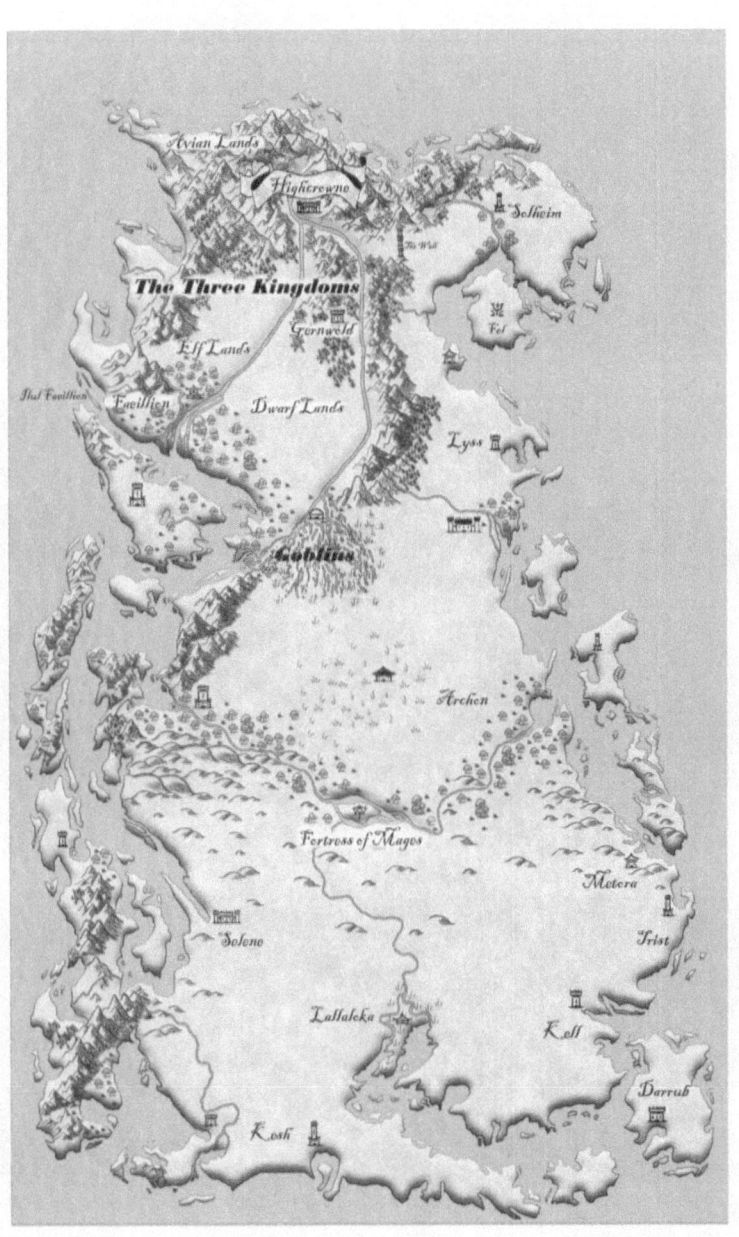

ACKNOWLEDGEMENTS

Thank you to all our readers, new and old, but especially to those who have waited six, long years for a new Eva Thorne novel. We are so grateful.

HOMECOMING

A flash of lightning sent shadows looming, blocky figures in dark raincoats, as they hefted my steamer trunk from the hold and onto the deck of the airship. Rain pummelled them, driven sideways by the wind. Crew scrambled to tie ropes after several corroded brass moorings tore free of the old dock. The deck swayed beneath me, so I widened my stance. I shifted into a fighting pose and pulled the serrated sword from its bone sheath. My Ashur was the weapon of choice for Solhan ladies, but I was no lady.

"Where do you think you're taking that?" I asked, my ominous tone punctuated with thunder.

The thugs in raincoats froze, surprised to see me. Someone had drugged my meal and barred my cabin door from the outside. Fortunately, I had invisible Bogle companions following me everywhere, always the first to eat my meals, not because they were official food testers but because they were eternally hungry. They also removed the metal bar from the outside, so I escaped without needing to cut through the cabin wall, which I would have done. I would do anything to protect that trunk.

"No pithy comeback or plausible excuse?" I said, disappointed. "You two really are thick. Who do you work for?"

The deckhands saw my drawn blade and froze too. This old dock was not Highcrowne, likely a pirate mooring off the usual air routes. Either they were trying to find refuge in the storm, or they were in on it too. I didn't think they were pirates, else they would all be armed and coming at me with swords, but something was off about them. That's what I got for eschewing the premier airship liners with their security protection, courtesy of Rose Industries. I'd been trying to lay low, but it looked like I would need to be laying low a few bad guys instead.

"We don't want any trouble," one of the crew said, raising his hands.

"Untie us and get us back underway and there won't be any," I said. I didn't know how to fly this thing, and so I couldn't kill them, as tempting as it was. The two holding my trunk, however.... "I told you both to set that down. Gently."

They obeyed. Never trust anyone who complies so quickly. Not in this line of work. I ignored the crew, their hands full of ropes, their bedraggled clothing too threadbare to hide any weapons, and I went for the raincoats.

One whipped out a flintlock pistol. Fool. It was too wet to fire. The other was slightly smarter, revealing a bullwhip. He was fast too. He struck, wrapping it around the tip of my sword before I got to him.

The one weakness of a serrated blade was how easily it could be caught, but that usually worked both ways. It was fantastic for disarming an opponent, and if it was sharp enough—as mine was—it sliced right through anything, including leather. His whip lost a third of its length, and a heartbeat later I had the tip of my sword pointed at his eye. The one with the useless pistol donned brass knuckles and came for me, but I wasn't only a good swordswoman, I was a necromancer. Big mistake.

Necrotizing flesh was not one of my favorite tricks. I'd seen it used against friends of mine by people I hated, and so for a long time I had avoided learning the spells, but when I finally relented, I had to admit they worked like a charm. He dropped the brass knuckles as they cut into his putrefying fingers. He screamed a primal scream as bone shone through, which sent the crew running to obey my command to get underway again. That scream also gave the one with the whip pause. He'd drawn a dagger, but he dropped it, open mouthed, as his compatriot's forearm turned skeletal.

I waved my hand, and the spell stopped there. I couldn't restore what was lost, but he'd survive. He wouldn't believe it, what with the pain he was in, rolling and thrashing on the deck, but he had messed with me. He deserved it.

I snapped my fingers in front of bullwhip guy. "Listen up. I asked you a question. Who do you work for?"

"I dunno. They told us to get the trunk. We were to take it to Faellion."

"Did an elf pay you?"

"Who else has gold like that?"

I was curious how much gold and where they'd stashed it, but it wouldn't be on them. My elven pursuers were getting slightly cleverer, using human thugs as cutouts, but not smart enough. Typical elvish arrogance, thinking I wouldn't escape their trap or manage to interrogate their lackeys. I didn't need to interrogate further because I knew who was behind all of this.

Surely, she knew I was coming for her? I'd fought off all who dared cross my path, and I knew the only way to stop them for good was to cut off the head of the snake. That's why she wanted the trunk: Leverage so I wouldn't kill her—and her ultimate prize. Queen Hilja was getting neither.

"Go back to your employer," I told whip boy. "Take your skinless friend with you. Tell them I want to negotiate."

The airship was back in the storm, swaying and bucking in the winds.

"How?" he asked. "We can't get off now."

"Oh, yes you can." I felt for a runestone in my belt pouch and rubbed my thumb against it. Wind twisted around them both and carried them away, throwing them onto the dock we'd nearly landed on. Their contact had to be nearby, waiting. Maybe they would get the word to Queen Hilja before I got to her first. I didn't care either way. There would be a reckoning.

Of course, dealing with Hilja was only one reason I was returning home after all these years. The least important reason.

"You." I pointed to two of the scrambling crew, and they looked like I had marked them for Death. They would know it if I had. "Take this trunk to my cabin. Carefully."

They obeyed, terrified as they nearly slipped in the thrashing storm. When it and I were back inside, enjoying blessed warmth and relative dryness, I laid my head against the lid and said, "Soon, my love. It's almost over."

How wrong I was.

It was still night when my airship arrived in Highcrowne. The coach I'd hired from Distant Imports was waiting for me, black and ominous with a few dim lanterns aglow. Lightning and sleet laced with snow added to the melodrama.

The air dock had experienced a significant upgrade since I'd been away. It not only stretched across the cliffs above the river but had a six-story tower as well, where the huge airliners berthed. My skittish crew and equally apologetic captain—who had been paid off by my attackers without asking the right questions and practically bowed when he realized who I was—made sure we were moored as far from the authorities as it was possible to be without drawing undo attention. This section of the cargo docks was famous for making their guests languish for weeks, awaiting inspections because they were too poor to pay off the assessors and speed up the process. Only cargo not prone to spoilage dared be berthed here. I did not intend to stay meekly with the wool and lumber, however.

"Eva Thorne?" the carriage driver asked when I walked up to him.

"Yes."

"That is your real name?"

"Who else would dare wield it?"

He was human, dark skinned and well dressed. He tipped his hat and proceeded to professionally supervise the transfer of my trunk, making sure it was concealed in a lower compartment. He removed the black cloth draped over a glass coffin in the upper compartment of the funerary wagon, and the crew from the ship scurried away. They weren't transporting any other cargo, so they made haste to depart. No one wanted to be near a human corpse for long, fearful it would get up again.

These risen were not so bad as the Risen of my day when the Dead God made them powerful and lethal. These were lost souls, trapped in their bodies with Death away. Not on holiday. On a mission I had given Him. Although none knew that but me.

I climbed in back and sat beside the coffin.

"Foolishly fearless," the driver noted. "Don't worry, it's bound for a pyre when we're done."

"I wasn't worried." I placed my hand against the glass and felt the ghost trapped inside the flesh within. It was an older man, accomplished in the making of musical instruments. He had enjoyed a full life and died peacefully. Too bad he would never know true peace.

Fire was the closest priests could come to releasing their souls. It stopped the bodies from walking around at least, but it was no real solution. Those of us with necromantic power knew the streets were full of ghosts these days, and there was no release for them. Not yet. I was working on it.

Bribes were made at the gates to the city, and the wagon proceeded at a steady pace, the clatter of horse's hooves out of sync with the patter of rain on cobblestones. There were few streetlamps in the Outskirts, and so we travelled in near total darkness, until we reached my old neighborhood in the richest section of the human quarter.

I expected to find a small mansion perched atop a bookshop and instead found what I could only call a bazaar. I've seen the likes in the liberated South, noisy places full of craftsmen churning out bronze pitchers and plates, incense burning to hide the scent of old meat and vegetables, carpet salesmen loudly hawking their wares, while a snake charmer sits cross-legged near the entrance with a cobra poking its head from a round basket. There was no snake charmer here, as cold-blooded creatures didn't fare well in the North, but the building had expanded like the docks, bulging out with a makeshift structure three stories tall.

Porters with huge, bushy black beards silently removed the trunk and carried it into this new morass of mercantile frenzy. I fended off salesmen and held my belt pouch against pickpockets as I followed them through the narrow corridors between shops. At last, we reached the old wooden door with its glass window.

'Eva Thorne, Detective' was still written there, white lettering faded and scratched, but in bright gold above it was 'Distant Imports Ltd.'

We stepped into an office, and I indicated the porters should wait a moment. I looked around, noting the lack of books in Viktor's old bookshop. Now it was all ledgers and desks of clerks scribbling notes, shuffling manifests and invoices, or weighing coins on brass scales. At the back, behind the largest desk and reading some document so deeply I thought her furrowed brow would fracture, was Kali.

I can move silently when I want. I stood before her a full minute, studying her perfect black skin. Was that a laugh line? The smallest wrinkle to mark the years that had passed. Finally, I cleared my throat, and she looked up, startled. Her squint of concentration turned into one of annoyance. "Who let you back here?"

There was a clerk at the front desk newly returned from his break who never saw me pass. He cringed at Kali's dread gaze.

"You don't recognize me?" My face was shadowed by my hood, but my voice was unmistakable. I'd been told it was husky, sensual, dangerous.

Her eyes went wide with fear, the quill in her hand trembling ever so slightly.

I smiled, although she could not see it. I had planned to lay low when I returned but had changed my mind the moment I told these smugglers my true name. Kali must have known I was on my way—else, like her carriage driver, she believed it a pseudonym. Maybe every dark and shady character chose the mysterious 'Eva Thorne' as their nom deplume these days to instill a bit of fear?

Let Hilja tremble at my coming too.

When the silence stretched like starless night, I said, "I know what you're thinking. What kind of friend vanishes into the wilderness just when the dust of war begins to settle? What kind of friend stays vanished for six, long years. My kind? I hope?"

She sighed and set down the quill, although the tremor hadn't left her hand. "I've never been one for pen pals or weekly meet ups at the pub. Too busy for that nonsense. Six years, you say? Can't believe it. You won't recognize the old place. Come on up."

Her Lallalokan accent was gone, her elvish perfect, but the language was interspersed with dwarf-ish and various human words too. I had heard others speaking this new cant. So much had changed.

I gestured for the porters to follow us, and they looked enquiringly at Kali, who nodded hastily, clearly ready to throttle them for daring to question my authority here.

I wanted to ask about Nanny. Most would wonder if she was dead, being as she had raised at least three generations of Thornes from babes to grown, but a Solhan crone like her might never die. My own mother had been an undead lich.

I started to jokingly ask Kali is she had tried, and failed, to kill her yet, when I heard the familiar screech of Nanny's voice: "I smell death coming. That better not be Ilsa on our stair!"

Ilsa. My sister was dead. A vampire anyway. My fault? Hard to say. I'd worn long grooves of regret in my memory, too many to count. I had left Ilsa entombed, not willing to kill her. Had she come back home to Highcrowne? To hunt? Or did Nanny live in denial, like she used to after Viktor's death? Holding on to the memory of her beloved ward was one thing, but Ilsa? I supposed Solhans loved their enemies more dearly.

"You," is all Old Nanny said when I reached the parlor. The internal staircase was new, a direct route up from the office.

We had hugged the last time she saw me. Probably the only time in my life. I'd been heading off to face the Dead God. Of course, she would have heard how I addressed the Crown Assembly after I won. She would know I had left again without saying goodbye to her or to Little Viktor. Still, she seemed surprised to see me alive now. Only the doomed warranted her hugs, apparently.

"How is Little Viktor?" I asked.

"A teenager." As if that said it all.

"Can I come in?"

"Now she's asking, polite. Not like when she shoved her way in before, without a by your leave and bringing this one along with her. The one who never leaves. Who keeps building and hammering and growing the business like some merchant queen." She indicated Kali. Indignant. Nanny always spoke about those she disliked in the third person, even when they were standing right in front of her. Good to see some things hadn't changed.

"This has always been your house more than mine, Nanny." I assured her. "You deserve this and more, a small payment for all the Thornes you've raised, but Uncle's house is gone, ashes, and I need a place to stay."

Nanny's sour expression turned even more sour. "You don't sound like her. Not the scrawny, rebellious girl who hated her uncle and me, all of it. Not the good Solhan she became, remorseless, either."

"I was never remorseless. I just hid it well. I am Eva. Believe it."

I lowered my hood, revealing Solhan hair black as the void, skin as pale as new snow, and eyes white as death.

My eyes had seen Death, heard His name on my lips, felt His love. All that and more was contained in the depths of my soul, a glimpse visible in my gaze, but even that glimpse was too much for Nanny. I won the staring contest. A new first. She made a sign of protection against the Devourer, and for once I mimicked her. There was one thing I still feared. Two.

The bushy-bearded porters were shaking so much, I told them to set the trunk down and go. I didn't like strangers in my home, anyway.

"Why'd you send the porters away?" Nanny asked. "I'm not lugging this trunk. Kali's arms are too skinny to be much use."

"I can manage." Kali took one end while I hefted the other.

"Careful." I told her as we went up the next flight of stairs to my old room.

As it was, we bumped and banged more than I liked. Not that there weren't plenty of protection spells woven into the steamer trunk, but this was my only possession of value. Gems and gold and power be damned. This was all that mattered to me.

I think a little of that desperation betrayed me, slipped past my steely gaze, because Kali's curiosity finally raised its fanged head. "Now that I've done all this for you, my friend, you will show me what's inside?"

"Tomorrow. For now, I have spell work to do."

Kali could do the sign against the Devourer as well. She was practiced at it, living with Nanny, and justifiably wary whenever magic was mentioned.

"I look forward to breakfast then," she said.

"Nanny's not cooking, is she?"

"Only for herself. I have my own cook."

"Jorg?"

"I wish. He's a famed chef these days."

I knew, but it was fun remembering when I bought him his first pastry parcel and taught him to boil human food at Karolyne's Café, when he lived in our basement. A lifetime ago.

"Breakfast then. Goodbye."

Kali was slow to leave, and Nanny hovered in the doorway. I had to give her a little push so I could close the door and lock it. I bolted it in three places. Most rooms in the house had levels of mundane and magical protection.

My room hadn't changed since I'd lived there: still small and bare. I'd never settled into this house, never made it my own, so it was unsurprising to find no trace of me left. I had never wanted wealth, never wanted anything that I got, except for the one thing most valuable to me in the whole world. That which I would die—or kill—or lie to protect.

I waited, listening until Kali had gone back to work, and then I drew the bolts and stepped out again.

Nanny was waiting, eyes narrowed at me. Even a necromancer as great as her had nothing like the God-given soul sense I once possessed, but I knew there was enough power in her to read me a little. She smiled then, raising me a notch in her estimation. Maybe I was a good Solhan after all?

She followed, brimming with curiosity, as I walked the corridors, assessing.

Nothing had changed in Nanny's room either, hers only a little less bare, except for a few trinkets from Solheim and her prayer altar, but Viktor's room was transformed. After his death, Nanny was set to enshrine everything as it had been. Now, the space was filled with his son's, Little Viktor's, old toys from when he was seven, when I last laid eyes on him, but there were far more things I didn't recognize. It was a mess. Clothes everywhere. The books on the shelf made me smile, thinking of his father, my brother. They shared the same taste in histories and politics.

The half-written letters crumpled and tossed into his trash were more worrisome. Democracy. Not him too? Some politics should never be penned, never revealed to potential rivals. Little Viktor, Vikky, was still a boy in so many ways, although at thirteen he was near a man by Highcrowne law. And he was a Thorne. That and his connections to 'Uncle' Duane meant his adolescent fury and rhetoric were dangerous things to leave uncensored.

I burned the crumpled pages for him, as well as a letter that had made its way into an envelope with a wax seal, leaving the charred fragments of parchment on a silver platter atop his desk. Best he saw how close a stranger had come to reading it.

I felt like a stranger. I also felt more like Uncle Ulric than I liked: The wise one come to lecture about behavior, politics, caution, especially for Solhans like us.

"Harsh," Nanny said. "He spent days working on that."

"Not harsh enough."

I was glad Vikky wasn't home, else I might have unleashed those rebukes and ruined our reunion. Better to approach him calmly, later, in a place of my choosing. I recalled how Duane had curried his favor with ice cream and presents, trips to the Central city. I could do that and more. I would become the beloved aunt. I had to be for his sake. To save him from his own foolishness.

But that wasn't why I'd come. There were far more important things.

I set about placing wards around the house, from the attic all the way to the basement, protections far more powerful than Nanny's. She scowled, but then stepped aside, admiring a master at work. I scratched out her worn runes and etched new ones into wooden doorframes, stone lintels, and even the rafters and floorboards. Each I activated with a drop of my blood. Now no one, not even Kali, could enter without my leave. Nanny too was forced onto the stoop until I granted her admission.

"Knew you'd toss me out one day, girlie." Nanny was smiling wider than when Erick came to visit and pretended he liked her cooking. This was clear evidence I was the great Solhan necromancer she always wanted me to be.

I was more than that. I backed up the Solhan runes with other layers of protection, spells learned in the South, in Darrub ... even Lyss.

Nanny did not know what those paintings of ash and sand were before they fused into the hearth, sinking deeper than the house, into the very bedrock. No one had been to Lyss in millennia. And no one could erase my mark.

This had always been my home to claim, the younger version of me too weak to take what was hers, but now it was mine irrevocably. My protestations of simply needing a place to stay were lies. Oftentimes lies were simpler. No need to shout and argue as Old Eva would have done. New Eva was silent, implacable—and far more dangerous.

I locked Nanny out of my room again, which she didn't like. She thought I'd brought her into my confidence, but I trusted no one anymore.

After I'd covered mirrors to prevent scrying and the spyhole, which I knew full well was hidden in the wallpaper, and once the steamer trunk and I were finally unobserved by all things natural and unnatural ... I opened the lid.

A dark-haired child, skin like mine but with a golden cast and delicate elf ears, lay coiled, blissfully sleeping in magical slumber, like something from a fairy tale. I had not needed a fairy for this, being Death's bride came with some perks, including the power to induce an unnatural sleep.

She looked perfect, innocent, safe. She was none of those things. I ignored the darkness visible to my magical sight, the shadow creeping into her fragile soul and slowly hollowing her out, the same darkness digging into me. Instead, I let the warmth of my love fill my gaze.

I had spent the past six years trying to keep her and me alive, and then learning all I could to understand what the First Soul had done to us both—how to make use of the power and blunt the evil.

The First Soul was a relic of the primordial gods, their first, failed attempt at crafting a soul. They had created something immortal, yes, but also eternally hungry, full of despair and hatred and a thirst for power. It consumed light, love, hope ... and although it had been six years since I last held it, its claws had not left me or the child I'd carried in my womb then. It had dug in and would not let us go, reaching for us across the Void to which it had been banished.

We travelled the world like this, my child sleeping as we moved, never staying in one place for long, assuming false names and identities. Highcrowne was the first place I used my real name, at least the part not secret.

Now, once I released my daughter from her slumber, could I let her run around the house and meet Nanny and her cousin, Viktor? Could she play in the streets as he had done at this age? Could she finally find a home?

I would discover all that tomorrow. At that moment, I needed desperately to hold her, and so I touched her shoulder to wake her.

"Dawn," I said. "It's mama."

2 REUNIONS

Despite all the sleeping she'd done, Dawn drifted off in my arms on the narrow bed. I breathed in her scent, like jasmine, but my mind overlaid a whiff of cinnamon, remembering her father as I followed her into peaceful slumber.

Morning light woke me first. Angelic, she opened pale eyes, more sky blue than white, my favorite color, and smacked soft pink lips. Sunbeams slanted across her dress, which was plain brown overlaying a white petticoat. Her glossy black sandals glinted.

Then she sat bolt upright, raven hair sticking up. She screamed.

There was pounding, footsteps on the stairs, then fists on the door. "What's going on in there?" Nanny and Kali asked as one. They must have been nearby, hovering, waiting for me to rise.

"Where am I?" Dawn asked, her throat hoarse from the scream.

I was used to it. This was how she always woke during our travels. In other lands, I'd been sure to include privacy charms that dampened sound, but here, in our new home, I wanted to be able to hear her, wherever she was. But that meant everyone else heard us too.

"Is that a child?" Nanny asked.

"Child?" That was Vikky's voice. What was he doing here? He usually spent Sixth Day with Duane. I had his schedule memorized. Nanny must have summoned him, and I was glad I'd granted him and Kali access already, else he would have been full of the wrong questions.

"We need to freshen up," I told Dawn, pouring water into the washbasin and splashing my own face. "Today, you meet your family. Remember?"

"Oh, yes." She sounded even less enthused than me.

"Just a minute!" I told Nanny to quiet the banging.

I picked out fresh clothes for both of us, choosing comfortable riding pants and boots for the expected hike through the city today, and something elegant for Dawn—pale blue to match her eyes, with gold threads to impress elves. She would need it. If the negotiations went well.

"Alright," I said, pulling open the door. My words hadn't stopped the banging, and Nanny nearly rapt me on the nose before she stayed her hand in time.

"What the..." she began before spotting Dawn. She gasped. "Oh, precious."

"This is my daughter," I said. Dawn did a good impression of a dutiful child by standing straight and smiling before giving Nanny a curtsy.

Kali and Vikky were stunned.

"How...?" Kali asked.

"The usual way." There was nothing usual about her, but now was not the time to share the details. The less everyone knew, the better. "Her name is Dawn, and I'm sure she's famished. What's for breakfast?"

"I have stew..." Nanny began.

"And pastry," Kali finished. "Come along." She took Dawn's hand and led her down the stair, Nanny chasing after. Vikky stood dumfounded, and then he turned to me.

"Aunt Eva?"

"It's me." I hugged him before he could stop me, teenager or no. "I'm so sorry. I've been away too long."

Vikky hugged me back, a good, solid hug, and I felt even more terrible for leaving him. I tried to reassure myself, remembering he'd had Nanny, and Kali, not to mention Duane and Morgan. Even Ulric. All the ingredients that had made me who I was—all except my brother Viktor and Ilsa. One good, one evil. They negated each other really. I couldn't wait to see who Little Viktor had become. My eyes in the city could not know every detail.

"So," I said, pushing him back so I could look at him. We both wiped tears away. "I hear you are a Master of Mathematics and quite the intellect as well."

"You burnt my letters to the Crowns."

"Most were already in the trash. You knew they weren't quite right. I just made sure no one else saw the earlier versions. I'm sure you'll discover the perfect words one day."

"You don't disapprove?"

"How could I? You have so much of your father in you, Viktor. And he was the most true and good person I ever knew. I adored him. I know you are just like him, and I believe in you, just as I believed in him."

Vikky stood straighter, proud. Just as I hoped he would be at those words.

"Are you surprised to discover you have a cousin?" I asked.

"Yes. I thought everyone in this family was so old. There was no one young. Just me."

"Will you be a big brother to her? Look out for her? Dawn needs someone to look up to, someone like you."

Now his breast was puffed out like an exotic bird, he was so chuffed. "Of course."

"Good. She needs a protector. I've made many enemies. Not everyone is happy I sent the Dead God away."

"What? They're crazy. I still remember the walking corpse in the square in spring, how it took dozens of guardsmen to stop it, the caverns where they kept us during the war, the battle with all the werewolves … It was because of you, Aunt Eva, that everyone here is alive."

"You remember all that?"

"Yes, and when Uncle Rose told me what you did—"

"—Duane told you?"

"He doesn't like to be called Duane. Anyway, he told me all the stories. How you travelled across the wall together to face all the Dead God's hordes. How you went to Solheim …. I never tire of the tales. I'm proud of you."

Now it was hard for me not to be chuffed. I thought … had hoped, really, that everyone had forgotten. I was here to start a new life. A low profile one, if I could. Would that be impossible?

"Well," I said, "Duane does tend to exaggerate. It was nothing really."

"Uncle Rose never lies."

He'd told me the same. Would a liar admit they were one? The important thing was to keep Vikky on my side. "I know. A good story meant for children isn't lying, it's leaving out the hard parts. The sad parts. That's all I meant."

He saw the sadness in me. That was a truth I couldn't hide from anyone, and so he nodded. "I understand. A lot of people died. Uncle Rose glosses over those parts, I know. I know lots more than people realize."

I remembered his penchant for prophecy. Had it grown or diminished? Sometimes a magical talent in childhood was subsumed to the ego of adolescence. Another thing my spies did not know. "Tell me, do you still dream about the future? Did you know I was coming?"

"No. I mean yes, I dream. But everything is all jumbled, you know? Something about Dawn was so familiar, though. That blue dress ... I didn't know she was my cousin." He struggled, trying to remember something nearly forgotten. "I dreamt about her last night. She was ... surrounded by elves."

"And alive?"

"What? Of course. She was smiling and charming and they loved her."

I ruffled his hair. "Just what I needed to know. Thank you. Now, let's grab a bite to eat, and I want you to tell me all about your studies ... and your friends. You can't' hang out with the likes of Uncle Rose and us oldies all the time. What do you do for fun?"

I let Vikky talk my ear off, as I sat at the table, listening to all his stories. There were lots of 'Uncle Rose' this and 'Uncle Rose that'. I remembered how he used to call him Uncle 'Ane because I always called him Duane. There would be no getting around Duane, I knew. Still, I could put off our reunion as long as I could.

Nanny and Kali doted over Dawn like a doll they both wanted to care for. She had that effect on people—when she wanted to.

Finally, I said, "I must go. Can you look after her, Nanny?"

"I'm not letting this child out of my sight. How you could have produced … I'll ignore the fact she clearly has some elf in her, as she's Solhan enough at first glance. And so clever…."

Nanny pinched her cheeks, and the glare Dawn shot me made me riposte with a warning glare of my own. Behave.

"She needs to stay inside," I insisted. "She cannot leave until I return."

"You can't keep her locked in a house all day," Kali argued. "Children need to get fresh air, play…"

"No. Her existence must remain a secret for now. Understood? That goes for you too, Vikky. Her life depends on it. Can you keep her secret?"

Vikky nodded, serious. "Yes. I swear."

Kali looked more dubious, but Nanny said, "Oh, I can lock up anything if required. I like mausoleums myself and could go weeks without sunshine if need be. If she's as Solhan as she looks, Dawn is the same."

"Surely, we don't need to keep her secret forever?" Kali said.

"No. But I need to make some arrangements. If things don't work out … we won't be able to stay."

Nanny and Vikky looked stricken by my words.

"I do hope we can work things out," I continued. "But if we don't, Kali, can you get her away as easily as you helped her arrive?"

"In a trunk?"

"Yes."

"I suppose so."

"Good. I knew I could trust you." I took her hand, feeling her squirm and wondering if I could trust her at all, but that was what the wards were for.

Besides, Dawn had her own defenses. She never let me hold her when she was awake, so I shared a look with her, our unspoken communication. She would be good. For now. After all, there was more family for her to meet, and the darkness growing inside her wanted to be free. It knew this was the only way forward for it. It also knew I would fight it for control of Dawn's soul—but not today.

"Arrangement with whom?" Nanny asked.

I ignored the question. "I've got to go."

I left them all to their breakfast, having barely touched by own plate—the fluffy elvish pastry looked good but not the congealed lumps of fatty entrails from

Nanny's stew sitting alongside it—and set off for the Central City.

Coming home is strange, people say, not that I had a real home, but Highcrowne was the closest I'd ever known. It's supposed to feel smaller when you go back, but this crazy city had somehow grown larger.

The thousands of human refugees who once huddled in the Outskirts in canvas tents and mud shanties barely holding out the ice and snow had turned those walls to stone, those roofs to slate. While smoke billowed from a few chimneys, others had adopted warlock-fueled stoves of ever burning crystal, requiring a small magical recharge fee now and again of course, but so much safer. Even in a city of endless winter, fires can rage.

Areas I knew as a child, running through muddy streets with my brother, Viktor, while chasing after Duane were now paved with ash, the blackened skeletons of burned-out warehouses torn down and replaced with tenements teeming with life. Clotheslines stretched from window to window, sheets and wool socks fluttering among snowflakes, a few hardy plants clinging to life in the window boxes, warmed by the hearths within.

I looked like a country yokel in my tattered hood, gawking at the strange sights and smells, my feet no longer knowing the worn paths, stumbling and—crown of ignominy—even needing to stop to read the street signs. There was a dozen of them hammered onto a tall pole, pointing in different directions.

What was 'Ton town'? 'Begger's Block' seemed an odd thing to advertise, as they could usually be found on every street corner. Were there so many now they needed their own neighborhood? 'Market' district leapt out at me, and I almost headed there, but I was no elf and had no escort this time, not even Duane's thugs. No Conrad of the City Watch. There would never be another Conrad.

I choked down the lump in my throat and finally saw the faded sign for where I wanted to go.

"More immigrants," an immaculate elf with pale hair and disdainful gaze said, as I walked past him through the gate between quarters amidst a throng of humans from the southeastern region of Darrub. "Thought we killed you lot already."

Humans were hard to kill as cockroaches, multiplying like rats, and hungrier than locusts looking to pick Highcrowne and the Three Kingdoms clean at any opportunity. I knew all the racist stereotypes, heard them all growing up, often mistaken for one of them— but I wasn't human. I was Solhan and far, far worse.

"Killing is Death's job," I turned and whispered into the obnoxious elf's ear. "And mine."

With the slightest tug on his soul, I pulled it free of his body, and he collapsed in the street. I saw his ghost still standing, looking at me open mouthed with shock, while soldiers from the gate rushed over, shoving migrants aside. The elf was a Citizen, and they'd trample any old lady or child to make sure he was safe.

"Don't worry," I told his ghost. "I'm turning over a new leaf, all that drivel, so it's your lucky day." With a turn of my fingers, I allowed his soul, still tethered, to sink back into his carcass. He gasped and sat up, while I continued on my way.

Bigoted elves and sycophantic dwarfish guards aside, Highcrowne felt different.

It was the greatest city in the world, a center for trade and the capitol of the Three Kingdoms. The historic union of Avian, dwarf and elf kingdoms was nearly destroyed in the Dead God's war, with dwarves joining His ranks, elves willing to sacrifice the human refugees huddling at the feet of Avian magical power for protection, anything to sate the Dead God's wrath.

I had done what I could to patch things back together, but the real work had gone on in my absence. Highcrowne still existed because of people like Queen Calka, King Harley, Queen Hilja, and General Moore.

The eloquent general from the South counteracted the human supremacists led by Darrub mercenaries and terrorists in the guise of the Upside Down party. Moore had unified humanity, at least its newly minted Highcrowne Citizens, and was elected the first Human Crown. So, the Three Kingdoms was really Four, although humans held no lands here. At least they were no longer slaves.

There were also heaps of goblins running around, even more than before. Not just muck rakers and street cleaners, but merchants and Citizenry, with the mercenaries who aided in the war being granted rights as well. Maybe it should be called the Five Kingdoms? Not that the goblin Emperor had revealed himself, or the locations of their hidden cities. The goblins were conniving and untrusting by nature, so an open alliance would never happen.

Highcrowne was all about what existed in the dark. And Duane, A-K-A Mister Rose, was the Shadow King, ruling over all the illicit trade conducted in dark alleys, on hidden docks, and even in the air.

The more airships that travelled the skies, the more piracy was on the rise, and anyone who wanted their cargo, and people, to arrive safely had to hire Duane's protectors. There were airship guards, former caravan guards, usually, who had changed careers after the land routes became impassible because of the Risen dead, but none of them were as skilled at aerial combat as Duane's people. That's because he had Avian gadgetry to aid him, I knew.

I had no idea why the Avian Queen needed a Shadow King like Duane, but she was his not-so-secret and staunchest supporter. Not that Queen Hilja wasn't warm toward him—they had been lovers for a time before politics got in the way—and he had even charmed his way into King Harley's good graces after the two of them famously stole the silver crown from

Queen Gypsum and helped end the siege of Highcrowne.

I knew the tales too because I'd been there.

My informants told me that General Moore was the only one as wary of Duane as I was. Shadow Kings, unchecked, were one step away from claiming open power for themselves, from becoming dictators or emperors. The term depended on who did the naming—the victors or the losers.

I knew Duane better than anyone. I'd grown up with him, admired him, before I saw him get lost in the dark. Before I got even more lost myself. He had been good once, but so had I. I knew full well how little you could trust the ones you called friends, how you couldn't even fully trust yourself, and so it was a relief when he found me, as I knew he would sooner or later. At least the dread waiting was over.

"Eva," he said, appearing out of a shadowed doorway to walk beside me as though he had been there the whole time.

He didn't wear his street clothes anymore, no torn shirt revealing bronze skin, no hair hanging in his green eyes. I saw him as he had been for a moment, my breath catching at the memory, before his new image came into focus. Now, he wore a suit, all silver silk with a black satin collar and shiny buttons, a top hat to match. He'd stolen my cane idea and now carried one with a golden snake holding a rose in its mouth, a weapon surely concealed inside, just as my

Ashur cane concealed a Solhan blade inside its bone sheath.

"Don't you look the dandy these days, Duane," I said, just to set the tone.

I was happy to go back to our old sparring, happy to forget the war and all that was seen and said, or almost said between us. Last I saw him, he'd been recovering from a necromancy-induced coma. I'd sat beside him for ten days until he recovered, and then I left before he knew I was there. At least I hoped he didn't know I'd been there. It was good to see him healthy again. Like Kali, the years had barely touched him, a few more laugh lines were all.

He laughed now, and it was easy to see where the lines came from. Mirth still glinted in his eyes too. "And you're the same old, Eva. I think those are the same boots too, just resoled?"

"You can be sure of it. I like to keep things simple, uncomplicated, predictable."

"How's that working out for you?"

"Well … I was having a grand old time travelling the world, making up for all the dreary years spent locked in boarding schools or Uncle's house, finally getting a taste of freedom, on my terms, when I noticed myself being followed everywhere. I'm not as good at the observing game as you—"

"—admitting that for once? Something new—"

"—but I'm observant enough to notice elves slinking about in human lands, newly liberated to be sure, and yes fending off the advances of elvish slavers looking to continue their reprehensible activities beyond the laws and watchful eye of Highcrowne, but slavers have a certain stench to them I'm familiar with, or I should say lack of stench. They are a lower class than royal elves, whose privilege grants them the right to truly stink and strew their odor wherever they please. Now, I thought to myself, the only royal elves who would be wandering through Darrub and Kell, aside from those muscly ones wanting to slay wyverns, are Elven Elite Protectorate—"

"—EEPs—"

"—glad my name for them has stuck. Yes, EEPs following me, and so I thought, who controls EEPs? Why, only the Elf Queen. Hilja. Now, with Hilja being a good friend of yours, perhaps you can tell me why she has taken a sudden interest in me?"

"You've always been interesting, Eva. If I were the Elf Queen, I'd never take my eyes off you."

"Flirting. Now, I'm really worried. What aren't you telling me?"

I surprised him by pulling him into an alcove, one his flunkies weren't watching. I knew they were all around us, and there were startled grunts and running feet as three of them came to check on us, but Duane waved them back. His cane sword was half drawn, but so was mine, blades locked together. My blade had trapped his. It was serrated and made for disarming, but his was so sharp a fallen strand of my hair was severed by it.

"I thought you were happy to see me," I said, batting my eyelashes better than I had in my femme fatale days.

"I never said that."

"I'm happy to see you."

"Now, who's the one flirting? You have me worried." He stepped back, sheathing his sword, so I did the same.

Flunkies still lingered within earshot, and without looking back, Duane ordered them, "Go away. Now."

"Sir?"

"You heard me."

His shadows disappeared, really disappeared. I felt it. I no longer had the same soul sense I'd once possessed, which had allowed me to know where every fly and worm was in a five-mile radius, but I was a necromancer. That meant I knew souls, living and dead, and I knew I was now, finally, alone with Duane.

I turned off the femme fatale routine and crossed my arms. "Tell me what you know," I ordered.

He sagged. "Fine." Who knew a Shadow King could still obey? "I do know why Hilja sent EEPs after you: Dawn."

"Because she's the Elf King's daughter? Hilja's half-sister? Who told Hilja about her? How did she find me?"

"Like I said, Hilja has never let you out of her sight. You're too dangerous. You stopped the Dead God. Somehow. How?"

There was so much he'd missed, he'd been on the verge of death most of the time, and some things only I knew. I was the only living person who had been there—and I wasn't telling anyone.

I stayed on subject. "Does Hilja want to eliminate a potential rival? Dawn has no political supporters, no one should even know about her. Plus, she's more Solhan than elf. Hilja's Crown is safe."

"It's not." Duane looked around, and it seemed the secluded alcove I'd found still wasn't good enough for him.

He lifted his sleeve, revealing a row of bracelets, each one Avian made. I saw the leather and silver braid he'd used to unlock doors before, but this time he rubbed his finger against a pure silver band. Green runes glowed as he did so, and I detected the cool wash of a privacy spell, like being encased in ice. I felt a chill, not just from the cold but from the memory of such a spell Erick had once cast. Thane. Her father. I tried to keep the emotion in check, but Duane knew me too well.

"I didn't think you got claustrophobia," he said, probing.

"It's not that. Just say what you need to say. Please."

"Hilja does not want to eliminate Dawn—she needs an heir."

So, my information was correct. Good to have Duane confirm it. If anyone knew the truth, it would be him. This would make bargaining with the Elf Queen easier, but the more the odds were weighted in my favor the better. What else would Duane reveal?

"What do you mean?" I played dumb. "Hilja is young, for an elf. She has time. Besides, elves don't have children all that often. It's too soon to get worried. Who is she married to by the way?"

"No one. She doesn't want to give up power. She has ... concubines. Plenty." Duane soured at that.

Had he been one for a time? I didn't ask, as that would make Duane defensive, and I wanted to keep him talking. I knew Hilja had broken things off with him a long time ago—she couldn't have a half-human heir. Half-Solhan was different: we were one of the ancient races with more claim to this world than any save the Avians. I knew lots of things, but not how much it had hurt Duane. There was still pain there. I knew not to probe, as I had plenty of old wounds of my own.

"I'm..." I almost said I was sorry, but that would make Duane suspicious. I was pretending to be the old Eva, for his benefit. "I'm still not sure why she needs Dawn," I finished. "Did you know they tried to take her? I killed several EEPS and fought off plenty more, plus her latest human goons on the way here, which I'm sure Hilja is not happy about."

"Hilja is desperate. She's young, normally plenty of time to make an heir, like you said—but her enemies poisoned her. Some magic, some curse no one can break. She can't bear children. That means her line dies with her, so the quicker someone hastens that end, the quicker another elven family can rise to power. Probably the same one that poisoned her."

"Dawn is more Solhan than elf."

"Solhan sentiment is on the rise, never diminished in some royal circles I hear. Hilja herself carries Solhan blood. It gives her an even greater claim to power."

I knew more than most about true Solhan history. My people had not only subjugated dwarves but also elves to their empire. The Avians had been their only rivals. Solhans had nearly destroyed themselves, and Avians were nearly extinct. All that remained were their former vassals, elves especially, vying for shreds of ancient and long forgotten power.

"Dawn is only a child. How do I get Hilja to just leave us alone?"

"You have to understand Parties."

I rolled my eyes. "Surely, the elven political parties have no place in Highcrowne. They didn't even seem to be all that effective in Faellion when I was there."

"Elves think long term, and the lines of succession need to be solid," he explained. "Until Hilja recognizes one of King Fharen's bastards—"

"—what did you just call my daughter?" I asked dangerously. Was that an old wound too? Did he still disapprove? It wasn't like I had been with the Elf King; it was Thane in his body. Way too complicated to explain, and I wasn't willing to explain to Duane anyway, so I crossed my arms and gave him my dangerous look. That was old Eva and he seemed relieved by it really.

"I apologize. King Fharen only has one bastard, Dawn, which is part of the problem."

I punched him then. Not as hard as I could, but it felt good to hear his jaw pop. He might even have a bruise. That would clash with his fancy silk suit.

"Do you want my help or not?" he asked, exasperated.

"Is that what you call this? Helping? You were just dying for an opportunity to rub it in, to make me feel like crap. It's been six years, Duane, and Thane ... Thane is gone." I refused to tear up, no matter what role I was playing, so I tore past him.

I ran through the streets, a little more lost than I liked, whipping past teeming crowds of dwarves who looked ready to beat up anyone who'd make a lady upset. Duane's goons had to make a path so he could pursue me unhindered. A goblin muck raker looked shocked when I sunk down in the alley where he was working. It stank, as he hadn't finished with his raking, but I figured the extra stink wouldn't hurt and may actually be of benefit when I faced elves later. It would raise me a few ranks in their estimation, especially if I bought some perfume from the square and splashed that on too. I would need the perfume, just for my own olfactory sanity.

"Eva," Duane said, sitting beside me. Wasn't he worried about his suit? The goblin went wide eyed with terror—the Shadow King was more famous than a secret, underworld boss should be—and hurried away, leaving us alone, the privacy spell in place again with Duane so near. "I didn't mean ... Alright, I know I don't know the full story, but I was ... I am still look-ing out for you, just like Ulric—and Viktor—always wanted me to. I made promises, and I won't break them."

"Protecting me from myself, right? That's what you told me before. It's too late. I'm broken. But Dawn is innocent. For my sake, help her. I need her safe more than anything. More than life itself." That part was true, and the burning truth penetrated even Duane's dense emotional shielding.

He sighed. "There are several houses with a blood claim to the Crown. Hilja is certain one intends to assassinate her and derail the debates over democracy in the Crown Chambers. If she recognizes Dawn as her heir, then she can bring most of the other houses and political Parties to her side by assuring the future of the Elf Kingdom."

"And put Dawn in an assassin's sights as well!" I said. "No. Naming an heir won't stop an assassin. You should know that much."

Duane had been an assassin once, the trade he had learned while I was learning how to drink tea and walk with books on my head at finishing school. Our upbringing began to diverge even more wildly after that.

"Assassins don't get paid unless they do what their clients want. If we can find out who wants Hilja assassinated, she won't need Dawn for a long time. Ever, if she can lift the curse."

"She doesn't need her now. Can't have her! And what's this 'we' business?"

"You pointed out that Dawn means more to you than your own life, so you're going to get yourself killed protecting her, and if I'm to fulfill my oath to your brother, then I have to help you. I have no choice. So, it's 'we'. Or, I prefer, 'me' if I can get you to stay out of this? Just once?"

I raised an eyebrow. This was Eva Thorne he was talking to.

"It was worth a shot." He smiled, adding to those laugh lines.

"So, where do 'we' start?"

"I've already been looking into Hilja's enemies. I'll try and speed things up a bit."

"Who are they? Maybe I can help?"

He sighed. "Our old friends the War Party, plus the Peace Party, and even the Royal Privilege Party."

"No," I gasped. "Not Royal Privilege? I thought that was Hilja's favorite Party?"

"Very funny, but actually true, she was their leader until she became a Crown and had to assume neutrality. They're the ones who have the most to lose with democracy."

"You used that word before. What do you mean? Are the Crowns still disturbed by humans electing General Moore as their representative? By my reckoning, his final term is up next year, so do they want to keep him in power? No new elections?"

"Not as out of touch as I thought you were."

"Human activity in Highcrowne is the one piece of news that makes it all the way to Kell. Highcrowne is still home—or hell, depending on who you ask—to those who were once refugees here. Few natives survived the Dead God's hordes in the human lands, and the resettlement proceeds in fits and starts, with warlords and power brokers trying to rebuild in their own image, so everyone looks to Highcrowne for leadership. General Moore's speeches are shared over campfires and acted out by troubadours in town squares from here to Lyss."

"Moore is a damn good speaker. Scary how influential he is."

"Not as scary as his detractors in Darrub, and the Upside Down Party in Faellion: Our old friend Gas and his gang."

"I wished I'd killed Aguragas when I had the chance," Duane said.

"When was that?"

"A long time ago when I was young and stupid. I haven't had a chance since."

"You're still young and stupid, so there's still a chance."

He smiled again. I still had it.

"Okay, you see what the Royal Privilege Party is up to, and I'm going to tell Hilja to stay out of my hair."

"Giving orders to the Shadow King?"

"Who's that? I only see Duane."

"And I only see Eva brazenly taunting the bad guys, as usual. You can't just go and threaten the Elf Queen."

"Watch me. ... and why do you call Hilja a bad guy?"

"Just be careful." Was there more he wasn't telling me? Typical Duane. I would dislodge the truth in due order. Just give me time, and my good old, resoled boots to do some kicking.

"See you around." I tossed my hair and cast a smile his way as I strode out of the alley and into the market, looking to buy perfume.

I saw him watching me when I looked back. Duane was still in there, somewhere. Good. I wondered if the old Eva was in me too. Or were we both just ghosts summoned by a good necromancer?

3 ONE OF THE BAD GUYS

I stood at the gilded gates to the Central City. As much as I'd always hated the garbage pile that was the Outskirts where my family lived, with the pretty layer cake of Highcrowne resting atop it like a flamboyant weight slowly crushing us lesser races, I hated the lumpy, mountainous Central City, representing the wedding topper in the middle most of all. Nobles meant snobby elves, noses in the air, flower gardens in spring making my allergies go crazy….

Fortunately, it was autumn, nearly Highcrowne winter, which meant it was more like regular winter for the rest of the world. The plants were dead, the elves freezing and huddled at home by their fires, and so it would be the perfect time to visit. If they'd let me in. I didn't have friends who could give me a visitor pass anymore. Only enemies.

Sometimes they were just as good.

"Haven't you heard? You don't need a pass to enter the Central City anymore, Citizen." The guard was a dwarf, not an elf playing games with me, but I still blinked at him a few times. I forgot humans (and thus us, nearly indistinguishable, Solhans) were no longer the sewer muck of Highcrowne society. At least not officially.

"What if I want to see the Elf Queen?" I asked.

"We don't give out passes for that. Doesn't matter who you are."

An elf marched up to the gate, just behind the dwarf, jackboots shining, beret canted just so. An EEP.

"Certain people do matter more than others," the elf said, making the guard half jump out of his oversized armor. "Let her through."

"I was goin' to, sir. I was just telling her she can't see the queen is all. Elf Queen, I mean. No one sees the Avian Queen either, but the Dwarf King and Human King are really friendly both and do see petitioners every second day. Maybe she can go to them?"

The EEP looked weary of the conversation already, so he turned to me and said, "This way, Miss Thorne. Queen Hilja is expecting you."

"Why didn't you say so?" The dwarf grumbled something about no one ever giving him the list for special visitors and how was he supposed to read minds? He was a werewolf not a magic worker.

I frowned. While I liked feeling special, I didn't like EEPs. This one didn't like me either.

"I was there in Darrub," he said, "when you unleashed those rope vipers on my team."

"Darrub is a dangerous place, rope vipers even more so. Maybe you shouldn't have been there in the first place."

"I go where I am bid by my queen. You should do as she bids as well."

"She's not my queen."

"She's a Crown. She and the other Crowns have graciously allowed vermin like you residence in this city, so you had best sound more grateful than that when you meet her."

"Oh, I've met Hilja before, tried on dresses with her, girl to girl chats over ex-boyfriends too, so I daresay I know her pretty well. I also know the way, so I'll be seeing you." I had my good boots on and had gained stamina while on the run from my past, so I quickly outpaced the EEP as he dealt with ceremonial armor and swords tripping him up. I waved back as I rounded the corner of a hedge on the path to the Crown Assembly.

I didn't know if that was where Hilja would be, probably not, but it was good to be temporarily free. I dodged and weaved through more doors, halls, and stairwells until I was good and lost, assuming my escort would be too.

I stopped in a massive gallery with lots of flying buttresses and decorative arches, tapestries taller than most buildings in the Outskirts hanging around me, so I felt I was wrapped in a giant carpet. The tapestries were embroidered in silk, depicting scenes from dwarven, elvish, and Avian history. Well, not Avian so much, as they were secretive, but there was the occasional winged bird swooping into a scene to rescue some beleaguered dwarf army or to bestow a gift on some elven hero. I stopped in my tracks when I saw a human hero for once—and she looked all too familiar.

The tapestry was a blend of scenes over time. The girl in a black dress first a supplicant at the foot of Queen Calka receiving a white feather, the embroidery so detailed, I even made out the Avian script written on the haft of the feather, spelling out Truthspeaker. The same girl later stood in a red dress, green claws of magic emanating from her hands as she faced an army of werewolves, then she was beneath the sea in an azure gown, cleaving off one of Leviathan's heads with a sword. I was pretty sure it had been a rusty dagger. I had been wielding a silver serving wedge in the other hand which the artist had left out entirely. In another section, I wore Ilsa's sapphire blue dress—entirely inaccurate as I hated dresses and had been wearing my riding pants at that part in the story—when I stood before the entire Risen army of the Dead God at the

Wall with Highcrowne's armies battling in the background. There were goblins throwing themselves at the enemy, dirigibles ablaze, a dragon swooping through the sky. Olyvandra, my dragon godmother, had definitely not been there that time. It did look impressive, though.

The last scene was of me standing in a dress I swear I've never even seen before, addressing the Crown assembly, with humans, elves, dwarves, goblins and even a grall in the audience, rapt to my every word. There was a beatific glow of light around me, like some saint, and I held the proclamation of Citizenship in my hand, granting rights to the downtrodden. Citizenship was granted long after I addressed the Assembly, and after much debate among the Crowns. I heard about it after I fled for the Wall. I was deeply disappointed, realizing how much they'd gotten wrong with recent history and thus worrying the other tapestries were equally inaccurate. Surely, someone somewhere had recorded history truly? Or was everything always glossed over so much?

"Remarkable, isn't it?" A familiar voice said. I looked around and finally spotted a goblin who had blended into the tableau of the Assembly scene with the embroidered goblins. He wore brass spectacles, tufts of gray hair sticking out his ears, but otherwise cleanshaven, his suit very scholarly with a cravat and robes over his vest and trousers.

"Doctor Ghunnan," I said. "In disguise again?"

"If you mean I'm disguised as a professor of history overseeing the tapestries as well as updating the Crown archive to ensure a certain Solhan lady who has been extremely valuable to my research, a travelling companion, and I daresay friend, is adequately recognized in the history books? Then yes, I am here 'in disguise'."

"So, I have you to blame for all this? Of course, you weren't even there when I fought Leviathan, so I can see how you got that wrong."

"The Avian, Kerrik, was there, watching, as well as many other sources I've drawn on heavily. Of course, it would have been so much simpler if you had been accessible for interviews, Miss Thorne."

"Is that disappointment in your tone, Doctor? Did you miss me?"

"You didn't even say goodbye."

"I suppose I have a lot of apologizing to do, as I didn't say goodbye to anyone. Best I not start then, else it will never end. Instead of 'I'm sorry' how about 'good to see you'?"

He pushed his spectacles up on his pug nose and snorted. "Very well. I suppose that must suffice. It is good to see you as well. What brings you back to Highcrowne?"

"Surely an old spy like you must know?"

"I retired from the Emperor's service after the war. More time to pursue my research. The blood you helped me obtain from Harbinger alone has yielded more questions than answers, stimulating years of work, not to mention my progress with the Avian's green lubricant. It has grown rarer and more expensive of late, and so this historical work for the Crowns is also a means for me to obtain a more reliable supply. There is not a legitimate vendor in Highcrowne who sells it anymore, but there is an allotment for vital Crown activities."

"I did notice that. More warlock magic in the city instead, and Southern technology." I hated human inventions and preferred magic.

"Warlocks," Doctor Ghunnan snorted. "Necromancers too, now that the ban on followers of the Dead God is lifted, are crawling out of the woodwork. Charlatans one and all, taking advantage of the simpleminded. And there are far more simpleminded in this city than you can imagine."

"I did grow up here. So, I know." I didn't mention that the Doctor's insistence that there was no magic, just fakery and hallucinations, was the naivest perspective I had ever encountered on my long travels. But he was endlessly entertaining. Soon he would start talking about science. Hilarious.

"My scientific pursuits..." Told you. "...include creating the glowing pigments you see in this tapestry. The 'magic' so many interviewees insisted I include in the depictions. I didn't weave it of course, but I did produce an auto-loom to aid the artisans the Crowns hired. Some of them have grown sick from the pigments, hair falling out, teeth too. Best to stand a bit back from the tapestries."

I took a huge step back.

"All scientific pursuits have their price," he continued, "but I daresay it is worth it. The glowing green pigment, my first attempt at recreating the Avian goo, and which I call 'radiant'—"

"—radium?"

"No, 'radiant'. It produces some fascinating invisible particles I've been studying. You can cook with them to be sure, although I would not recommend eating anything exposed to the substance, and I daresay I am also close to creating a machine that can peer inside the human body, without killing and dissecting anyone, which is my usual method. I do believe we will one day be able to look at functioning hearts, lungs, the flow of blood...."

I was already getting bored. Science wasn't as hilarious as I remembered. "I need to find Queen Hilja," I interrupted. "Do you know where she is?"

"I do." It was the EEP soldier. He'd found me.

"And what is your name?" I asked. If he was going to be following me around and 'escorting' me, I might as well know.

"Lieutenant Tibald Uanal."

"The bald urinal?"

"No, Tibald—"

"—I heard you the first time. Any relation to Captain Uanal of the City Watch?" My dear old nemesis.

"He is my father. And he's Lord Marshall of the Guard now."

"Very impressive. I will have to say hello. He owes me for solving some cases for him."

"That's hard to believe."

"Not so difficult," Doctor Ghunnan argued. "This is Eva Thorne, Savior of Highcrowne." He indicated the tapestries.

"Propaganda," Tibald said. "Everyone knows the humans needed some appeasing to get them back to work, so a hero was fabricated. My father told me the truth, and as much as the good old days of human slavery sound like a better idea to the common elf, I daresay getting humans to willingly work for 'hope' of earning their fortunes, the mere 'chance' of bettering themselves, while really paying them less than it took to clothe, house, and feed them as slaves is actually a stroke of brilliance. Amazing what the right propaganda and turn of phrase can do. So, now, Miss Eva Thorne, Savior of Highcrowne, I heard you want to see the Queen. So, may I escort you? I think offering you the choice gives you that semblance of free will you so desperately need."

This one was even more annoying than his father.

"Fine. Lead the way." I almost gave him the slip again, just because it would be so easy, but I did want to get the negotiations started.

At one point, I thought I might never return to Highcrowne, never have to deal with the queen's interest in my activities, but Dawn was running out of time. I had done all I could, looked everywhere I could for answers, and those answers led me home. Ulric and the Avians were my last hope, which meant dealing with annoyances like EEPs was required.

I couldn't get one of the images from the tapestry out of my mind. When I faced the hordes of Solheim there was more than the green glow of necromancy about me—there was the black shadow of the First Soul reaching out to kill. It had been visible to everyone then when it nearly consumed me. The First Soul was the flawed attempt of the Primals, the first gods, to craft a soul. Its shadowy claws had dug into me and thus into Dawn when she was in my womb. I thought I had sent the First Soul away with the Dead God, thought we were safe, but I made a mistake. A big one. I was wrong.

Now was not the time to start worrying and replaying history. I clamped down on my fears, preparing myself to face the most formidable foe I had faced in years, worse than Darrub raiders, Kell sorcerers, or Lyssian serpent priests.

Queen Hilja.

She was not in the Crown Assembly chamber or even the Elven Palace—just one of several palaces. Instead, she had taken over a Central City boutique and lounged on a gilded chair like it was her throne, legs crossed, revealing petticoats and perfect satin slippers. Nearly a dozen guards, courtiers, and servants, not to mention the proprietor of the boutique, surrounded her, holding up samples of rich cloths, strings of pearls, and intricate brocade.

"Oh, my darling Eva!" Hilja declared, rising and shoving them all aside. "You are just in time to help me decide. I have worn every gown of every color it seems, and nothing piques my interest. What fabric should I choose?"

Despite the inaccurate tapestry depictions of me, I was not the person to ask about gowns. I thought Duane and I were good at pretending no time had passed, but Hilja acted as though we had never parted ways in Faellion, or fought a war, or ever argued about executing my friend Gypsum's entire family. Hilja was all for executing innocent husbands and children, by the way. She feigned flighty better than I did and was far more dangerous than she appeared.

She didn't hug me, which meant she was not happy, and I was not happy to be having this conversation with an audience of sycophants. How to get us alone?

"Perhaps we should all vote on it?" I suggested, indicating the gathered servants. "I'm sure you each have an opinion on which color suits Queen Hilja best? Raise your hand if you think it's sage with silver threads." I raised my hand to demonstrate the process. Nothing. None of them dared twitch. "Looks like I'm outvoted then. How about rose satin? Mauve?"

A guard raised her hand.

"Excellent! That's one for mauve. Anyone else—"

Hilja grabbed my hand and dragged me into the dressing room to shut me up, saying, "Sage it is, as I wanted your opinion, Eva. Come along and let me show you."

The change room was as large as the salon outside, and it had a lock. She bolted the door, pressing her back against it. "Democracy. Yeck."

"Goblin curses," I noted. "You speak the new cant also?"

"Yeck. I mean 'damn'. Oh. that's human. What is the elvish equivalent?" she pondered.

"Lisht," I said.

"No wonder I prefer yeck. And yes, as much as I have embraced a new Highcrowne with equality for all—I do not actually want equality for all. Understand? Voting turns my stomach."

"So much you don't want the humans to vote for General Moore's replacement? Is that what the Royal Privilege Party stance is?"

"I don't control the party, and I don't care who or what humans vote for. The real issue is elves. And dwarves, especially dwarves, are catching the plague of democracy. I think I preferred the undead plague that turned them all into walking corpses."

"That plague is still around. And another thing on my long to do list."

"Yes, but it was so much more fun when there was less aimless shambling and more focused brutality under the Dead God's command. Command. How I miss it. I tell you, even the undead are too democratic these days."

"Well, it sounds like you are quite busy too, trying to balance the Three Kingdoms on a knife's edge between the illusion of freedom and actual freedom," I said. "With General Moore being democratic and Queen Calka being Avian and preoccupied with who knows what, I suppose it comes down to bringing King Harley to your side?"

"His new wife makes that impossible. She's as democratic as they come."

"A Matriarch? Why?" Female dwarves were rare and held the reins of power—or they had when they were the representatives of King Rutgard's ghost. My destruction of the king's body had sent ripples through dwarven society.

"Guilt of the conquerors. Which I cannot understand in the slightest either. As Queen, I try to put myself in the shoes of goblin mercenaries, slavers, dock workers ... good statesmanship requires it, and how else am I to remain at least a dozen steps ahead of their petty schemes? But I cannot for the life of me understand why anyone would willingly give up royal privilege. Surely, you can explain it to me? You did give up Solheim and ruling over all the Risen hordes after you defeated your mother, the lich queen? How do you really, truly give up that kind of power?"

That's why Hilja never stopped watching me. Sure, there was Dawn, but there was also fear. Of me. Good.

"I suppose you don't, not really. But you can refrain from using it. Unless someone forces your hand."

Hilja's eyes narrowed at my less than subtle threat. Not that I could carry through. I couldn't command risen hordes—well, some risen, but certainly not what you'd call a 'horde'. She didn't need to know that.

"I can't just forget about my father's other heir," Hilja said.

"Your sister. You have a sister, Hilja. I thought you always wanted that. And Fharen never knew about her. She's as illegitimate as they come and no threat to anyone." That was my biggest lie. The First Soul had changed her into a threat greater than anything imaginable.

"We elves have magical protections against pregnancy," Hilja said. "The fact you even have Dawn means my father recognized her, even after his death. He is dead?"

"I don't know. He was taken by the Dead God, so he would have to be." Her father, King Fharen, that was. What mortal could survive the Void? And the Devourer? I only hoped Thane, my Thane could.

"Know that Dawn's existence, not to mention the lack of a body to produce for my father's state funeral, this is all … a problem for my own dynasty."

I didn't like how she said 'problem'. Maybe Duane was wrong about Hilja needing an heir?

"What do you want?" I asked. Time for negotiation. I had a straightforward barter in mind—Hilja's life for my daughter's, but I knew things were never that easy.

"Same as everyone. To feel safe, secure."

"Difficult with an assassin after you," I said.

"So, it's true?"

"It's not?" I was about to tell her Duane would know, but I thought it better not to reveal my source.

"There are always threats against every Crown, irate citizenry who don't make it past throwing things at the gates, but I have made enemies."

"Big surprise there."

"I don't mean the unimportant ones, like humans and dwarves. I mean elves. Real people." I rolled my eyes but didn't bother to interrupt. "Without an heir and with my father gone, it leaves only me to represent our family name. My mother and everyone else is dead. If I were too, then other houses would have a clear claim to the Elf throne."

"Like your old fiancé, what's his name?"

"Gallan? Oh, I had him poisoned. He was too easy, too exposed. My worry is the older clans with their deep, hidden roots in our society. They are like pulling giant oaks rather than weeds from your garden."

I shuddered. I hated gardens.

"Cut to the chase," I told her. "You want Dawn so your dynasty doesn't look as weak as it is, but I don't see how a six-year-old will frighten anyone off."

"She will remove arguments against me, destroy fragile alliances, offer hope for new ones. Someone to marry..."

"Stop right there. My daughter is no pawn in your political games. I was going to offer to find your assassin for you—"

"—and I was about to order you to do that—"

"—but it sounds like your giant oak of a rival ... and which clan are we talking about?"

"The Leyllans are my greatest concern."

"Sounds like dealing with these Leyllans is just too messy, and I will not place Dawn in danger just to get you off my back. I'll disappear off the edge of the world first."

I was set to turn on my heel and get Dawn out of Highcrowne right there and then—when a horn blew. It was a sound I had never heard before, the note pure as crystal, never growing louder or quieter but stretching out for heartbeat after heartbeat.

Hilja's eyes went wide.

"What is it?" I asked.

"Avians." She unlocked the door and dashed out.

All of us poured out of the boutique and looked up at the sky. Four Avians—the only four who existed, I knew, with the species on the verge of extinction—hovered above the Central City. They were weaving some magic, strands of light like straw held in their talons, creating a tapestry of magic, which grew larger as I watched. The golden cloth they constructed fell over the city like a covering for a bird's cage, blocking out the sky. I saw a dirigible pressed down by it and forced to land in snow-covered gardens, the crew shouting and cursing as they smothered their burners and expelled air.

"The Central City is in lockdown," Hilja said. Her bodyguards had abandoned cloths and decoupage to array themselves protectively around her, swords drawn.

"What's happened?" I wondered.

"I don't know, but this is not good."

I thought of Dawn, protected by wards in the Outskirts, but with only Nanny and Kali to care for her. Neither of them knew what to do if things went wrong. If the darkness came to her … and why had I even granted them access to the house? Sentimental stupidity. Could one steal her from its protections? Had I warded it well enough to specify Dawn could not leave, not even in their care? Like being unsure whether I'd turned off the stove or locked the door, I fretted that I had left some loophole in my protections. I couldn't be stuck here.

I needed to discover what was happening. Fast. I didn't bother to say anything to Hilja before I took off running. I headed for the innocuous garden shed on the eastern side of the palaces, where Duane had taken me before, and the rendezvous point for Avians to take the few people they allowed to their roost. I didn't know if I was one of those people, but I'd soon find out.

4 NEST OF THORNES

The Avians had locked down the Central City, home of the ruling elite, treating queens and kings like nothing more than disobedient children. Just as Hilja pretended to offer democracy to the masses, the Avians pretended to offer co-rulership to elves, dwarves, and humans. Their display showed there was only one real power in Highcrowne.

As I ran, I looked up to see lights dancing across the golden barrier. Elven mages were trying to break through, their attempts blunted and absorbed into the weave. The telltale signs of fizzled spellcasting were visible to both the naked eye and my third eye. Not that I had a third eye in the middle of my forehead,

but figuratively speaking, my ability to sense and identify magical workings had grown the more I practiced.

I knew better than to try and attempt to break
through the Avian barrier—their magic was too alien
to me—so I had to appeal to their reason. Surely, little
old me could be let out?

Duane was there beside the weathered garden
shed, waiting for an audience too. Doctor Ghunnan
came running up next, his mechanical legs whirring.
Was it just us three who knew about this place? It
limited the suspects. I didn't know what I was
suspecting yet, but something had ruffled our Avian
rulers' feathers.

"Were you following me? Yourself, not just your
flunkies?" I asked Duane.

"Following you? I got here first."

"Right." Unless he'd already been in the Avian
nest for some nefarious purpose.

"What do you think you're doing?" he asked,
interrogating me now.

"Investigating."

"Me too," Doctor Ghunnan chimed in. "Such a
barrier would be incredibly useful for protecting goblin
cities. I must learn more about it."

The professor had been an accomplished spy since
before I was born, so I didn't buy his innocent act.

"So," I asked after an uncomfortable and
interminable silence had set in, "how does this work?

Is there a way to summon an Avian or do we just stand around all day, hoping they see us here?"

"I called them already." Duane revealed another bracelet, this one pulsing with white light. "They're just not answering."

"Do they speak to you through that thing?"

"You can say that." He was as tight-lipped as ever when it came to his secrets.

I didn't like relying on other people, they always let you down, so I pulled the white feather Queen Calka had given me from my belt pouch and held it before my eyes, saying "Yusha kalal."

Last time I'd been here with Duane, we had needed an Avian escort to fly us up the mountain peak to their sanctuary. With the feather's ability to reveal the truth of objects, I saw that there was a hidden way up, a crevasse in what appeared to be a blank rock face, leading to an ancient, stone staircase. I started climbing.

Duane was right behind me. "I didn't know about this."

"Me either!" the goblin chimed in again as he took up the rear.

Right. I had a small fragment of Avian magic in my possession, while Duane was adorned with far more, flashing it like bling, and the doctor had been studying their goo for years. Was it any wonder I had trouble believing the two of them?

The staircase grew narrower, so tight it pressed into my shoulders, and I had to wiggle through. Avians could fly, so who had the stairs been made for? There was writing on each step, or ornamental scratching, hard to tell, because I didn't recognize the language. There was something slightly Solhan to it, though, with odd dots thrown in, but the thin lines were more like the Avian script on the haft of my feather. Was this some ancient language, a blend of the two oldest races? Did it predate them? Or had Solhans and Avians dwelled together at one time?

When I stopped to wipe away dirt from a rune that was more recognizable than the others, definitely related to the Solhan for 'star', Duane took note of my interest.

"I've never seen you read anything except mass produced mysteries, Eva. How is it that you are suddenly an archaeologist?"

"Ooh, that's a big word for you, Duane," I said, not answering. I climbed faster, hoping to keep him too out of breath for conversation. I heard a few seams on his fancy suit split as he hurried to catch up, and I smiled a bit at that.

I wasn't smiling when I reached the top of the stairs, sweating profusely and wishing I'd brought an adventurer's pack with water and supplies, and found the way blocked. I tried the Truthspeaker feather again, but the stone wall was just a wall.

I sighed. "Looks like we need to head back. Will you stop pushing and turn around."

Duane was trying to get around me.

"Stop. Shoving." I grunted, finally pushed down one step while he pressed on the stones with his palms.

"What do you think you're doing--?" I began when the stones rumbled and shifted.

"Classic hidden latch," Duane explained.

Right. Interesting he figured it out so quickly, as though he had been this way before.

It was a relief to leave the tight space and sweaty, stagnant air. We emerged in one of the larger Avian caves. It was empty, except for the ruins of nests and furniture that had decayed over centuries. The Avians had been more numerous sometime in the past, abandoning extra living quarters like this as their numbers dwindled. Because of what I'd seen on the stairs, I was on the lookout and noted more writing on these walls, as well as the remnants of beds, not just nests. Interesting, but I couldn't allow myself to get sidetracked. I needed to find a living Avian and get out of here.

"This way," Doctor Ghunnan said, leading us to a side chamber.

"You've been here before?" I asked.

"While conducting my studies, I was, shall we say, 'detained' in this area, as my work was unsanctioned. I had been granted an audience to discuss the tapestries and chose to take a slight detour on the way to the bathroom to investigate the pipes the goo is pumped through. I may have also tried to open the door to where it is manufactured, but with nowhere near the success Mister Rose had opening that last door. I will have to make note of that pattern for pressing on the stones next time."

"Next time?" I supposed he had a direct route now for his illicit research. Not my problem.

"Ah yes, here we are," he said, leading us up to a gate.

It was newer than most of the place, gilded and very elvish in design, and I realized locked. We were in some sort of makeshift prison.

"So," I asked the doctor, "when you were 'detained' last time, how did you escape?"

"I didn't. They let me out after my very genuine and heartfelt plea of innocence, or mere scientific curiosity anyway."

"So," I said. "We're back to waiting, aren't we?" I really hoped the Avians checked their prison from time to time, else we'd end up decaying here like the ancient furniture.

Doctor Ghunnan and Duane were both working on the door, one scientifically approaching how best to remove the hinges from ancient stone with acid phials and other items available in his pockets, the other picking the lock with well-worn thieves' tools, while I reached out with my magic.

I held Calka's feather so my soul sight could track her anywhere. She and the other Avians had returned and were within earshot when I called out, "Queen Calka!"

"Truthspeaker," she said when she came to me. It was the one nickname I liked. Duane and Bell had always called me less flattering things like 'dark evil necromancer'.

"Could you please let us out?" I asked. "From this prison, yes, but also from the Central City? I can't stay here."

This time Duane was the one who squinted at me. I hadn't hidden the desperation in my plea well enough, and he suspected something.

"How did you come to be here?" Calka asked. "Never mind. The fact you discovered the old passage proves you are just the one I need."

She touched the lock and it opened, but she raised her wings menacingly and gestured for Duane and the goblin to step back. "The Truthspeaker only. Her I trust."

"How long have we worked together?" Duane asked. "You know what I'm capable of, what Aguragas asked of me. What I refused."

Calka's menacing wing display abated, and she seemed to deflate. "You are right to remind me, and it is good to have one other I can trust." When the doctor tried to slip out with Duane, she slammed the door in his face. "Definitely not you."

"What's all this about?" I asked. "Why is the Central City locked down?"

"Come. I will show you."

She led me and Duane through ancient tunnels to the outside. The air was thin this high up the mountain, despite the chill wind. Avian runes emblazoned on obelisks flared to life all around us, providing air, warmth, and wisdom. The wisdom part was especially nice I recalled, as it helped when trying to speak with enigmatic Avians. Although Calka was being far less inscrutable than usual. Something was clearly wrong, and it had her as discombobulated as I felt being away from Dawn.

We reached her throne, essentially a chair sat in the middle of a Magpie nest of sticks and shiny trinkets, like worthless beads and unpolished stones. Calka was black and white like a Magpie too, so the setting suited her. Behind her throne was a more tightly woven nest of sticks lined with downy white feathers. She gestured to it.

"What am I supposed to be seeing?" I asked.

"My egg."

"Egg?" Avians were near extinct, so an egg meant ... "Your child?"

"The only child born in centuries now that the threat of the Devourer and First Soul no longer weigh on me—and a female. A queen. Our hope for the future. And someone has stolen her." Tears formed in the corners of Calka's eyes; thick gunky tears that didn't fall so much as congeal.

"I am so sorry. Who would have ...?" I began then answered my own question. "Wise to keep Doctor Ghunnan locked up. Still, I think if he had stolen it, he would have vanished into a goblin swamp by now, locked in scientific enquiry, and we wouldn't have him in a cage. Who else could have taken it?"

"No one. Only Avians come here, and the few non-Avians, like Mister Rose, who we escort. I had forgotten about the old staircase, and besides, it leads into the caged off area. I am always sitting in my nest and only rarely called away for affairs of state."

"When were you last called away? When did the egg go missing?" I didn't need this. I needed to get back to my daughter, not help find Calka's, but I burned with questions. I could never let a mystery go.

"Less than an hour ago. King—General Moore as he prefers to be called—begged I meet him in the Crown Assembly Chamber. When I arrived, no one was there. I waited as long as I could before returning here to find my egg missing. We shrouded the Central City immediately, so no one could escape with it."

"Who sent you the message from Moore?"

"It was a sending, an ensorcelled piece of parchment all the Crowns use to contact me. It is kept locked in a case in the Assembly. Each Crown has their own key."

"That limits the suspects. Unless ... General Moore genuinely needed to see you, but someone delayed him, thus making you wait." I was about to head off to question him but stopped myself, telling Calka: "I want to help you. I will help you. But I need to get out of here first."

She shook her head. "I cannot lift the shroud until the egg is safe."

"You can't make a doorway for me?"

"No, that's not how it works. If I take it down, then everyone goes free. I can't allow that."

I understood. This was her child and the future of her kind at stake. Exactly what was at stake for me too.

There would be no placating her, and I would waste precious time trying to argue further.

"Then I will find your egg," I said. "Tell me exactly where you were and when, who you suspect would want the egg and why. I also want to speak to the other Avians. They are the next most logical suspects."

Calka looked horrified at the thought, but she nodded. She would do anything—and so would I.

5 More Bad Guys

I would normally glare, ask probing questions, walk away, then turn around with more probing questions ... all to throw off my suspects as I sought the truth, but there was no time for that.

After I bailed Doctor Ghunnan out of the Avian prison—I had reasoned he was low on my list of suspects since he hadn't run—I got him to help me brew truth serum. It was an old Darrubian recipe I'd learned, which he already knew, and the necessary equipment and ingredients were simple enough. It was a steady pair of hands I needed most, someone to patiently drip thistle extract into the main concoction.

"How much can you make in the next hour?" I asked.

"A handful of doses."

"Good. I need this ready before I talk to the Crown Assembly." That's where I was headed next, after I finished interrogating the Avians.

I doubted the serum would work on them, as drenched in ancient magic as they were, so it was probably best I questioned them the old-fashioned way. I lined them up in Calka's chamber. Was that embarrassment on Roosal's face? It was hard to tell with Avians. It would make this more difficult.

While I was looking for signs of guilt on feathered faces, Duane stood behind me, fingering a dagger and looking menacing, which he still managed despite his silken suit. Calka drooped on her throne, awash with misery.

I made sure everyone else was facing the empty nest.

"An egg, after what? Two centuries?" I asked.

"Three," Kerrik said. He was the gray colored one, a ring of feathers around his neck fluffier than the others. I detected a note of fear in his soul, even if his voice betrayed nothing. A scared Unmentionable was something to worry about.

"Are you still an Unmentionable?" I asked.

None of the Avians flinched, but Duane dropped his dagger.

Kerrik went still. "Be careful, for you may have survived one judgement, but they are always watching, and they do not like their secrecy disturbed."

"Very well. I will talk to you separately, later."

Unmentionables included dimension-hopping fairies, invisible Voidwalkers, wall climbing spiders ... plus they were known to toy with the fates of nations, to obliterate cultures ... ending the Avian species sounded exactly like something they would do. I itched to question Kerrik but mentioning the Unmentionables had shaken the others. They obviously knew Kerrik was one, but they too were suddenly wondering, like I was, if they had been marked by that capricious group for annihilation. Scared Avians were easier to question.

"Naren," I said instead. "We haven't spoken before."

"No, we have not."

"While you helped with the protections during the war and over the Central City this morning, I suspect you spend all your days in the chamber that produces the green goo. Why is it running out?"

"That has nothing to do with Calka's egg."

"Doesn't it? Perhaps if you told me more, I could judge for myself?"

"I cannot."

"I'll use logic then. One magic weakens, the green goo, and then something miraculous happens, an egg. Perhaps Avian magic is limited and there's not enough to go around. Perhaps you and Calka want different things. Did you take her magic to feed your own?"

"No! I---" he didn't say it, but I sensed a burst of love in Naren. He loved his queen. I wished I had my old, more reliable soul sense back. My own diminished version of the magic was frustrating at times. Was it love for a queen, romantic, sisterly? How related were Avians? Was inbreeding a problem?

"Calka," I suddenly thought to ask. "Who is your mate now? Who is the father of your child?

"Roosal," she said. She reached out to him and held him in a feathery hug. Avians were usually not demonstrative to each other, at least the few times I'd seen them, but it was clear she needed the comfort of his embrace. Roosal nibbled at her neck with his beak.

While they snuggled, I bore down on Naren. "You love her. Does it make you angry she chose Roosal?"

"I never said..." He fought for his composure. "My queen and I are too genetically similar to have mated."

"So, you're her brother?"

"No." He fidgeted, which I liked, but being flustered made him struggle for words. At least the other Avians knew to leave me to my game and not intervene.

"A son? First cousin?"

"Our relations are not like yours," Naren finally said. "There have been so few of us for so long ... Once there were many lineages, strong families, when males would fight or, in more civilized times, display their prowess in magic, to win the affection of a mate. We are immortal, but time destroys even mountains. We are not immune to death, to accidents or murder."

Like Calkas's old mate. Saral. He'd been assassinated.

"Before elves and dwarves came to these lands," Naren continued, "we had been weathered down to only a hundred. At that time, we began monitoring the lineages, to prevent inbreeding yes, but more to strengthen our magic. Immortal beings require magic to reproduce, and so you were close in guessing we are limited, but the 'goo' as you call it is a form of magic separate from our own. We began studying it to reverse our demise, to discover a way to save ourselves. So, you see, the work I toil at every day and night for centuries is to accomplish what Calka has. To generate an immortal Avian. Losing the egg would be akin to losing myself."

I was learning so much. Good thing the goblin professor wasn't here, else we'd be well off on a tangent.

"So, Roosal was the superior choice in a magic compatibility test sort of way?"

"Superior is not the best word," Naren began.

"Why was he chosen then?"

"Because I love him," Calka cut in. "Kerrik's magic is the most potent of all of ours, and he would have been the 'superior' choice, but love creates a magic of its own. It amplifies, combines, blends ... I was at a loss after my mate Saral ... but Roosal returned a semblance of joy. Then real joy as my heart opened. Then love. Greater than any I have known. No amount of magical research could have achieved the egg without that, I realize it now."

The way Calka and Roosal looked at each other ... I suddenly missed Thane with such a chest tearing pain, I had to turn away. Unfortunately, that put me face to face with Duane. He could see the tears welling, my mask dropped for a moment. I was a much greater wreck, even after six years, than I pretended with him, with everyone.

There is a type of love that overshadows all others. That changes your own soul. I'd had it with Thane. And he had given it to me again, with Dawn, but losing him had meant losing the greater part of myself.

I think Duane finally really saw that in my gaze, which was why he turned away this time around.

I found my composure. No good for the detective to show weakness. "That's beautiful," I told Calka. "Do you feel the same, Roosal?"

I knew that sometimes love could be one sided. I had known Thane's thoughts and his mine, so I had not had that worry, but could Avians read minds or souls? I had no idea.

Roosal, always the sweet enigmatic one, gave me a look that made me feel shame. I knew his answer before he said it: "Yes."

And I knew a dead end when I saw it.

"Time for our private chat, Kerrik." To Duane I whispered, "Stay here and see what you see in my absence."

"Leave the observation game to the master, Eva." He tried to sound light, joking, but I could tell the emotions running high among the Avians were disturbing him.

The Unmentionable led the way, taking me to one of many deserted rooms carved into the mountainside that led off the main courtyard and its circle of obelisks.

A stone door rolled aside for us then closed behind with a noisy sound of stone against stone and the deep finality of a tomb being sealed. Messing with an Unmentionable always ran the risk of putting one in their own grave—if there was anything left to bury.

Unmentionables were the boogeymen of bogeymen, not even myth to the younger races, but the stuff of legend to ancient Solhans. I'd been raised on nightmarish bedtime tales, and then I had met them. They were even more frightening in reality. I was brought to judgement before them because of my poor handling of things, of nearly destroying the world by falling into the Dead God's trap. Like I could have stopped any of that. I was really in trouble for not obeying their summons, for not jumping when they said to. And protecting the world had not been their true motivation, while retrieving the First Soul and its power for themselves was their real goal.

When I said 'they' I meant a score of unique and often ghastly creatures, each a survivor, each a powerful representation of their species. I trembled when I was first brought into their presence. Now, Kerrik was the one who trembled ever so slightly. Several of those Unmentionables were dead now, two of them by my hand.

"All this secrecy because of Duane? The other Avians seem to know what you are."

"They do not know everything, for they are too polite to ask," he said.

"Truly? You four can spend centuries together and never get curious? I'd have thought you'd know everyone's dirty little secrets."

"I do, for secrets are what we Unmentionables collect. The others respect Avian customs. Solitude, contemplation, privacy is their way."

"You almost speak as though you are no longer Avian yourself. The Unmentionables are just a glorified club."

"We are more than that. Harbinger grasped too much too soon, but Trickster showed you our ultimate aspirations."

"To become a god? Trickster was kicked out of your club for that."

"Not for that. For not sharing. But none of this is relevant to the here and now."

"I find it very relevant. You would turn on your own people for power because you are an

Unmentionable first. What power would stealing Calka's egg give you? Or did one of your wanna-be god buddies do it with your help?"

"There is no power in the egg, aside from the power to arrest the extinction of Avian-kind. Freed from the danger of the First Soul, of protecting this world from the Devourer, they were able to achieve new life, finally. I am happy for Calka and Roosal."

"Avians did a crap job of 'protecting' the world, although better than the Unmentionables," I had to point out. And the First Soul was still a danger, especially to me, but there was no need to share that with Kerrik if he didn't already know.

"Are you seeking praise for your role? The hammer does not expect gratitude from the carpenter."

"You calling me a brainless tool? So nasty. Not very Avian. You must be feeling especially inadequate.

"I feel nothing other than regret that the power of the First Soul could not be harnessed before you sent it away."

"I see. You're bitter. No godhood for you."

"All things are possible with time and patience, and I have an abundance of both."

"Very well. I will assume you have no need for the egg, but you never answered me about your Unmentionable friends."

"We are not friends, merely allies, and there are none I would steal for. We judge, we kill, as needed."

"And imprison. Where is Olyvandra?"

"That I do know, but I will not tell you. She betrayed us for you, and so she must be judged."

"I suppose if you did know an Unmentionable had stolen the egg, you couldn't tell me anyway. That would make you a traitor, right?"

He stayed quiet.

"What can you tell me?" I asked. Questioning the Avians was going nowhere, especially Kerrik, so I was keen to seek out some weaker links.

"I do not know who stole the egg. Like you, I have suspicions, some I cannot share for fear of judgement, but I can tell you it was not Calka. Protestations of maternal devotion aside, I am a creature of facts. I saw the egg was safe, as she and it were with me all morning before Calka was summoned to the Assembly."

"'With you' with you?" I raised my eyebrows, hoping he wasn't saying what I thought he was, not after Calka's beautiful speech about love.

"No, but I am unsurprised by your bestial suspicions. We were performing a channeling. Magic. She needed to borrow my power as is often the case."

I sighed, doubly relieved. My faith in love remained, and motherhood. I had not wanted to suspect her, not as a mother myself.

"What was this magic for?"

"You would not comprehend it, but it is most simply explained as 'protection'. The Dead God and

Lili of Solheim are gone, but more enemies remain on every front and even within our own borders."

"Any of those enemies with motive, means and opportunity?"

"Several. You do not need me to tell you who they are."

Once again, not much help, other than confirming my thinking. I didn't thank him. What would have been the point? Instead, I said, "Can you unseal this tomb now? I'm keen to converse with more lively company."

As the door rumbled open, and I found my own way, I mulled over what I had learned so far.

Naren had basically said the Avians were using the green goo's magic to aid their efforts to create an egg. While they didn't mind it being used up for that, someone else might. Quite a bit. Once again Doctor Ghunnan came to mind, with his goo research and general curiosity. While he might not have done the deed himself, his known associates weren't above trying to steal Crown property, or Crowns, namely Miss Kissel, a goblin spy and commando. Was the doctor being truthful when he said he no longer worked for his Emperor? Was he still sending reports? Or could they simply be watching him?

I tried not to betray my suspicions when I went to the goblin to retrieve the vial of truth serum he had prepared. I wanted to try it on him first, but using his scientific parlance, a 'control' was required. He was surprised when I drank the first vial myself. It tasted bitter and seemed to cling to my throat.

"Now, ask me something," I told him.

"Do you trust me?"

"No." But that would have been my answer no matter what. "Ask me something I won't want to reveal."

"How did you defeat the Dead God?"

"I didn't. I took command over Him, the power Lili of Solheim once possessed and which I claimed when I killed her. I sent Him away with the First Soul to save us all from the Devourer."

"I do hope I formulated the serum correctly, for that was all nonsense." He sniffed a few of his ingredients and checked the residue at the bottom of a flask. "It all seems to be in order ... you must deeply, delusionally believe these things you are saying."

"I do. Now, your turn."

"I'm afraid goblin physiology is such that the effects of a veracity serum are blunted."

"Let's try anyway." I poured a vial on his tongue myself so there could be no sleight of hand. I gave it a moment to take effect, and then asked, "Did you steal Calka's egg, aid anyone else in doing so, or are you aware in any way of who is guilty?"

"No. Isn't this fun?"

"Yes, actually. And frustrating. And terrifying. What's happening to Dawn while I'm trapped here? You have no idea what damage she can cause."

"Who is Dawn?"

"My daughter and possibly the next great danger to this world. Wait. How long does this serum last?" I belatedly asked.

"Several hours."

Oh crap.

I headed for the stairway, a pouch of the goblin's truth serum jingling against my hip. Mechanical legs whirred as he hurried to catch up. I wanted to avoid the Avians for now and instead get the serum down the throats of my next suspects before I started babbling all my secrets. At least we knew the serum worked.

I wasn't to be allowed to sneak away, however, as Calka and Duane were waiting for me on the obelisk platform.

"Mister Rose suggested we fly you to the Crown Assembly. That way everyone knows you are working with my authority."

I nodded, not daring to open my mouth and start telling her there was no Mister Rose, only Duane, as he had no last name that he could remember, his parents killed before he was old enough to talk. 'Rose' symbolized his aspirations, beloved, desired yet still dangerous, while to me it represented the fake ostentation of elvish flower gardens poorly hiding the jagged truth beneath. Yep. Better I didn't open my mouth.

Duane noticed my quiet as he stood beside me while the levitation rings the Avians used to counteract our weight were placed around our waists. Looked like Roosal was flying him down, and I got Calka. Very authoritative.

"What is it? What did you learn from Kerrik?" he asked.

"Nothing I didn't already know." I changed the subject. "I need Doctor Ghunnan also. Can Naren carry him?" I asked Roosal.

"Naren has already returned to work. I will carry the goblin as well, since he and Mister Rose will not want the attention Calka will bring you. I will deposit them in a more secluded location where they can join you shortly."

"Perfect." More time for the serum to wear off.

Unfortunately, Calka had to fix her hair or fluff her feathers, whatever, and don her tiara for this display, while Roosal took extra time to prepare the goblin, so Duane and I were standing around together longer than I would have liked.

"Do you have any new leads besides the Crowns with their keys to the sending scroll?" he asked me.

"Yes." I would try to keep from elaborating on my replies. "What about you? Did the Avians tell you anything in my absence?"

"Naren left right after you did. I don't think he's comfortable around Roosal and Calka. Odd, to have only four of your own kind left in the world and not being able to stand one another."

"I know what that's like. There are not many Solhans left either. Morgan dislikes my diplomatic association with elves, Nanny and I argue ceaselessly, Ilsa didn't survive me, neither did Erick, Viktor didn't survive himself, and Uncle Ulric won't even see me. I expected him to be here to greet me."

"Ulric has become a priest of the Dead God. The Avians cannot appear to support him because so many Citizens still hate the god for the war, despite His worship no longer being outlawed."

"But I know my uncle still comes here, using Avian power to keep tabs on that plant creature you all so unwisely bargained with."

"How do you know that?"

"I have spies." I pinched my lips shut then. Really wanting Calka to hurry it up. No one knew what a beautiful and regal looking Avian was supposed to look like anyway. She could wing it. "And I can't very well go to him." Why were my lips still moving? "I can't walk into that temple and gaze up at a larger-than-life statue of winged Death without it breaking my heart again. It never heals. It just keeps breaking over and over..."

Shut up, Eva!

I practically leapt onto Calka when she drew nearer. "Let's go!"

I thought I heard Duane say, "So does mine," before we were off, flying.

We descended through the cloud layer, trading sunshine for a dreary, overcast Highcrowne midday.

Roosal deposited Duane and the goblin near the garden shed. Seemed this section of the Central City never had visitors, so no one noticed them. They both headed on foot to the main palace where the Crown Assembly chamber was located. It would take them a few minutes, while Calka and I reached it in seconds.

There was an opening in the roof of the Assembly, so high up it was in mist, the bottom of the clouds that clung to Highcrowne's peak and which we had just passed through. I thought I had been privileged to enter the Assembly before, but only Avians had seen it from this height. I was a bit woozy, standing on a platform so high up that the people below were smaller than my pinkie nail.

"I knew they would all be here," Calka said. "They are curious to understand why I have sealed off the Central City."

Calka must have keener vision than me because I couldn't make out anyone's faces. I saw three people and assumed they must be the other Crowns. "How should we play this?"

"You are the detective. What do you propose?"

"Normally, I'd separate them so I can pitch them against one another, but I'm short on time and think I'll go for mass dosing with truth serum."

"I am urgent to reclaim my lost egg, but your urgency stems from something else. What is it?"

I didn't want her to know, but that damn serum was still coursing through my bloodstream.

"The First Soul dug its way into me when I wielded it—dug its way into Dawn when she was inside me. Before she was even born, she was corrupted by it. Her soul is still there, beautiful and innocent, but something darker is too. It whispers of power and lends her its own dark magic to sow discord. I can resist, but when I do not keep her asleep, she is open to its suggestions. I wandered the wastes of Darrub, slipping into villages only when she slept to gather supplies, ever since she destroyed a town with her infant cries. I sought out magical knowledge first in books, and then from cautious hermits, far flung sages, and finally in the long-lost writings found in never-visited ruins. I dared the dangers of Lyss…. I gained what I needed to control her, perhaps even free her of its influence soon, but I worry when we are separated for too long. What if the First Soul fights for control of her when I am not there to counter it? What will she do to Highcrowne if she listens to it?"

"I see now why you wanted to leave. If she is such a danger … then yes, I will lower the barrier so you can check in on her. Once the Crowns have been questioned."

"Good. Thank you." Maybe telling the truth wasn't always a bad thing?

"But how is the First Soul exerting its influence over her? I thought you sent it away with the Dead God?"

"I did. But the god is returning—because I called out to Him."

"What?"

The truth wasn't that great after all.

"There is no time for this," I said, trying not to reveal more. "It was a mistake, and I will fix it, but first things first." The goblin doctor was tentatively opening the Assembly door and peeking in with spectacles glinting in the torchlight. "Take me down."

Calka seemed to be at war with her worries, but worry for the egg superseded all others, and she flew me down to the dais. There were four thrones, but none of the Crowns were in them. They stood in a circle, speaking to one another in hushed tones which turned angry when they noticed the goblin.

"How did you get in here?" Queen Hilja demanded to know. "No one is allowed entrance."

I saw the doctor hide one of his mechanical lockpicking devices behind his back as he stepped further inside. "Apologies, but...."

"But..." Calka took over, her commanding voice echoing in the vast and empty chamber as she landed beside them. "...One of you has something to answer for."

Good start to the interrogation. Couldn't have done better myself. I removed the magical ring around my waist that made me light enough for an Avian to carry and pulled a vial out of my bag. I held it up to the light. "This is truth serum. You will drink it and answer my questions."

"What is the meaning of this, Eva?" Hilja seemed surprised to find me with Calka. "What is going on?"

"First. Each of you drink. Then we talk."

"Hand it over," General Moore said, quickly assessing the tactical situation and realizing it was simpler to just go along. King Harley followed his example, reaching for his own vial. They each downed theirs without complaint and without cheating. I'd been watching.

I was even more relieved when I realized Duane had crept into the room unnoticed, in that thief's way of his, and was observing too. He nodded to indicate they hadn't palmed the serum.

So, Hilja remained. I held out her vial. "Take it."

"No. Never."

"Then I will assume you are guilty and rend the meat from your bones with my own beak," Calka said.

"Wait a minute! Guilty of what?" Hilja was good at playing dumb, and it could all be an act. She had fooled her father and former fiancé for years. She was cleverer than all of us, save Calka I suspected.

"I command you..." Calka began, but she didn't get a chance to finish.

Duane had crept forward and took hold of Hilja, pinning her arms behind her back. "Give her the serum, Eva. You can't trust her to take it. Her glamour could fool even me."

I had seen elven glamour at work. Fharen's had been able to conceal the First Soul. If Hilja had a tenth of his power ... I strode forward and force fed the truth serum to her.

General Moore looked offended, but he kept shifting his gaze to Calka and followed the Avian's lead. Harley followed his lead, only saying, "That is no way to treat a lady."

Hilja glared daggers at me, especially since I might have chipped one of her teeth on the glass phial. Time to test it.

"Tell me what you think of me," I told her.

"You are a heartless Solhan witch who not only beguiled my father, just like your harlot of a sister did before you, only worse. Now, you have placed some hold over the Avians. I don't know what you are playing at, but I will not let you control Highcrowne or the Three Kingdoms. You can't be trusted."

"So, I'm not the sister you always wished you had? Someone to try dresses on with?"

"I hate dresses. And you." Hilja seemed as surprised by the things she was saying as the other Crowns were.

Good. It was working.

"All right," I said, my gaze darting to each of them in turn. "Which one of you stole, or helped to steal Queen Calka's egg?"

"Egg?" Harley looked really confused, and then his swarthy, dwarfish face lit up with joy. "You mean, like a baby? Avians are birds, I suppose. This is fantastic! I would love to see a baby Avian. They have to be precious. Once they get feathers. I saw a hatchling once that was actually kind of scary, with big, sightless eyes, and gray blue skin. Wait, stolen? That's horrible."

So, it wasn't him. I hadn't thought so.

"Wasn't me," General Moore said, curt and to the point. Where were his usual, rousing speeches? Seemed he saved them for the troops and Citizens.

"Or me," Hilja said, smug. "Although now I think it's clear what all this commotion is about."

Maybe I had phrased the question wrong? They could be unwitting accomplices. "Which of you summoned Queen Calka to the Assembly this morning then?"

"That was me," Moore said. "I wanted to talk to her about the democracy debate."

"Why weren't you here when I arrived?" Calka asked.

"There was an attack. An elven airship was downed before it reached the docks, crashing into the south tributary of the river, the section under supervision of my defensive forces. I suspect Darrub terrorists. I went to handle things as quietly as I could before the City Watch or elves got wind of humans being involved. Although, they would have accused us anyway, even if it weren't true."

Darrub terrorists. Aguragas. I knew where this was headed.

Duane and I exchanged looks. "Is Bell still with them?" I asked him. I couldn't keep things flying off my tongue any more than the others who had taken the serum. It was annoying.

"Yes."

"And I bet you know how to reach her."

"Yes."

"That's where we go next. But first," I turned to Calka. "Take down the barrier."

She nodded. "Search the ends of this world if you need to but find my egg. And protect your own."

"I will. I swear it."

Even More Evil

While Calka and the other three Avians were shredding the barrier with their talons— and it looked like messy magic, not the elegant way they had draped it over everything in the first place—I was running.

I knew we had left a trio of truth serum-dosed Crowns behind us, and yes there were questions I wished I'd asked, especially Hilja, while they were vulnerable, but I had the worst feeling about Dawn. I had to get to her quick. So, I headed for the dirigible I'd seen forced down in the rose gardens.

Do not get me started on the irony of speeding full tilt toward a mass of my most despised flowers and with the eponymous Duane, aka Mister Rose, by my side.

"I'll find you later," I told him for the umpteenth time.

"First, you said we needed to find Bell, and you need me for that. Now, you're off on some random tangent? And what did Calka mean by 'protect your own'?"

"As if you don't know everything, with your spies everywhere."

"Know what?"

I had no time to spar with him. The dirigible was just ahead and beginning to rise, as the barrier, which was more like shrink wrap for the Central City than a dome, pressing down on its balloon disintegrated.

"Wait!" I called out, but I didn't wait myself before scrambling up the rope net hanging off the side of the thing.

Part of me wondered why an airship had something made for nautical boats (Tradition? Were there airborne uses, like scraping jollups off the hull mid-flight?) but the greater part of me wondered what had possessed me. Rope nets were awful to climb, swaying, catching on my Ashur as I tried to hold it in one hand, and we were gaining altitude.

Duane climbed the net like he had wings, and it wasn't even there. He reached down for me when he was at the rail.

Old Eva would have slapped that hand away with a scowl, ignored it at least, but new Eva was wiser and more focused on what really mattered, so I took it.

I would not say 'thank you'. That was just going too far.

A bored sailor watched us as he coiled a rope around his arm. No one else seemed to notice we were there.

"Where's the captain?" I asked. The rope guy gestured to the big cabin with his chin.

I hadn't brought enough gold to bribe him, so I'd use intimidation to get him to drop me by the Outskirts. I banged on the cabin door.

A huge troll with tusks stuck his head out. Bodyguard? "What do you want?" he asked.

"Passage to the other side of the city. Please?" Intimidation didn't work with gralls or trolls.

"You have coin?"

"I..." I felt in my belt pouch, nothing but truth serum now. "A silver or two, maybe?"

Then the troll noticed Duane, who was hard to notice unless he wanted to be. "Shadow King. We're under attack!" he shouted, pulling out a massive scimitar he had stashed behind the cabin door.

More armed sailors emerged from below decks and the crew quarters, more than I swore the small boat could hold: Ferocious goblins with grinning mouths of teeth and no brains and thus no fear, plus several dwarves with suffragist red armbands, desperate looking humans with jaundiced skin and too much gold on display, as though their greed had colored them, and two more trolls. I thought they hated their own kind. Who heard of trolls working together?

"Trust you to find the one pirate ship in disguise daring to pass over Highcrowne proper," Duane hissed.

"And trust you to piss them off for no reason whatsoever!" I shot back.

"Oh, they have good reason to be angry with me." He pulled the blade from his cane.

I did the same with my Ashur.

Always cut off the head, was my motto. Not literally, but as in take out the leader first. Since trolls were almost impossible to kill, I did the next best thing and shoved the captain back into the cabin, locking him in.

When I say 'shoved' and 'locked' I mean in the sense of using magic to do it. I'm tough, thanks to my Solhan height, reflexes, and wiry strength, not to mention training since I was old enough to hold a sword, but no one is tough enough to take on a troll without a siege weapon.

Necromancy is the ability to talk to and manipulate souls, of the living or dead, but mostly dead. Solhan necromancy also lends itself to nasty curses that rot or necrotize the flesh of the living, so they become dead. It is not pretty, so I instead called on some more elegant Darrubian magic I'd picked up in my travels. A gust of wind, a conjured sylph that pulled planks from the ship and rearranged them into a barricade in front of the cabin door, before turning to the second troll and shoving it over the side. It was a long way down already, but the troll would probably survive.

The sylph had got overzealous and thrown itself overboard also, and was now outside my range, dissipating back into mindless wind.

I pulled off one of the knotted cords I wore around my wrist. It was woven horsehair, not some showy, glowing, Avian thing like Duane wore. I tossed the cord at the remaining troll, scoring when it caught on a tusk, and with an incantation, the cord enlarged itself enough to wrap around the troll's throat. Even trolls needed air. This one toppled to his knees. That put him at my height finally, so I gave him a kick to the head. It took a few more whacks from the head knocker on the pommel of my Ashur to knock him out.

It was an old habit, trying to knock out bad guys rather than killing them. Sure, murder was technically illegal in Highcrowne and punishable by death or imprisonment, but in reality few saw killing trolls as murder. Only elves, dwarves, Avians, and just recently humans counted on the list. Not sure if Solhans were on it yet.

The troll wasn't about to make it easy, fighting to regain consciousness, striking out with massive claws on pure instinct, making me leap and dodge. Another incantation and the cord around his throat dragged him over the side of the boat. I loved cord magic, and I got nostalgic, remembering the first time I'd seen Erick use it. He had been so mysterious, attractive. Had Thane been possessing him even then? I was sure he had to be. I sighed.

Only then did I realize that while I'd been happily fighting trolls, Duane had been fending off a few dozen more ordinary pirates by himself. Mostly by disarming opponents with a flick of the hidden rapier he carried, swinging about on ropes to avoid clubs and axes which were impossible to parry, and even scurrying up to the crow's nest to drop some heavy objects on people. I had no idea how he'd carried some cannonballs with him. He'd lost his top hat, his silk jacket was torn and sleeveless on one side, revealing lots of muscle, and his fancy shoes long gone. He wasn't injured, but he was looking winded, hair disheveled, a glint of fun and fire in his green eyes. I thought he looked much better this way. More the Duane I had grown up with.

I supposed I should help.

Magic on a mass scale was always tricky because anything powerful enough to affect so many was usually powerful enough to destroy an area around them too. I really didn't want to damage the airship which was keeping me from plummeting to the ground. As much skill as I had gained over the last six years, I still couldn't fly.

I had gotten very adept at putting Dawn to sleep, however. I grabbed the nearest pirate, a dwarf with a red armband over a tattoo of his mother with her eyes crossed out, and told him, "Sleep." He crumpled like a toddler.

I reached out to one after another, needing to parry a few sword strikes with my Ashur in the process, especially after they caught on. My other rule was 'take out the wizard first' even before the head bad guy, so I understood why I was their new target. I distracted them enough to allow Duane time to climb down and join the fray, wielding his rapier cane in one hand and a pirate's cutlass in the other.

He had never adopted the non-lethal method, and so everyone he faced died or at least lay unmoving on the deck with severe wounds to livers, lungs, and other vital organs. We met at the mast, a swathe of snoring cutthroats behind me and a mound of bleeding cut throats behind him.

It really had been too long since I'd had so much fun. I was just thinking I should go out with Duane more—probably some other weird side effect of the truth serum—when he made the mistake of speaking.

"I could use someone like you on my crew," he said.

"On your crew? Do I look like a petty thief? I will never work for you, Duane. Not if you offered me the Star of Darrub or a dragon's hoard."

"Never say never." He tucked a stray lock of hair behind one ear and winked.

The troll captain roared and splintered the cabin door as he tore free. "Oh yeah," I said. "We still have him to deal with."

I took control of the ship's defensive mangonel, spinning it around and skewering the troll before he made it across the deck. He fell back, eyes teary looking at the giant arrow poking through his heart.

I got teary eyed myself, remembering Thane, how he'd helped me kill my first troll by draining its soul. Too many romantic memories everywhere I went.

"I thought you didn't kill anymore?" Duane said.

"I'm hanging off the wagon with my feet dragging the ground, falling off now and then before climbing back on. Now, do you know how to drive an airship?"

Duane sheathed his sword. "No."

Why was I always getting myself into these situations? Back when Thane and I could read and reap souls, we were a dangerous duo, able to absorb anyone's life memories and put them to use. It had been a heady, god-like feeling. I missed it, even after all these years, and it was part of the reason Dawn and I were in the trouble we were in. Why had I opened the door to the Void? I'd like to say the First Soul was already
exerting its effects on us, blame it, but I knew the worst reason was how much I missed Thane, how much I missed true power.

Duane had always worried I was destined for the dark, and I'd hate to confirm it, so I fought against the truth serum as hard as I could and simply said, "Oh. I guess it's time we bail out then."

I managed to find a parachute. I was tempted to take it and go, but I kept looking until I found one for Duane also.

He'd been adjusting rigging while I searched and then tied the helm off after setting a new course. He knew more than he let on. He took the parachute I handed him then said, "I think this is headed out of the city where it won't do any damage in case it crashes. I'll send some people to recover it. I need more lessons. Never quite got to landing."

"You had airship lessons?"

"I do run the largest airship protectorate service in the Three Kingdoms."

"Putting it that way—now I'm more disappointed you didn't learn enough."

"I do my best. Or worst, as the case may be." There was that wink again.

I suddenly realized he'd distracted me. I was supposed to be terrified for Dawn, but there was something about Duane that always circumvented my reason, that led me to do foolish things. He blames me for freeing caged pixies and other live food from the markets when we were kids, for trying to help the downtrodden in my sappy way, but he'd been there encouraging me the whole time. Just like now. He could tell me I was crazy and an idiot. He did—but he should repeat it more, so I listened.

I did know how to use a parachute at least, so I readied it, and before diving over the side said, "Don't follow me this time."

Of course he did. I was steering my chute towards the unmistakable spires of the Outskirt's temple district, while really hoping I turned before getting skewered, when I noticed his chute paralleling mine.

"What!?" he called, air whipping the sound away. "I live in the same neighborhood you do."

I swooped to avoid the spire then landed at a run in the wide, cobbled street leading to Kali's bazaar, goblins, humans, and elves slumming it dashing out of my way. Duane went to a side street, so I hoped that meant I'd lost him. I didn't bother rolling up the chute but cut it loose to drift across the square and catch on someone's upper story. Then I ran to Nanny's house. My house.

Seemed the truth serum even worked on my thoughts, and there was no playing coy. The house was mine, Viktor gave it to me, and I would never let it go. Dawn needed a home, and I needed a safe place for those I loved. If anyplace could be called safe for the likes of us.

I avoided the bizarre bazaar and took the back stairs to the house. The dread only built as I drew nearer. I slammed open the kitchen door, expecting to see Nanny's perpetually boiling entrail soup in the cauldron over the fire, but there was no fire. The room was cold. Empty.

The sitting room was next. Silent. Empty. A darkness like starless night creeping in at the edges.

I tore up the stairs, fighting through suffocating dark, devoid of air, until I reached the guest room. Dawn had been a good girl and stayed as I'd told her, but curiosity killed more than cats—Kali was lying on the floor beside the bed. She was cocooned in a ball of shadow that left only the top of her head exposed, Nanny stood beside her, casting every protection spell she could remember, while Dawn sat cross-legged on the bed, looking down at Kali's inert form like a spider looked at the fly it was about to devour.

"What is that?" Duane asked, slipping in behind me.

There was no way he could have crossed my wards unless I had invited him, and I remembered I had put him on the short list of those granted admittance. Why had I done that? Some part of me must have wanted him here to witness something just like this—I could never explain without him seeing it for himself.

I felt Duane's shock. Despite all his spies, his knowledge of Dawn's parentage, he hadn't known about the First Soul. Good. Then there could still be secrets between us.

"Stay back," I warned. "Or you'll be next."

I stepped over Kali and sat beside Dawn, petting her hair.

"What is she?" Nanny hissed.

I ignored her. "Dawn, honey. Are you there? It's mama."

Spider Dawn was still, the cold seeping from her the same cold as the Void. So instead, I spoke to the First Soul.

"Oldest one, darkest one, beloved one," I whispered. "I have returned. Come to me. Release Dawn. Release Kali. Come to me." It was a chant, a song, a spell to draw the First Soul's attention to me.

Before, when it had been present on this world and not countless miles away through the Void, its power and attention had been overwhelming. Now, with just a tendril of its dark radiance enveloping us, the First Soul was still overwhelming. Like being drowned in a pool instead of an ocean.

Duane and Nanny fought to breathe. It was going for them too. It always did this, resisted what I asked. I wrapped Dawn in my arms and pulled the First Soul in with my will, repeating the words I'd sung in an endless whisper until I knew nothing but the words, nothing but Dawn and me, clutching one another against the cold, until the cold was inside us once more and no longer threatening the world of heat and light all around that was so foreign to us.

Dawn was asleep again. I ached at the sight. She was like an enchanted princess in a fairy tale, and I was the witch keeping her in perpetual slumber. I didn't want her like this forever, she needed a childhood. I wanted her to be free.

I should attempt the Lyssian ritual soon. There was no other choice. But I needed Avian magic. That meant I needed the egg.

"I forgot to search that pirate ship!" I told Duane. "What if they were sneaking off with Calka's egg? None of them looked like masterminds, but maybe they were working for someone else? I suppose if I find the motive I'll find the head bad guy, so it doesn't matter."

I scowled when Duane put a hand on my shoulder to quiet me. "You're babbling, Eva. What is going on here? Really?"

"Just another detective case. Can you show me to Bell now? That's all the help I need from you, and then you can be done with this."

He stubbornly refused to change the subject. "I thought your daughter in danger because she's King Fharen's—"

"—No. She's Thane's. Mine. That's what matters."

"But this darkness ...This cold. I remember it... Is it the First Soul?" I had never heard him so afraid before.

"The First Soul is far away, but not yet swallowed by the Devourer. Their cat and mouse game continues. It's coming back unless I sever its tie to us. I need Calka's egg to do that."

"Did you steal it?"

"What? No. But I need all the power I can get, and the Avians are all too distracted until I get their one hope for the continued existence of their species back. And as you can see—the sooner the better."

Kali coughed as she climbed to her feet, and Nanny sunk back into a chair, rocking herself as she watched Dawn. I had never seen Nanny so afraid either. The First Soul had that effect on people.

"What did you do to distress Dawn? Why did this happen?" I asked Kali.

"I just wanted to take her outside."

"I told you, no, and Dawn clearly did as well. Were you trying to steal her? To sell to Hilja's agents and bypass me?"

Kali darted a look at Duane.

"Were you in on this?" I confronted him.

"No." He always feigned innocence so well. Could I believe him? "Kali doesn't work for me—she works for Bell."

That made sense.

"So, you and Bell are back together?" I asked Kali.

"We never parted. She's my love. I'd do anything for her."

"Including work with that terrorist, Aguragas. Get out of my house."

"You said," she argued.

"I said this was Nanny's house. She's always welcome here, but you are not. I remove you from the protection of my wards. Go."

I spoke to the magic I had infused into the house, not her, because she looked too stubborn to move. Maybe she wanted to argue Bell's side, maybe she wanted to call me an elf loving Solhan devil, whatever it was, I didn't give her the chance. The wards took over, and she vanished.

Nanny looked strangled. "Where did she go? Did you disintegrate her?"

"I wish. No, she's out on the street somewhere. Disintegration kicks in when someone openly attacks me or Dawn. Or just pisses me off too much." I gave Duane a dangerous look.

"I'm on your side, Eva."

"You don't even know what my side is."

"Only because you won't tell me what's happening to you."

He was right. But I couldn't tell him the First Soul was coming back because of my mistake, because I had called out to Thane. There was so much I couldn't tell. Especially not him.

And I couldn't trust anyone.

"I'll see you outside, Duane. Now, go." The wards vanished him too.

I looked at Nanny and part of me wondered if it was weakness to allow her to stay. Someone had to feed and care for Dawn when she woke, however. I took the fire poker from beside the fireplace, after first coating its tip with ash.

Nanny's eyes went wide as I drew near. Too much the Solhan necromancer she had always wanted me to be. Be careful what you wish for.

She didn't try to stop me when I wrote runes on her arm with ash or whispered the incantation that sunk them into her skin, into her soul. This was like the slave mark used to subdue whole bloodlines to the will of their masters, but my mark was slightly different. Nanny would only obey me.

"Stay in this house and keep Dawn safe."

"Yes, mistress."

I found Duane leaning against a lamppost on the corner of my street. He looked very annoyed.

"That was not an enjoyable experience."

"Wards are supposed to keep people away. You never want to go back to my place now do you?"

"Never say never."

Maybe I needed to make the warding even more unpleasant. I'd adjust it later.

"It won't help that Kali went through that too," he said. "You have her offside now. A disadvantage when speaking to Bell."

"I won't be speaking to Bell. I'll be questioning her."

"You have changed. It's not just the kid." He seemed uncomfortable at the thought of me being a mother, not the girl he had known, but there was more. "I thought you were the same brash rebel clomping about and causing trouble, but you've got a working brain in there."

"Do you really want to piss me off? Because that ward is the one I use for my friends. I have less pleasant spells for my enemies."

He smiled. "Now, you're just trying to derail me, making me think you are still you, with your easy threats and anger barely held in check."

"That part is definitely true."

"No. It's not. You're scared."

Duane knew me better than anyone living, but he was no soul reader.

"It's never just fear, Duane. It's anger, self-hatred, fear, hatred of others, love, desperate love, fear for your own child which you can't comprehend—"

"—I have Vikky."

"Maybe you know a little, but it's not the same. You have no idea how dangerous this cocktail of emotions makes me," I told him.

"Or what you've learned while you were away," he finished for me. "You are more cunning. And you are using the intelligence I always knew you had. I'm starting to fear you may almost be one step ahead of me."

"Only one?"

"I said 'almost'. More like half a step. You don't get to be the Shadow King without seeing your enemies' actions laid out on the board, every move and countermeasure they will take."

"You sure like to make titles for yourself, 'Shadow King'. What's next? 'Court Jester'? What about your friends' actions? Enemies I find predictable, but friends can surprise you."

"There are no friends in the game. Only enemies, pawns, and would be enemies."

"So, how can you ever be on my side?"

"There are shared enemies. Factors that can create allies, for a time."

"For a time. So, allies always end up as enemies?"

"Look at Bell and Kali. They were your friends once."

"They still are. That's where I haven't changed, Duane. You are on my side because of our shared history, your vow to my brother. I am on no one's side but my own, but that doesn't mean my friends stop being my friends, even when we are enemies for a time. I am a complex creature."

"Ok, maybe only one quarter of a step ahead of me. Friends are trouble."

Feelings too. I knew what he really wanted, his weaknesses, as much as he tried to hide them behind his tough exterior. It was when his enemies learned them that I worried for him.

"Bell. Now." I reminded him. Someone had to keep us on track and not pondering our navels forever.

"This way." He headed for one of the narrow alleys off the bazaar, one so darkened by overhanging window boxes and crisscrossing clotheslines that soggy laundry refused to dry in the minimal sunlight.

Not the type of place I'd have thought to find Bell. Then again, her old workshop had been buried in a junkyard to hide it and provide material for her gadgetry.

Duane whistled, and two gutter rats shimmied down from an upper story. I didn't mean 'gutter rats' in an entirely dismissive way, it was more descriptive, as they were scrawny and hairy as rats and used the rain gutters as a ladder. They were twins, identical in every detail, down to the same stains on their clothing. I blinked, wondering if the serum was now making me see double.

They even spoke as one. "Boss." They bowed in an equally gangly way that was almost creepy. I began to wonder if they were being puppeted by that alien plant thing my uncle and Duane had made a dark deal with. I shivered.

"You are to escort Miss Eva Thorne," Duane said, and he spoke in such a commanding, proper voice I shivered again. Was the cold underworld leader the mask or the rakish flirt he showed me? I thought I knew, but in that moment I doubted.

"Where to, boss?"

"The Upside Down headquarters."

The twins suddenly went skittish, putting their greasy heads together and whispering in a secret language of their own.

"You will need this," Duane told me as he handed me one of his bracelets, not Avian, but something made of copper wire.

"What is it?" I asked.

The creepy twins looked suddenly hungry to hold it, twitching their fingers, reaching out and pulling away, so it must be valuable somehow.

"My marker. The only one Bell was willing to give me, what I was owed for all I did before she turned on me and ran to Aguragas. Markers are favors, and this one is now yours." He fastened it around my wrist.

"Bell owes me already—I did invest in her crazy schemes. Plus, it would be dangerous for her not to do as I ask."

"I like this new, threatening tone in your voice, Eva: less bluster and more real danger. But you will need this. She's changed as much as you, and this has been the only thing keeping her from trying to kill me with one of her mindless automatons."

"Then you keep it. You need it more."

"I said she would try to kill me, not that she'd succeed. Aguragas is another matter. If we face one another, one of us will die, and it is best not to risk that. I assume you still want us both for questioning?"

"Tempting. I would like to see Aguragas dead. You sure you can't come?"

"Missing me already?"

"Yes." Damn truth serum. "Who else is so easy to pick on?"

"I'll see you later." He went to tip his hat and stopped, forgetting he'd lost it in the pirate fight, and turned the gesture into a salute.

I watched him go, finery torn and hair hanging over one eye, and it seemed like no time had passed. I felt like the little girl who wanted to go chasing after him to find a new adventure. I fought the feeling and focused on my new 'friends'.

"Milady," the twins said, indicating a wheelbarrow half filled with junk.

"You want me to sit in there?"

"If you please."

"No."

"It's a bit of a trip and it's best if no one sees you visiting. Best if no one sees us, as we don't have that shiny trinket the boss gave you to keep us safe, so only way we're getting close enough to show your marker to the Upside Downs is if we pretend to be tinkerers."

"You just made up this cover?" I asked, impressed.

"We are tinkerers—to most who see us around the city. They know no different. Must be why boss chose us. We are so honored. So honored, Miss Thorne." They gestured again, and I reluctantly climbed into the wheelbarrow.

I regretted it when an oily cloth was thrown over me. I could only make out a few shapes and colors and movement through frayed patches. I saw there was another wheelbarrow with another identical cloth covering. Then they set off, and I suddenly disliked this ruse even more. Cobblestones were bumpy, and being jostled against rusty, sharp, and broken pieces of metal and machinery was a lot less enjoyable than my unenjoyable airship ride had been.

I began to think my twin escorts were mindless automatons themselves, or plant possessed for sure—that idea had yet to be disproven—the way they moved through the city in a synchronized dance of deception. If anyone was trailing us, they'd be confused as one twin headed one direction with his wheelbarrow of broken parts, and my wheelbarrow went another, only to meet up here and there and trade places in a three-dimensional shell game.

I missed Grim and Gormless. And the good old days of just waltzing into enemy territory and fighting it out. All this subterfuge was no fun at all. Okay, a little bit fun.

It was a long trip. We went out past the stage line, and I was added to a pile of junk in a larger wagon, which the two of them climbed aboard side by side. I still wasn't allowed to show myself, so I had to peek through slats in the wooden sideboards to see where we were going. We were on a dirt track, a shortcut between the coach line and the train line, which only highwaymen were likely to use. I thought cobblestones were bumpy, but this was worse.

Then there was no road. We stopped where the cliffs rose high above the Serpent's Ribbon, an impassable section of river that also served as defense for Highcrowne. When Lili of Solheim's army had attacked, they'd been forced to use boats, as the riverbank along this stretch was impassable to all but werewolves whose claws could cut handholds in stone.

I couldn't help remembering Thane and I on that river. Our boat drifting on the water like it was another world that belonged to just the two of us. Yes, we were on the run from the aforementioned army of werewolves and liches—but it was the best time of my life.

"Sorry," I suddenly asked the twins, as they helped me out of the wagon of junk. "What's your names?"

"We're Sten."

"You both have the same name?"

"Yes. Short for Stendarion, the famous elven hunter. Our mother loved elvish stories. She read to us before bed every night after she got home from washing sheets at the laundry. Her hands were chapped, red, when she opened that book and read to us by candlelight. She looked ready to sleep herself but kept going until we dozed off. Sometimes I did see her sleeping in the chair beside us rather than her roll on the floor. She always gave us the one bed. Then the war came when we were twelve. They hung her as an elf-loving traitor. Bell and her humans-first rabble did it."

"I'm sorry." I was. The whole war felt like my fault. I was born to bring the Dead God into the world, to enable Lili of Solheim to reign over a dead world. I stopped her, but not before so much damage was done. So many people hurt. Killed. Changed.

The twins glared at the cliffs. "Kill Mistress Bell if you ever get the chance. She's in there."

"In where?"

"There's a hidden entrance. Look for a crack in the rockface. We've seen people come out, but never get closer than this ourselves." They dumped the wagon of junk and lifted a stone beside the track. There was a small pouch of coins inside, which one of the Stens pocketed. Payment for the junk delivery, likely parts for Bell's automaton work.

"Thank you," I said, waving as they rumbled away in their rickety tinkers' wagon.

I stared at the cliff, layers of sediment full of grooves and cracks, searching for where to start. I headed for a dark crevasse at ground height and knew it was the right one when an automaton stepped out and pointed at me.

It was brass, human in shape, no hair though, and eyes that glowed green. I thought it was pointing a finger at me until I realized its hand was a cone. One of those blunderbuss guns that turned flammable powders into propellant for balls of lead. I'd seen them tear through people more messily and noisily than a crossbow bolt. Bandits in the South felt powerful wielding one of those—until they realized they'd crossed a necromancer and that their one shot, poorly aimed, only pissed said necromancer off, and they were usually dead before they got a chance to reload.

I hadn't killed in front of Duane. I'd tried to keep up the pretense that I was old Eva, but he was catching on. Soon Bell would too.

And we would come head-to-head. I was the ultimate elf lover, having born Fharen's child. Bell would want me dead as much as Duane.

How best to approach this?

I had changed, focused on bigger things, but it didn't mean I didn't still bumble my way through a detective case. It was part of the fun.

And this search for Calka's egg was just a distraction. Important for Avians and Highcrowne, but insignificant in the grander scheme. I needed Avian magic, but what I needed even more was the willpower to complete the ritual and sever my and Dawn's ties to the First Soul—to Thane. That meant giving up on him, on us, on what we'd had.

Much more fun to face down an angry blond with pigtails who had bombs hanging out her pockets and dynamite in the fridge.

At least, that's how I remembered Bell. The Bell that stepped out and stood beside her automaton was another beast entirely.

Friends, Enemies, and the Real Enemy

B ell was still short but far from perky. Her pigtails were gone, replaced by a frenzied array of dirty blonde dreadlocks sticking out between patches of shaved skull. She wore an eyepatch, which made her look like a pirate. Any good mage could create an artificial eye, so maybe she wanted to look like a pirate. That explained all the black leather and knives on display.

"You're trying too hard," I told her.

"Excuse me?"

"To look tough. The most frightening person I ever met looked as dull and ordinary as the priest of the Sun Temple's second cousin. The next scariest person on the list liked pink bunny toys, and the third, well he's not at all scary to me but makes plenty of others tremble at his name."

"Which one of those was the Dead God?"

"None. I was never scared of Him—more tempted."

"So, you didn't defeat him, Miss Savior of Highcrowne?"

"Been reading Doctor Ghunnan's historical propaganda have you?"

"I was there when the Crown Assembly celebrated your glorious return."

"Then you probably remember I asked for human freedom. And they granted it. So, why are you sore? All dark and broody like a wannabe Solhan teen? Aren't you a bit long in the tooth for that?"

"I'm only twenty-two."

"Way too young to be so upset. Murdering Sten's poor mother? Plastering graffiti over Karolyne's café? Letting dwarves suffer in camps? Now I hear you and Aguragas run the local terrorist cell that stole something from the Avians which they very much want back."

"Who's Sten? Doesn't matter. What we stole from the Avians is ours. Takers keepers."

Well, well, well. Was the egg here? I doubted it, really. Bell probably stole something else, was guilty of something, many somethings no doubt, but it didn't mean I couldn't shake loose information that might lead to the real culprit. I was sure Aguragas told her nothing about what he was truly up to.

"Avians are kind-hearted, enigmatic creatures," I explained. "Part of being immortal, I think. We must all be like puppies to them, running around biting each other and chewing on things, making a general mess. I think we're more like vicious, homicidal puppies, but that's my perspective. Point is, we're insignificant and kind of cute to them, so Avians tolerate a lot. They've just turned intolerant. And if they start adopting my perspective on things, they're likely to rain down destruction on us or at least toss us out of their house. You get my meaning?"

"What's suddenly got them all worked up?" Bell sounded flippant and obviously did not get the full depth of my meaning.

"You tell me. Better yet, let Aguragas tell me. I want to see him."

"He doesn't just hand out audiences to any vagrant tossed here in the junk heap. He's very important, and he's—"

"—Eva," Aguragas said, stepping out of the shadowed crevasse behind her. He put a hand on Bell's shoulder to calm her. She was looking very tense and angry, but there was more to it, an intimacy. Wonder what Kali thought of that?

"Gas," I said by way of hello to one of my most hated acquaintances.

"So nice of you to visit after so long. How was Darrub?"

"Better than expected, probably because they drove your family out a generation ago. Lovely, talented people with a genuine warmth when you get to know them. Not at all like you, so I understand why you're no longer welcome there."

"I don't have to be welcomed to rule them, and I will someday. Mark my words."

"If Highcrowne is your recruiting ground, I wouldn't be too sure. You've attracted," I emphasized the word, "the likes of Bell and Kali and others, uniting them with a shared hatred of elves, but hate only goes so far. You'll never get them to march to war with you."

"That's the messiest and most foolish way to take a kingdom. Far better to sow fear and distrust, erode it from within, until there is nothing but me left to rise from the ashes and show the shaken masses where to bow."

"And you really think that will be easier here in Highcrowne than in Darrub, don't you? This isn't just your recruiting and training ground but the first domino on your path to empire. I see. Trouble is, you're not the only one playing that game. The elves will win."

"Elf lover." Bell spat. If she'd had a bit more thrust behind it, it would have hit me in the face but landed at my feet. Even so I didn't like that drop I saw on my boot.

It took the greatest effort of will not to snap. Snap her in two. Aguragas too. End his violent dreams right here with a taste of true violence, with fear in his eyes.... That was the First Soul. I had calmed the tendril of it in Dawn, but a tendril tied me to it as well. Across vast stretches of space, its darkness was deeper than Void, and it spoke to me of power and hate and destruction.

That tendril of darkness whipped out, a living shadow swirled around Bell's boots, which were trying to look as tough as her with their black leather and buckles, but in a moment, she was on the ground, the shadow wrapping itself around her like a python.

I saw Kali then. She had crept out to watch, and I thought she would yell and fight me, but there was only terror. She had been cocooned in that same shadow herself a short time ago. It was hopeless, soul-sucking. She couldn't fight it. Bell couldn't fight it. Not even I ....

The look of desire on Gas's face squashed the anger in me. He was getting off on this. Power was like musk to him, and I suddenly hated myself for doing anything he would approve of. I felt sick.

The shadow dissipated, but I pretended I had control of it and did not let the self-disgust tinge my voice when I said, "Now, Gas. How about us grownups have a few moments? Why don't you show me around?

Or am I to remain here on your doorstep like a travelling salesman you fear to let in? What could I possibly sell you that you don't want?"

"I have always wanted you, Eva." Very turned on. I felt a ball of vomit in my lower throat but choked it down. He gestured for me to follow him, and I stepped over Bell and brushed by Kali on my way.

I could sense Gas wanting to take my hand, caress my shoulder as he had Bell's, but he knew me well enough not to try.

Aguragas was beautiful in the way a viper was. A sleek, perfect specimen, skin dark as night while mine was pale as moonlight. His white hair was tied in a sleek ponytail, while my sable tresses tumbled crazily over my shoulders. He was my opposite in every way. He killed for power, while power compelled me to kill.

The crevasse in the cliff zig zagged before opening up into a small cave. This is where the guards were, more toughened-looking rebel fighters with their dirty leathers, scars, and sharp weapons at the ready. They glared like they hated the world, and I was the world come to call. Puppies. I understood Avians better than humans sometimes.

A thick metal door had been set into the cave wall, and a soldier removed the bar at a gesture from Gas, allowing us both to pass. There was a mixture of that rebellious glare at war with adoration in the gate guard's face. One of Gas's converts, no doubt, willing to blow themselves up for him fighting elves or Darrubians he had never met.

Once through the door I saw there was a honeycomb of natural caves, most widened or connected with human made tunnels. The stone of the cliff looked like it was full of interconnected air bubbles, and some of those bubbles had popped, revealing windows to the outside that looked down on the river far below. I supposed they could escape by rappelling down if needed, or reach boats on the river that way, docked pirate airships even. Good way for an Avian to attack too, not that they'd risk themselves on a frontal assault. If they had to, they could command dwarven werewolves or EEPs to do it for them.

I was surprised this terrorist cell hadn't already been attacked. Duane and his cronies knew about it, so the Crowns had to also. Was there benefit to someone allowing Gas to sow discord? Benefit to elves maybe? Probably. They were just itching to start outright war with one another. Captured humans could be magically marked and turned into obedient slaves, so let them come, Hilja or at least her frienemies thought, I was sure.

I heard sounds of fighters training in other caves, unified shouts about 'elven scum', the clatter of dishes where the cafeteria must be, but Gas steered me to his 'office' a perch looking down on the river with some knives and other weapons hanging from hooks on the walls. He had a desk and a chair, but there was no paper, no letters, just a brazier with a lot of burnt scraps of parchment. Very clandestine.

"Are those pigeons?" I asked, noting an adjoining cave with several cages and the cooing of birds.

"Messengers."

"Ah." While the rest of civilized Highcrowne communicated long distance through linked scrolls, fire sendings, and other magical means, humans used birds. Figured. I should let King Harley know Highcrowne would strike an easy blow against the insurgents if his werewolves simply developed a taste for carrier pigeon.

"I don't have what you're looking for," Gas said, sitting behind his empty desk.

"You brought me all this way just to show off your pigeons then?"

"I have something else you'll want." He showed me Calka's coin. The death mark I'd returned to him. Giving it back had pissed him off, which led to Conrad's death. Conrad was all my fault, but Gas had a real role to play in that, and I would never forget.

"I'd prefer to see your face stamped on that piece of silver. I'd happily seek that bounty. But I'm no assassin, and even if I was, I'd never touch an Avian."

"They are a dying race, what harm in hastening their inevitable end? They are the ones who prop up the rule of the Crowns, who allow the elves to enslave our kind."

"Your kind. Solhans are not as human as we look, and I know you were a slaver, Gas, so don't give me the high-minded drivel you use to brainwash the likes of Bell. The Avians are the only real power left, the only ones who could stand in the way of your dream of empire. That's why you want them gone."

"I can't hide anything from you, we're two sides of the same coin." He flipped the death marker and this time I noticed the Avian face etched on the other side had its eyes scratched out. When I'd held the coin before, I hadn't realized one side was Calka and the other her old mate, Saral.

"Let me guess, someone took your offer after I threw the coin in your face. They killed Calka's mate but never managed to get to her. That's why you need me, or Duane. We've been closer to the Avians than the Assembly."

"Thank you for confirming."

"And" I continued, to keep him from thinking he'd scored any victory against me, "that means you can't possibly have what I'm looking for. It would have been harder to steal than Calka's life."

His dark eyes locked on me. "I'm intrigued. Tell me more."

I'd hoped he would be. Aguragas had more resources than me or even Duane. The Shadow King was a force to be reckoned with in Highcrowne, maybe even the entire Three Kingdoms, but the last of the royal line of Darrub had loyalists from Ilul Faellion to Kell.

"It's not worth wasting any more breath on you. You don't have what I need, so I'll be going." I stood up, and I knew he was hooked when he grabbed my wrist.

"You didn't ask me why I thought you'd want the coin." Here was the evil smile I knew so well, the one he probably wore when torturing kittens or whatever he did for fun.

"You're right. I didn't." I pulled free and strode out of his office. He darted up to me and, in that deadly quick way he had, pulled me into an alcove that looked out on the river. Highcrowne autumn meant winds tore down the Serpent's Ribbon from the ice fields of the north, and a particularly chill blast tossed my hair around and made me cinch my jacket tighter.

"I know why you came back. What you keep in that trunk you had Kali fetch for you," he said.

"Because Kali told you. Don't go there. I warn you."

He raised his hands innocently. "It doesn't matter. I'm good at keeping secrets. I'm just saying that family is clearly important to you, friends too. A weakness I am glad I lack. I happen to hold the fate of several of your friends in my hands. It took time and patience, but I have a way of seeing Gypsum released."

"She betrayed me. You've got to do better than that."

"I can also free Karolyne."

"Karo? What's happened to her?" Last I knew she'd been rebuilding her life. None of my own inform-ants had said anything about her being missing—oh, this had to be new. Gas had taken her as soon as he discovered I'd returned. Simple blackmail. Predictable and easy enough to deal with.

"Nothing will happen to her for now. But she will feel pain if you don't take Calka's head. More pain than I could ever inflict. You see, your sister has her, or she will once the sun sets."

"Ilsa." Now I was surprised and, for the first time in a long time, frightened for someone besides Dawn. Karo did not deserve my sister's attention.

"I'm not giving you Calka's head, but if you help me retrieve what was stolen from her, I'll give you that instead. Believe me, it's a far better deal."

"What was stolen?"

"The future of the Avian race. Where did you think all the green goo had gone?"

SWEET LIES

The best lies were half-truths, even better three-quarter truths. I convinced Aguragas the Avians had been toiling for centuries, creating a magical working of which the green goo was an integral part, as was Ulric's Solhan necromancy, which explained why Duane, and then I, was given access—all to resurrect the thousands of Avians who had died over the millennia. They were entombed atop Highcrowne's peak, mummified, awaiting power only one of the Nine, one of those who had helped bring the Dead God into the world, could wield to resurrect them.

It was all nonsense. Liches, shambling mummies, and risen were all possible for the likes of Ulric to create, but not true resurrection. That's where this 'mystical orb' created from Avian goo came into it. I should really write my own dime novels. Gas was rapt, listening, clearly terrified at the thought of not a dying Avian race but a reborn one, a race of powerful immortals at that, who would reshape this world in the wake of Lili of Solheim's great war.

He was trembling in his boots and might have even peed himself a little.

"You see how this is far more important than Calka," I said. "I don't want them to die off, but I'm not sure I want Avians becoming a new pantheon of living gods to deal with either. Look what one god did to us? Can you help me find this orb? It's been attuned with Solhan necromancy but shielded against me. If I could hold it, I could undo the magical working. I'm sure of it."

"Shouldn't we destroy it?"

"And risk merely setting it off? I understand they were done. It was ready, so someone who was just as afraid of what it could do as me took it before that happened. I'm working on my suspects, Crowns, Duane, Ulric, and the goblin, but I don't think it was any of them. There's an external factor at work here. An unknown player."

"I can't believe ... I didn't know."

"Few did. That should make the hunt simpler." Fooling him was just too easy.

"Yes. I'll get started now...."

"Wait." I touched his arm this time, pretending vulnerability, pretending I was as scared as he was. "Can you please get Karo to safety at least? I can't focus while worrying about her."

"I—" The pause was too long.

"What?"

"I gave her to Ilsa, figuring you wouldn't do as I asked, or if you did, I'd kill Karolyne anyway."

"You bastard. I should just set that e..." I almost said 'egg', "...orb off. Perhaps I can attune from a distance...."

"Wait! I'll send Bell and Kali to get her back, whoever else I can spare."

"Ilsa will eat them for a midnight snack. Literally. I'll go. Where is she? Where is my sister?"

"I worked through a broker."

"Who is this broker?"

"Another friend of yours. You see, getting her free from prison would be no effort on my part, and the bargain I made with her for that freedom was that she was to turn her extensive connections to my purposes. Handing Karolyne over to Ilsa was a test of her loyalty to me."

"Gypsum is a traitor. Loyal to no one."

"You'd best hope you're right. Hope that Gypsum betrayed me and spared your other friend. If you're wrong, then take your ire out on her. Kill her if you want. I will ensure her guards look the other way. Do what you must, but soon, for this orb is what we need to focus on."

"There is no 'we'. But I agree. I'll return to the search as soon as I can."

As much as I didn't want to see Gypsum, even less did I want to question my next major suspect about the stolen egg. I'd been avoiding him in every way imaginable, but soon it would be truth time.

Bell was the one waiting to escort me out of the hidden Upside Down terrorist base. She was extra unhappy looking now that a tendril of the First Soul had touched her. She was brave, though, to face me again after that. Kali had been more wary.

I missed Bell's enthusiasm and nerdy preoccupation with all things mechanical. She seemed aged now, dark circles under her eyes, a constant scowl adding lines to her face, and her only preoccupation was the dagger she waved languidly in front of me, like it was something living and looking for its next victim.

I held up my wrist and showed her the copper bracelet Duane had given me. "Point that thing somewhere else. Besides, Gas and I are allies for the moment."

"For the moment."

"Not surprised, I see. Eavesdropping were you?"

She showed me some metal box and with a flip of a switch I heard Aguragas in his office, whispering angrily to himself about Avians and Solhans and damned necromancy. Seemed she still liked gadgets.

"I'm sure Gas won't like it if he finds out you're spying on him."

"He knows. He only speaks to people in his office when he wants me to overhear. Saves him needing to repeat himself."

"Clever. I can find my own way to Gypsum. Why don't you join the search for the Avian orb?"

"Do I make you uncomfortable?"

"Sad, really. Remember when I bankrolled your whole automaton operation, back when the dream was helping this city, not destroying it?"

"You destroyed it. You and your lover, Fharen."

It was way too complicated to explain Thane. But for Bell I had to try.

"Necromancers know about souls. Fharen's soul was not in control of his body when I was with him. Sure, up until that point he'd done all sorts of horrible things to humans and dwarves and was a complete asshole. Totally agree. But after another soul, who I happen to love very much, took over, I got 'Fharen' to defend this city, hand his crown over to Hilja, and set the scene for humans being granted Citizenship. I really should be getting a medal."

"I hear you got a mural and a statue."

"There's a statue somewhere?"

"Which you don't deserve. Hilja is no better. Nothing has changed. Elves still hold slaves in Faellion, and while they may call us Citizens here, they treat us no different from slaves. Humans are smarter, more creative, while the elves are holding back progress. We deserve to run things. The old should die and make way for the new."

"With that attitude I don't suspect you'll be helping any old ladies cross the street soon. And what about the dwarves? What did they ever do?"

"All the old races and the Crowns are complicit. Not to mention the dwarves served that Solhan lich, the one who obliterated all the human kingdoms. Solhan, like you, right?"

And that Solhan lich was my mother. I'm sure I hadn't let too many people know that. Hilja. Duane. Doctor Ghunnan. Nanny. Kali had been there, had she overheard? Maybe too many people knew. Still, I wasn't going to bring it up now. Bad time.

"I guess once you give racism free rein there's no end to it. What about short humans versus tall humans? Maybe those with dark skin are superior, like Gas? Or is it blondes like you? Where does it end, and who decides?"

"I decide. And I've decided I despise you, Eva. And Duane and everyone who aids you."

"Kali helped me out the other day."

"She was following my orders."

"Do you order your lovers around now?"

"I don't have to explain myself to you."

"No. You don't have to talk to me either. I already said you can go. Now, shoo."

She really glared at me for dismissing her.

Not a good time to ask for my share of the money from the automaton investment. I didn't think she would pay up.

We were at the exit, so I waved bye and strolled back out to the junk pile the twins had left. I should have told them to wait right here. I didn't want Bell riding up in an auto carriage or some even more bizarre contraption and feeling all superior, making me ask for her help, so I whistled.

Roosal himself alighted next to me.

"I thought the Stens would have been hanging back within earshot." I knew Duane would never leave me totally alone. "Isn't it dangerous for you to be here, Roosal?"

Maybe it wasn't common knowledge among Avians that Aguragas and the Upside Downs wanted them dead. I lost track of who knew what sometimes. I needed a system.

"Queen Calka thought you could use our support for your investigation."

"I do need a ride. And something that will get me into Northcliff Prison, no questions asked."

"That I can arrange."

Roosal deposited me at the front gate and left me with a shiny piece of green glass, one of the trinkets Avians valued. I was hoping for an official looking writ with gold seals and ribbons, but the glass seemed to work when I flashed it at the prison guards and to the warden inside.

"What an honor to have a visit from an Avian representative, and the famed Eva Thorne as well," the warden said.

"I'm famed? What have you heard? Never mind. I need to see Gypsum."

"The Traitor. Of course. Whatever you require."

The warden was an elf but unnervingly friendly and accommodating.

I didn't see any dwarfish guards like the last time I was here and no humans either. Seemed they wanted only hardliners watching over the dangerous prisoners. How was Gas so confident he could get her out of here? Surely, no elf, even a strangely obsequious one like this, would be foolish enough to work for him?

The fact that Gypsum was a 'broker' and somehow in communication with Ilsa and others, while in prison, showed how corrupt the system was.

I raised an eyebrow when the warden held out his hand. I was not bribing anyone. I drew my Ashur instead. "And I'm keeping this with me."

With a little less enthusiasm than before, he showed me to the prison tower. The lower ground entrance anyway. He left a lesser guard to escort me the rest of the way. "Enjoy the climb," he said, smiling unctuously once more.

Gypsum's accommodation had been upgraded since I was last here. The tower was reserved for the political prisoners likely to live out their lives in isolation. No wonder she wanted Gas's help.

I was in better shape than I used to be, going on the run can do that for you, but I was still gasping like a landed fish when I reached the top. The guard was only red-faced and obviously did the climb regularly. He'd been wise enough to bring a pitcher of water. I had assumed for Gypsum, but I guzzled half before he had the door unlocked. I wiped my face and tried to look like a terrifying Solhan necromancer as I stepped into the small, round chamber.

There were lots of windows at least. Great view of the city. All too narrow to escape through. I had escaped from prison via a castle window once, so I had some experience, and escaping here would require shrinking to the size of a pigeon, and growing wings. I sensed the wards all around to dampen magic, but that didn't explain why Gypsum didn't turn werewolf and tear her way out, either through stone walls or her guards' throats.

Then I noticed the collar around her thick, dwarven neck. Avian. It kept her from shifting.

"Hello, Eva," she said. "It's good to see you."

"I can't say the same." She had aged, her muddy hair streaked with white, expression tired. I had always assumed it was her hordes of children who wore her down, but now I realized she had always been older than she pretended. She had been working for the Dead God when she befriended me in finishing school, and so she had lied about her age, about being my friend, everything, and anything to fulfill her mission. Only her brilliant, amethyst eyes remained unchanged, assessing.

"Aguragas must have told you about Ilsa," she guessed. You didn't become the favored servant and spy for a god without being shrewd. "Vampires can turn into mist and visit more regularly than my other friends."

"Since when do you have any real friends? Especially my blood sucking sister? I see. Like attracts like, and you're both evil, conniving, backstabbers."

"I didn't give Karo to her."

"You want me to believe that? Don't you want out of this tower? Your freedom?"

"Yes, but there are other ways."

"Why so unwilling to sacrifice one friend, but not another? Why did you turn on me?"

"I worked for Him not Lili. She was the one who wanted to ruthlessly sacrifice you for her own power. You were the Dead God's chosen bride. He wanted you protected until the time was right, honored when your death came, and your soul joined His. I have always held the greatest respect for you."

"Neither I nor the Dead God chose this marriage. It was forced upon us both by Lili."

"Our Lord did choose you. Thane is testament to that."

I wanted to believe Thane and the Dead God were different, but not really, especially not since Thane had rejoined Him. I didn't want to go into all of that right now.

"Just tell me where Karo is then."

"She's safe," Gypsum said, cagey.

"You can understand why you don't fill me with confidence?" I held out the stoppered vial. "Drink."

"What is that?"

"Not poison, so why does it matter?"

She took it, pulled the cork, and sniffed. "How did you get truth serum? Never mind. You are no end of resourceful. So, have you heard anything about my husbands and children?"

"I just came back to Highcrowne myself. Wait. They don't write to you?"

"No."

That was sad. They must have felt betrayed too. Surely, they knew Gypsum had been trying to protect them as well as herself? The Dead God was bound to win, all the odds were on Him. Not everyone knew you should never bet against a Thorne.

"Well, I don't think Hilja killed them if that's what you're worried about. She's forgotten you entirely as far as I can tell."

"I wouldn't say that."

"Well, I hope you start saying, and saying it all soon. Drink. Now."

"My secrets are dangerous."

"Aren't they all? Would you prefer I pull the answers from you like last time?" I wasn't sure I could do it, now that the Dead God was gone, and I was stuck with regular old necromancy—and the Shadow of the First Soul. I didn't want to use such unpleasant tactics if I didn't have to.

"No. I'll drink." She swallowed and handed the empty vial back. "I'm not allowed glass. They don't want me to harm myself. Whatever for, I have no idea. Not even my family cares if I live or die, so why should they? ... Oh, this works quite quickly and really loosens the tongue much better than even a rowdy night of dwarven drinking and song."

"Where is Karo?" I repeated.

"In EEP protective custody. Probably some lovely lake house in the hills or a shack near the beach in Faellion. At least that's what I imagine. It's got to be better than here. They promised she wouldn't be enslaved—they are the Queen's enforcers of laws, so they should follow the rules, even if other elves don't."

"Why would the EEPs protect Karo?"

"Alright, I admit it. I'm working for the elves. They want me to help Aguragas, win his trust, and then learn all I can about his networks, so they can destroy it all in one fell swoop. In return, I get my freedom, or at least a better sentence. Another lake house for me, I hope."

"So, the warden didn't really want a bribe?"

"Part of his cover. He's an EEP. They all are here."

"Now this double and triple crossing I do believe. Finally, a glimpse of the real Gypsum. Once a traitor always a traitor."

"Ouch. It does come with my upbringing, you know? My sister the Baroness knew she would inherit, but I always knew I'd have to lie, cheat, and steal for the power I wanted. I did fairly well, don't you think? I was the Dwarven Queen for a short time, and my sister was imprisoned in the tower then. Gernwold towers are even worse than here, so I can't complain."

"Turned on your own sister, no wonder you're buddies with Ilsa. Or did you lie about that too? Do you even know where she is?"

"I know. She came looking for you. She really doesn't like you very much."

"Being turned into an evil undead thing didn't change her at all."

"But you have changed." Gypsum looked into my eyes, and I wondered if she had something akin to soul sense, or did she gauge me with those predatory, werewolf instincts, looking for weakness, for prey?

"I'm not the one being questioned here. I have things to do, but it's good to know Karo is okay. I can mop up later when it comes to her, all this stuff you're entangled with. It's not as important as—"

"—your child."

"Ilsa or EEPs tell you that?"

"No. I can just tell. You're a mother now. It changes everything when you have a life more important than your own to worry about. I've been a mother enough times to know. They never understand the sacrifices you make for them, the lines you will cross, and they will never say 'thank you', but it doesn't matter. Nothing matters as much as them."

"What about power and being Dwarf Queen? You gave them up for that, which is probably why they're not speaking to you now."

"I did it all for them, and worse than blaming me, I know I failed them. Instead of making their lives more secure, I've made it worse, tainted their reputations before they had a chance to discover who they will be. That's what I regret the most."

"Not attacking Highcrowne alongside Lili and oh, I don't know, killing a bunch of people? You don't regret that?"

"That's war. And politics. Get used to it."

"I don't want to. But … I might have to. My Dawn is technically the Elf King's daughter."

"Technically? You mean Thane possessed his body. And you and Thane...?"

"Doomed, tragic, amazing love." Why did it feel so comfortable sharing with Gypsum? "Is this your spy craft? Drawing secrets from me without resorting to truth serum?"

"I'm not being a spy now, Eva. I'm being your friend. I was your friend when I wasn't supposed to be, when I saw it as weakness, and I fought to be cold-hearted before I turned on you. But I wasn't a very good spy, because I fell for my own story. It became real. Even if I had known where you were or what you were doing with your life, I would never have told Ilsa. I don't want to hurt you. I never did. Sounds like Thane did though."

"No. He changed me even before I knew about Dawn. In a good way. It's my fault he's gone, and I want him back more than anything, but it's complicated. Dangerous to try again. Not just for me, but for Dawn and the whole world. I have to let him go, but I don't know how."

"All I can say is think about your daughter. Anything you do that could hurt her is not worth it. You might rationalize, but your gut knows right and wrong. Don't ignore it. But also know you can't lock her in a tower to keep her from the world." She indicated her own prison. The beautiful elven architecture and slim, curved windows with golden sunlight slanting through did make me think of the enchanted castles from fairy tales.

"I've kept Dawn in an enchanted sleep to protect her when I needed to, which is much the same."

"Take it from a court-bred, second child turned queen turned traitor—there is no protection anywhere for royals. There is only learning the game well enough to survive. You can't hide Dawn away. You must teach her, help her learn to protect herself."

"Can I do both? She's only six."

"I started learning at four."

This was the side of Gypsum I hadn't known before. This was why she had chosen politics and power, why she had ended up here. What you are taught when young molds you, whether you want it to or not. Look at me, fighting my whole life against being Solhan, and now I was the epitome of my whole doomed race. What had I been teaching Dawn? To fear, run, hide? Is that who I wanted her to be?

"I do have to go," I said. I went to the door but turned back and said, "Thank you for the advice, Gypsum. I'll be seeing you."

"I hope so. I miss you."

Truth serum was a wonderful thing sometimes. If only we all told the truth to one another, how much pain could be avoided? How much easier to discover who your true friends were?

I had a few vials of serum left but not enough for the whole town. Two were needed for the two people I needed to question the most. Both equally unsettling.

Always do the hardest thing first they say, so I went looking for Duane.

Dread Truth

I knew Duane would find me. He was there as soon as I crossed the bridge over the prison's moat. He'd changed his clothes, but no top hats and silk waistcoats this time. He wore plain, undyed linen, something homespun, and instead of the cane and hidden sword, there were daggers craftily concealed in sleeves and boots. No twins or other flunkies in sight. I'm sure they were around, hovering at the periphery, awaiting their master's call.

Many saw the Shadow King as an object of fear. Duane had transformed himself from a street thug and petty gangster in my uncle's employ to the purveyor of secrets the Crowns depended on to keep their subjects, and each other, in line. He controlled all the gangs now, all the organized thieves and assassins, and woe to anyone who acted without his sanction. I had to admit he'd turned murder and larceny into an almost civilized profession. He even siphoned from the powerful and cruel to help the sick and poor. I'd kept myself informed.

That's how I knew he had not transformed himself at all. He was no 'Mister Rose' or 'Shadow King'. He was still the Duane I remembered, feeding refugees in the Outskirts and helping me free pixies from cages. He had a gooey soft center, and I worried for him. It's also why I dreaded this.

"You're my next suspect, Duane." I held up a vial of truth serum. "Where you want to do this? Is there someplace safe for you?"

"To reveal my secrets? The Crowns' secrets? No. But you have never been safe, Eva, and I have a place in mind. Come with me."

He had an auto-carriage, and before we climbed in, he brought out a device not dissimilar to Bell's eavesdropping box and waved it over everything. There was a squeal as it passed by the warlock crystal-powered steam engine, and so he brought out an Avian ring next, double checking.

"All clear." He held the passenger door open for me. Some of those manners he'd learned to impress the likes of Hilja. It had the opposite effect on me, and I almost leapt into the driver's seat, except I didn't like abominable contraptions and definitely didn't like driving them. Instead, I let him play whatever role he wanted while he could.

"Thank you." I sat down without complaint.

"You're really creeping me out." He smiled, but I sensed he was genuinely off balance by my uncharacteristic behavior. Good. No, bad. I was not looking forward to this.

"I suppose your gadgets and magical jewelry detect listening devices?"

"And bombs." Sounded like he worried about those a lot.

"Best you check me too then. I was as close to Bell as I am to you."

"I did as you climbed in, but it doesn't hurt to be extra thorough." He passed the squealing box over me, a few inches from my skin, moving slowly from head to toe. That one made me nervous, wondering if it would blow up itself. I hated gadgets. When he used the Avian charm, the hairs on my body stood up, an electric tingle at the nearness of magic.

"It must be hard," I said, suddenly. "Not having magic of your own. Do you even feel what you're missing?"

"You feel it?"

"That answers my question. I do. And you missed a spot." I took his hand and directed the charm along my left thigh. He was so close, leaning over me, my hand on his, and I noted the goosebumps on his arms. He felt something, even if it wasn't magic.

The silence had grown charged, so I gave his hand back and said, "So, where to? Is it a secret? Do you have to blindfold me?"

It was hard to tell with his bronze skin, but I may have made him blush. He focused on starting the auto-carriage and said, "No. You'll remember the place."

He must not trust anyone in or out of his employ, because he drove us farther away from Highcrowne than I expected, away from the train line, and over frosted fields of grass to the edge of the forest.

It took us about twenty minutes in the auto-carriage, but it must have been hours when we first travelled this way, our merry band of adventurers headed to Solheim. This was the spot where a lich had attacked us, Duane and me, Jorg, Grim and Gormless, the doctor, Roosal … Thane.

"Where is Jorg?" I asked, avoiding the painful subjects. Why had Duane chosen this spot?

"You know where Jorg works. I've gathered you have some of the same informants as me."

"You use bogles too?"

"Tricky but truthful creatures, unlike most others I deal with who are just tricky. Or accomplished liars."

"Truthful is a rare thing. … I suppose it's that time." I held up the vial.

"Why do you look like you dread this more than I do?" he asked.

"Because I'd like to trust you, but I can't trust anyone, and this proves it. This proves how heartless I am." That was a nobler explanation than saying I dreaded hearing what he was going to tell me. And it forewarned him.

"You'd like to trust me? That's unexpected. Are you still under the influence of truth serum too?"

"Yes," I lied. "So, it's an even field. Now, drink up."

He looked around, as if there might be watchers all the way out here. How could he exist always on edge, always worried about spies, a blade against his throat when he slept? I supposed it was the same way I existed with the First Soul, with dark magic always lurking and hungry for me.

He swallowed the potion, no attempts at subterfuge. He wanted this.

Oh no.

"Did you take Calka's egg, or aid whoever did, or do you, in any way, know who was responsible?" I asked quickly.

"No. If I did, they would be dead. Calka and the Avians gave me the only safe home I've ever known. Where do you think a Shadow King dares to sleep? I owe them everything."

That answered my unspoken question.

"Great. We're done then. Best we head back. Or maybe I should leave you here until the serum wears off? I'll start walking and you can catch up later. Should be a few hours, and I could use the exercise." I got out of the car. He followed.

"Eva. You haven't asked why I chose this spot, besides the remoteness."

"It's not relevant, not to this investigation. You deserve your secrets."

"I don't want them. Secrets are survival, but they are chains too. I crave freedom, especially with you. I—"

"—Don't. Please."

"I chose this spot because it was where I first truly feared losing you. I realized how close you were with Thane, I knew you were going to Solheim without me if you could, then seeing that lich wanting only your death, seeing the First Soul digging into your chest, and you fighting not just for your life…. You've always been so tough, so foolishly brave, but I realized you might die. Everything was against you. So, I vowed I would never let that happen. It's not the vow I made to Viktor when we were kids that keeps me watching over you, it's that vow I made to myself as a man. I would rather die than lose you."

I froze, trying to think but failing, and idiocy poured out. "…That's so sweet. I really appreciate it. But I'm good. And going now."

Before I managed a step, he took hold of my wrist and spun me into him, like we were dancing. He'd always been fast, his hands invisible when he pickpocketed someone, and I was just as surprised to find myself in his arms. He had put on muscle, no longer the scrawny street urchin, and I felt something unexpected in his embrace: sheltered, safe, home. How could I feel something I'd never truly known? I touched the top of his hand and his grip loosened so I could turn, face to face with him.

"Duane...." I began, wondering what I could say.

"You know I don't like that name."

"It's your real name. Why do you hate it so much?"

"It's the name of the boy whose family died, who became someone he wasn't to survive. He's not me."

"Then how come you answer when I call you by it?"

"Because it's you. It's yours, that name. You make me want to be that boy again. That's why only you get to say it."

Heat emanated from him. Just as his bronze skin never paled in Highcrowne winter, no matter how cold the outside world. He burned, like he carried the desert of his homeland with him. There was a sort of fire inside him, a fire to fight, to live. While I was death, he was life. I felt his life filling me, spreading from where he held my hand still. It moved along by arm, reaching for my heart, but that is where the black miasma of the First Soul drove it back.

He leaned in, perfect golden lips, green eyes like peridot, black hair hanging long over one side of his face, as though a part of him always wanted to hide. I felt his lips brush mine, ever so gently.

I stepped back.

My heart was drumming in my chest, my breath coming in gasps, like I'd just fought off a dozen foes.

"I still love Thane. Will always love Thane."

"Why can't you love me too? I think you are the only one who ever knew me, who knows me now, the only one who could love me if you tried. Love is the one thing I've never been able to steal. It can only be given, and no one has offered, so I'm asking. Try to love me even half as much as I love you."

This was all I'd feared it would be. More. I couldn't ... so I ran.

I dreaded hearing the motor carriage, worried Duane would pursue me. He didn't, which was even worse. I had wounded him.

He'd been vulnerable, raw, and exposed, stripped bare by the serum, thinking I would be too, but I had lied. The serum had worn off by the time I'd managed that whopper of a tale for Aguragas. I'd had all my defenses up, while Duane had none. And I'd rejected him. He couldn't help but believe that I didn't care.

That hurt. More than I thought it would, but it had to be done. There was too much at stake. I couldn't ....

Tears came, but I walked so long they had dried by the time Roosal found me.

"Need another lift?" he asked, clearly curious how I had managed to get so far from the city.

"Yes. I have one last horrible thing to do."

"What is that?"

"Talk to Ulric. Can you take me to the temple of the Dead God?"

Roosal was more in tune with the rest of the world than most Avians, and I sensed his curiosity, but he still knew how to keep his mouth shut. He was quiet as he wrapped the magical band around my waist that made me light enough for him to carry, and he didn't say anything when we flew over Duane's auto carriage, headed away from the city, sturdy wooden wheels tearing up dust on open plateaus of dried grass.

"Where is he going?" I wondered.

Avian hearing was keen despite the rush of air as we flew. "Mister Rose seems to be on a mission, travelling at such speed."

Or he was running away. I knew all about that. Just when I didn't think I could hurt anymore, the universe managed another punch to the gut that sent me reeling. There goes blessed numbness.

As we approached the Central City, Roosal said, "I must leave you here in the square. Calka does not want me to visit your uncle's temple, for why we know the Dead God saved this world from the Devourer in the end, all everyone else knows is that He nearly destroyed it. We must avoid controversy."

"I think temporarily locking down the Central City was pretty controversial."

"Calka reacted; we all did. Wisely or unwisely, we cannot know, but we are not without emotion. We cannot keep our feelings from affecting our actions, I cannot ... It is my child you seek, and I am glad we have given you this task, Eva, for I know you will not hesitate to go wherever you must, do whatever you must. I wish I could be so free to act."

As soon as Roosal set me on the grass, I hugged him. A perfect example of how I didn't give a damn what the masses thought. There were people all around, surprised and murmuring elves and a few dwarves, but I ignored them. I looked Roosal in the eyes and said, "I will not fail you."

"Thank you."

He flew off, and I strode toward the eastern side of the Central City, the side closest to Solheim. It was a trek and almost didn't count as 'central', but I was sure my uncle fought hard for the location. Where in Highcrowne one resided was a symbol of status. He had started in the Outskirts, and all he had done in the war to aid the Avians meant they dare not dishonor him by sending him back. Even the lower tiers where most craftsmen and temples could be found was an insult to someone as powerful as him, but as Roosal had pointed out, the Dead God was controversial. They must not have known Ulric would turn his mansion, his reward for service, to such a purpose, but now it was too late.

A line of EEPs formed in my path before I made it to Uncle's front door. They had been waiting. Queen Hilja was with them, sitting in a covered litter held up by four, muscular 'servants' who looked a shade shy of slaves. Probably freed and not knowing what else to do but take up their old employment.

Hilja beckoned me over, so I climbed into the litter and sat across from her. She lowered the gauzy curtains, which didn't appear to provide much concealment, but they were ensorcelled and cut out all sound, providing us with complete privacy. I sensed other protections woven into them. This dainty and ornate litter was really a defensive tank.

"I am not happy about having had that truth serum forced down my throat," she said. "The gall of Mister Rose. I am a Crown. I can't lay full blame on him, however, as he has no will of his own when it comes to you, much like my father who also became your puppet."

"Duane does what he wants."

"Hardly. That's beside the point—your lazy approach to investigation destroyed years of political maneuvering. General Moore and King Harley both thought I was aligned with them on the democracy debate, and that the Avians were the ones stalling, but my tongue lost all control. Talk about setting back negotiations ... it's a shambles."

"They realized you hate democracy with every fiber of your being," I guessed.

"Yes."

"How is this my problem?"

"You and I are still in the throes of our own negotiation, are we not? In your spree of chemical-enhanced questioning, did you learn who seeks my death?"

I wanted to say it was low on my list of priorities, but really, I'd entirely forgotten. Who didn't want Hilja and most elves dead, really?

"I can tell you who it's not. You can trust Duane, and even Gypsum is working with your EEPs in good faith."

"EEPs?"

"Has no one told you?" I guessed only my little circle had taken up the abbreviation I coined. "Eleven Elite Protectorate."

"The Protectorate reduced to 'EEP'. One more example of what I hate about democracy. Trivializing what is sacred, what should be feared and respected, means all becomes trivial and without meaning, including their own lives and purpose. The rabble."

So, I was rabble in her eyes? I supposed I'd never really doubted it.

"I will help you, Hilja, but finding Calka's stolen egg is more important right now. The longer this takes, the farther away it could be. Aguragas' networks could send it to Darrub before we know—but I don't think it was him, not directly."

"What about that disgusting goblin professor friend of yours?"

"Not him." Although the goblin Emperor and his other agents weren't off the list. I had so much work still to do.

"Are you any closer to solving this?" Hilja's question echoed my own worries. "Were I and the other Crowns so rudely questioned for nothing?"

"You three were the most likely suspects, but my uncle is not excluded. Now, if you'd let me continue, I can question him next and then get on with helping you as soon as I can." Maybe I needed to give her a ticket with a number like they used at the butcher shop? Some sort of priority system was needed.

"Crowns as suspects in some vulgar police matter? We are not criminals. Life and death, war, genocide … all is politics."

"If I hadn't cleared you under duress, I'd still suspect you with an attitude like that. Whatever happened to that progressive, tolerant princess I first met?"

"Politics." She sighed. "You have been away for so long you see the accumulation of the slow changes in me as a sudden shock. My politics do not defer overly from that of the common elf these days. I shirk at the forced comradery of the Three Kingdoms. The Dead God is gone, thanks to you, and there is now room enough in this world for each of us to stretch out and expand our respective nations, be they elven, human, or dwarf. Why must we squabble within the confines of Highcrowne? Because Avians demand it? I know they are too few to matter anymore."

"Once again—real suspicious rhetoric there, Hilja. If you are so aligned with the common elf, then why do you fear for your life?"

"Because, publicly, I side with unity and democracy and all that rot."

"Maybe telling the other Crowns the truth is the first step to telling everyone what you really think."

"Then the Upside Downs and Harley's supporters will want me dead. There's always someone."

"Isn't it better to be hated for what you truly believe?"

"No. Then people can manipulate me. Standing for something I don't care one whiff about means it's easier to make concessions, bargain, switch sides even. Believing what you say is the nail in your political coffin, oh naïve one."

Sometimes I wished I was as naïve as everyone presumed. Over the course of my short life, I had gone so far past jaded that bitter and resentful had turned to despair and terror, only to be replaced by grateful appreciation that I and his entire world weren't already dead. Things can get so bad that genocide barely makes you blink, but here I was worrying about far more devastating consequences than political upheaval that I appeared to be a guileless simpleton.

I didn't care enough about Hilja's opinion to correct her. If anything, it served my negotiating stance better when the time came for it. If Dawn and I lived, if EEPs or even assassins following me all over the known world became my biggest worry, then it would be time to prioritize Hilja.

"Well, thank you for the education," I said. "Just one more reason I never wanted to be a queen. Of course, I was offered rulership over the dead, which is even less appealing than Crown politics, so that might have been a factor also."

I hopped out of the litter, declining to use the muscled, ex-slave's bent back offered as a step stool, and waved goodbye as I climbed the massive stone steps to Ulric's.

Unfortunately, my progress was impeded once again when Doctor Ghunnan pulled me into a darkened alcove shrouded in ivy, servos in his mechanical legs whirring in such a way they conveyed his fear.

"Did Queen Hilja mention me?" he asked, a tremor in his voice.

"I believe she called you 'that disgusting goblin professor'."

"Oh good, she remembered my academic title. Nothing else? Like how she would be sending someone to kill me slowly after having me cast in irons and displayed naked in the town square?"

"No, nothing that detailed, although there was real distaste in her voice when she said 'goblin'."

"I am quite accustomed to elvish racial expletives, so I can imagine. She knows I concocted the truth serum, and she is displeased with me. She had been one of my staunchest supporters when it came to updating the histories, and paid a significant portion of the tapestry costs, but now I fear I have forever lost her patronage."

"She'll get over it."

I headed for the main door, a massive wooden thing adorned with carvings of ghostly figures and Solhan writing warning the uninitiated away, when the goblin doctor grabbed my shoulder. The heavy gloves he wore had some mechanical enhancement and internal heaters to ward off Highcrowne's ever present chill.

"You will put in a good word for me, won't you? It is imperative that I be allowed to stay in my current role, as there is still so much to be done. I haven't even commissioned half of the works I imagined."

"I'm not really the best person to represent you to Hilja." This time I got the door open a crack and managed to step inside. Doctor Ghunnan was right beside me.

"Surely the savior of the city has some pull—whup!" he cried unexpectedly when an imposing figure shoved him back onto the stoop.

It was Uncle's bodyguard, manservant and overall enforcer, Morgan, who then closed the door in the professor's face saying, "Only believers allowed."

Doctor Ghunnan was certainly not one of those.

I wasn't sure I qualified, either, as I did not pray to the Dead God, to any god. I knew He existed, had heard my name spoken in His voice, had felt His embrace, but that was not the same as worship.

"Morgan," I said. "It's good to see you."

I hoped he felt the same. Tensions had been high all around when I left. Morgan was like a father to me, my protector and trainer in all things Solhan, but I had disappointed him by turning out how I'd been raised rather than the rebel he'd secretly hoped for. I liked to think I was still a rebel, but one who understood what to fight for.

Morgan grunted, which could be a good sign, and gestured for me to follow. He was deathly pale as all Solhans were, shoulder length black hair graying ever so slightly, tall, but where most Solhans were lithe, he was thick with muscle, shoulders like a bull. He stalked as he walked, a predator aware of every shadow in the darkened room.

The ground floor of the mansion had been turned into a genuine temple. Rows of stone benches stretched before a massive statue of winged Death. I froze, entranced by it. The statue was huge, ten feet tall and black, but it wasn't that which impressed me so much as the gaze. I had met Death. I knew the Dead God's eyes were glowing orbs that seared your soul, His voice reverberating through your bones, but these eyes were mortal, full of love. They were Thane's eyes.

I was drawn inexorably, not sure if Morgan had spoken, if any of the supplicants bowed forward on the pews—and there were more worshippers than I expected—had said anything. It was like the world dropped away and only those eyes, that face remained.

I didn't know how Uncle had managed it. Had he even met Thane? I couldn't recall. But somehow the face of the statue shifted, just as Thane had shifted forms, a bit of Fharen in one angle, Erick in another, a slave girl, the elven priest he'd inhabited for a time, and the merman with a line to indicate gills along one jaw. There were the canonical dark robes and black, feathered wings stretched out behind the statue, the scythe, all the trappings of the Dead God I had grown up with, but the face was alive, the eyes following me. I climbed the base of the statue and stood there, captured by Thane's gaze. I sank into the statue's out-stretched arms, and it felt as though they embraced me back.

Eva.

My hairs stood on end and there was a gasp from the worshipers that pulled me from my trance. They murmured and pointed, awed as the statue's arms released me and returned to their former position. The face seemed hidden in shadow again, the eyes nothing but darkness.

Dazed, I stumbled back towards Morgan.

"A miracle," he whispered, warily assessing the crowd, as if wondering if they were now overexcited and in need of expulsion just as he'd tossed out the troublesome goblin.

The worshippers returned to their quiet and reverent poses, hands pressed together a bit more tightly than before, their expressions exultant.

Not me. The ache in my chest, the ball of anguish in my throat was worse than ever. Thane had reached out to me. Did that mean my connection to the First Soul was pulling Him back?

I needed Thane. The world needed the Dead God to bring peace to the dead. No one needed the First Soul, because it meant the Devourer and destruction would follow. Thane couldn't return until the Soul was no more, and He would never find a way to destroy it while Dawn and I were connected to it. We had to extricate ourselves.

"Where is my uncle?" I asked Morgan.

"This way."

He unlocked a door and led me into a private wing that looked more like a home than the temple did. Ulric's idea of a home, anyway: mahogany bookshelves, tables inlaid with shell, elaborately painted ceramic vases, velvet upholstered couches, a massive clock ticking away time, time that barely touched someone as powerful as Ulric.

He looked the same, sternly bent over his desk, reading by lamplight, ignoring my presence. I felt like a little girl again, come to face a lecture for my misbehavior.

"Hello." I wouldn't let the silence take over. I wasn't a girl anymore.

"I felt the Dead God's presence." He was still not looking at me.

"A miracle," Morgan said. "The statue moved, said Eva's name."

"A disaster," Ulric corrected. When his gaze met mine, I knew he knew. "What have you done, Eva?"

"I was alone..." I began.

"You chose to be. You left." He wouldn't let me make excuses.

"I made a mistake. Many mistakes."

Morgan smiled. "At least we know it's you and not some doppelganger from Lyss."

"There are no monsters in Lyss," I corrected. "Only shadows and light. And power. Just not enough power, or I should say, not the right kind of power for what I need. That's why I've come back."

"You reconnected with the First Soul before you entered Lyss. It's the only way you could have survived," Ulric reasoned.

"Yes. Although it's more the First Soul reconnected with Dawn and me. I have a daughter.

Thane's daughter. I wanted to know if He'd succeeded, if the Devourer had consumed it, if He could return and meet her. If the Dead God could return and put an end to the risen."

"You think I do not seek the same? That is why I built this temple. He needs our worship. He is made stronger by it. You should have spoken to me first." Uncle's disappointment seemed different than before. Always it had been because I was not Solhan enough, but we had come to understand one another, and now I think he was disappointed that I did not trust him.

I trusted no one.

"All I did was find one of Doctor Ghunnan's portals. I didn't even step through. I reached out with my power, a thought, a message, but the First Soul reached back. It had left deep marks in Dawn and me both, like a brand, and I could not stop it from reclaiming us. Not this time. It entangled itself with us, and I recalled too late what that felt like, how hard it was to resist. I eventually remembered how to fight it, how to remain myself, but Dawn is too young. It is taking her over."

"I'd like to meet her," Morgan said. His voice was the only warmth in the room. I was grateful for that small gesture. I could not possibly describe to Ulric what the First Soul felt like, the chill now buried inside me, eating at me. I needed whatever warmth I could get.

"I'd like that when this is over. She's with Nanny. I'm surprised Nanny didn't join you here, with all this space."

"She needs her own space—and she's been waiting for you. She missed you even more than I did."

I hugged Morgan then. It was not the Solhan thing to do, hug, and that made him even happier, his arms wrapping around me. "I missed you too," I said.

Ulric was very Solhan: unmoved and unshaken in his focus. "That was one mistake. What else did you do? Why do you need my power?"

I reluctantly let Morgan go and faced my uncle. "My second mistake was using the connection the First Soul had established to reach out to Thane. It strengthened the link. But He spoke to me. Just a few words."

I remembered how He said my name, as the statue had just now. A few words were not enough, and my yearning for more, for Him, only fed the First Soul more. He had known it could not continue, and so He had told me what I needed to know and then went silent. The wound was raw, unable to heal, and so I could say none of that to Ulric. I could barely think it.

All I told Ulric was, "He directed me where to search, reassured me there was a way to sever the connection, remove the First Soul's brand, so it could never link with Dawn and I again. It was the hope I needed, and so I spent years searching for the pieces. Knowledge of magic, spells, and rituals scattered on broken tablets, etched in the walls of ancient ruins, sometimes only carried in someone's memory, in ancestral songs. And I found a way into Lyss. I have gathered all I need to do this, to fix my mistake, but I need the power of you and your worshippers. More than you have here if that's possible. And I need the Avians."

"Why them?" Morgan asked.

"Different magics affect each other, like different colored glass alters the light. Avian magic is crucial, but they won't help until I find Calka's missing egg. So, will you both take this truth serum so I can get on with discovering who has it?"

"I didn't know Queen Calka had an egg," Morgan said. "That's amazing. Why would anyone steal it?"

"Maybe they want the Avian line to end? Maybe they want Solhan power to return? Who can say what they think? Isn't that right, Uncle?"

"You know me better than any other, Eva." Ulric's disappointment in me grew worse.

"Which isn't saying much. And I can't possibly know you better than Morgan here, or Nanny who raised you."

"They have power but nothing like ours. They don't understand ... the temptation."

"I know temptation well."

Not for power, like Ulric thought, but for love, for annihilation of self in order to join with something greater, to be greater. Power was a side effect in my case. Being Death's chosen bride gave me abilities no other necromancer possessed, as muted as they were now. Being linked to the First Soul would give me even greater power, the power to become a god myself if I wanted, but that would mean losing myself to it. Thane had tempted me, and I'd lost. I would have done anything for Him. I would not allow the First Soul to win me over like that.

"Morgan, please give us a moment." Ulric's request did not sound like his usual commands. Morgan nodded and left, and Uncle held out his hand. "Give me your truth potion. You already know the truth, but like me, you do not trust easily. If ever."

I was more like him than I wanted to admit. I handed the vial over and watched him drink.

10 SORRY

I learned more from Ulric than I imagined or ever wanted to know. About my parents, about Solheim before the fall, about Ilsa and I … but he had nothing to do with the egg. Neither did Morgan. I'd run out of truth serum until the goblin doctor could make more, not that he was likely to with Hilja raining wrath on him, but I didn't need it. Ulric had soul marked Morgan, and he could not disobey Uncle's command to answer me truthfully. Who knew Morgan was more slave than devoted manservant?

When it was all over, I ached for Morgan. No wonder he was always at Uncle's side, no wonder he encouraged me to fight my nature, to be who I wanted to be—because he couldn't.

Even Ulric was shaken. He didn't always wield the power he had, didn't always give in to temptation. Did that mean there was hope for me too?

"I will help you when you are ready," Uncle said before shutting the door on me. His Lord of Death might have embraced me, but Ulric now feared me and the knowledge I could hold over him.

Good.

I felt more a Thorne than ever after that experience, privy to the family's secrets, its deceptions and hypocrisy. I was the hypocrite for demanding truth and not giving it myself.

I was out of obvious leads and would need to use my wits from here on. And allies. If I still had any.

I sought Duane out, hypocrite that I was. While I couldn't tell him my truth, I needed him. The Shadow King was my greatest ally of all. But where to look?

I now knew Duane slept in the Avian sanctuary, when he needed sleep, which wasn't often. Duane was a machine of human invention, forged in war and loss and infused with survival as his sole purpose. Ulric was born with power and tempted by it, I acquired mine unwillingly and would as soon be rid of it, but Duane pursued power for the most selfish and noblest reason of all—because he didn't want anyone worse to have it.

The old phrase 'knowledge is power' always sprang to mind, but my recent experience just highlighted how wrong that was. Secrets were power. That's why Ulric guarded his and Duane hunted others' out. Everything shameful, selfish, and cruel was kept hidden, not because it would invariably hurt others, but because it had caused hurt, and those who protected their secrets wanted to project a mask to the world. They wanted to be respected, to rule.

Someone as selfish as them would use others' secrets for leverage or simple blackmail, but Duane was not so shallow. The secrets he kept were like a cloak around him, shielding but also drawing the eye. It was a kind of wealth, an undeniable magnetism, like darkest night: People wondered about its mysteries, what it might reveal, but most were scared to be swallowed by it. It was that fear of the unknown that allowed him to keep his enemies off balance, which made competitors pause and doubt during negotiations. It made Duane untouchable.

Except to me. He gave me his secrets like other men gave flowers. I pretended not to know how precious they were to him, but after our motor carriage ride, it would be impossible to dismiss, for that had been a grand gesture, the equivalent of a bouquet of roses offered on one knee. And I'd thrown them in his face.

I sighed. I was so tired. All my work protecting Dawn, searching the world for the ritual I needed to correct my mistake, staying alive ... all was made more difficult here. Highcrowne was a crucible of pain for me, but Solhans loved our pain.

"Psst," I whispered to a smelly corner in a darkened alley near the marketplace. Vegetables too rotten to be hidden under the fresher wares and sold were tossed here, and it was invariably where you'd find bogles. "I'm looking for Bitten Belly."

Rustling indicated there were probably dozens of camouflaged and invisible bogles feasting on the pile. Rats were still an issue in the sewers, but bogles were intelligent creatures and had taken over the surface of the city, even beating out the pigeons—or more accurately, eating them. They were relatively few, but on top of flight and magical invisibility, they spoke and organized their society with a strict code of behavior that ensured mutual defense, plus they were tool wielders. Other vermin couldn't compete.

When they risked revealing themselves, you could see they were like giant, leathery bats, with bulging eyes and huge ears. Each bogle was different, so I recognized Bitten Belly immediately when he dropped his camouflage: mottled blue with eyes like ripe cherries.

"I is here, Mistress," he said.

"Sorry to interrupt your lunch, but I need you to find someone. That man who I was walking with earlier, the one with green eyes." I knew Bitten Belly and other bogles in my employ had been watching me then, because I'd told them to. They were supposed to follow everyone who they caught following me and report back.

"I know where the rat meat man lives."

"Rat meat man? Has he been feeding you rat meat? You're one of his informants too?" When Duane had let me in on his bogle secret, I knew one of them could lead me to him. I just hadn't thought it would be my most trusted spy. I supposed 'trusted spy' was an oxymoron.

Bitten Belly looked sheepish. "So sorry, Mistress, but my bargain with him far older than my bargain with you. But I never tell him about you. Promise, promise. That sealed in blood. I never ever betray you!"

"Don't get worked up. It's fine. Show me the way." I knew the bogle code well, and any loophole in a bargain could be exploited. I thought I'd sealed them all, because Erick was the only other person I'd known who spoke to the creatures, but I should have guessed Duane would too. Maybe others. As I walked with Bitten Belly invisible on my shoulder and whispering directions, I asked him about any other prior bargains as well as for a report from earlier.

There was no telling if he would reveal all past bargains, they may have sworn him to silence, but nothing he'd agreed to previously could contradict the blood pact I'd made. It secured my privacy and safety. So, my probing was more curiosity than worry.

Bitten Belly's report from the morning was more interesting, however. Aside from Duane's goons, there had been other eavesdroppers to our conversation. No wonder Duane had been paranoid enough to drive us outside the city and scan for listening devices. While there had been Gas's Upside Down agents trailing us in person, someone else had been scrying us.

Did I mention bogles had magic? It was very natural and instinctive to them, a byproduct of their evolution. They were adapted for concealment and in turn could see through it. Anything hidden or surreptitious made their ears twitch.

I carried wards against scrying, Duane probably did too, but they distorted sound and blurred us from someone's magical sight. There was no way of preventing the mage who was snooping around from knowing who we were or where we were. If I'd had a way of doing that, no EEP would ever have found me in Darrub.

Bitten Belly led me to the dingiest portion of the Outskirts, a place I knew well. The old Slave Quarter was closed now, most of the abandoned buildings turned to housing, not for refugees but for those seeking an easier life than what reclaiming the human territories demanded. Not many people wanted to deal with risen, even if they were less dangerous than before.

I'd only been to the Slave Quarter a few times, all for heroic purposes like freeing Kali or fighting bad guys, but the abandoned factory there I knew too well. It's where I had uncovered my brother, Viktor's, darkest secret: He had worshipped the Devourer and created an abomination of metal and flesh in a failed attempt to resurrect his wife. This was the place where the last of my illusions had shattered, where I realized there were no real heroes.

The fact the building had not been converted to tenements screamed something was off: It was the Shadow King's office.

His informants watched me approach. They were good, but I spotted them looking out the windows of nearby apartments, among workers building the new sewer system, even a few kids playing innocently in the streets were on the payroll. The kids were the first to give themselves away, looking a little too long or racing off to report. They'd learn in time, sadly.

No one stopped me or said a word, which was the equivalent of Duane rolling out the red carpet, so I was surprised when I knocked on the door Bitten Belly indicated and there was no answer.

He wanted me to wait. To feel regret building in me. Did he expect me to chicken out and run away again, or knock louder?

I waited.

Bitten Belly flew back to his lunch. I thought about buying some of the street food for sale nearby, the spiced meat wraps smelled good, but I wasn't hungry. A ball of regret filled my stomach.

I pressed my hand against the cold, metal door and let myself grow just as cold. It was easy here. Finding Viktor's secret workshop had hurt, had proven to me that there was no escaping my Solhan nature. I was evil, heartless, and drawn to death. That's what everyone thought about me and my kind, anyway.

Viktor's despair and love had driven him to the dark. That was not heartless. Uncle's efforts, as unsuccessful as they were sometimes, to resist the temptations of power revealed he too struggled with morality. The fact Nanny had not killed Kali already proved even she could control her murderous instincts. Even Ilsa had cried, missing the sister she had grown up with and who had turned on her because she chose to embrace her Solhan nature before I did. We were not what others saw—we were all more complex than that.

Duane was too. I heard a chain rattle, and the door squealed open. He stood there in a plain green shirt that made his extraordinary eyes stand out even more against his bronze skin.

"You only let me stew for about five minutes." I smiled. "You miss me that much?"

"No."

"The truth serum has worn off. Good. I'm sorry. About that. About…" I didn't want to say about running away because it had been my only choice. "I think Doctor Ghunnan spiked that stuff with something that makes you say things you would never normally say. More than the necessary truth. Hilja was livid after it blew her politicking to bits, and you have no idea what I just endured speaking to Ulric. It was weird and horrible."

"But you survived. The weird and horrible."

"I didn't mean…" I didn't want him to think that's what his confession had meant to me, but I didn't want him not to think it either, for that way lay ruination. Best to just shut my mouth.

He let a wing of straight black hair fall over his face again and turned away, leading me into his office. "Well, while you were busy, so was I. I caught up to that dirigible and brought it back to the docks. I have it under guard. Come on. I thought you'd want to search it together."

He grabbed his coat and brushed by me, heading back into the street where I'd just come from. The nearness of him was electric, and I paused a moment to give him some distance.

I took in the place. The warehouse had been renovated, but I recognized the wooden stairs where I'd had a sword fight, and the secret entrance to Viktor's workshop would be underneath the carpet behind Duane's metal desk. Like Aguragas, he had a desk with nothing on it. More a symbol, like a throne, than something used.

"This is the place I first killed someone," I said when Duane returned to see what I was up to.

"Fond, Solhan memories?" he joked.

He had his mask on, his armor, and there would be no penetrating it now, so I felt safe asking, "Why did you choose this place for your office?"

"Viktor. After you found it, Grim and Gormless told me about the workshop, the automaton. I didn't want anyone else to know, especially not Little Vikky. And how do you dispose of dark necromancy stuff and a shrine like that without accidentally cursing yourself with bad mojo? Best to bury it."

"And if any enemies come looking for you here, they might just bear the brunt of the curse?"

"You know me well." There was a tiny crack. A note of pain that echoed in me. I ignored it.

"And you know me. I'm dying to search that pirate ship. Lead the way."

I expected Duane to take me on another excursion, feared it, but we didn't have far to go. We rode one of the mechanical trams that ran through the Quarter and to the Docks, ferrying workers and supplies. He blended in easily, no one guessing who he was, while everyone stared at the Solhan necromancer. I wore a lot of black, yes, and my complexion gave me away, but it was my automatic glare that sent shivers through the crowd and made them stare at their feet the whole trip.

Our captured pirate ship was berthed at the farthest edge of the air dock on the cliff above the river. General Moore's soldiers surrounded it. When

Duane had said 'guards' I'd assumed his stealthy incognito kind, not these veterans in dented armor.

Duane was surprised to see them also. "This is my property," he said without preamble to the scariest looking one of them. "Go."

The soldier almost obeyed, automatically shifting to the side, but then he stood firm. "I have orders from the General himself."

"And my orders come from the Avian queen," I said, holding up the piece of glass Roosal had given me. The guard shifted again, but stayed where he was. He was a stubborn one.

"I'm sorry," he said.

"So am I." Duane turned and left, and I hurried after him.

"Not going to attempt more intimidation? You can be scary. Or let me try. This is my favorite part."

"There are easier ways." Duane reached into a nearby doorway and pulled a well-hidden spy in his employ from the shadows, saying, "Get me General Daniel Moore. I want him here, now."

The spy dashed off, but Duane slowly wended his way into the depths of the air dock. I followed him down a series of ladders, through passageways and underground storage rooms for handling cargo between ships. I had no idea this area existed.

"Not waiting for the General's permission?" I guessed.

"No. For me, this is the fun part."

In no time, Duane had stealthily made his way back to the quarantined pirate ship. I would like to say I was just as stealthy, but I'd cheated a bit. Not a professional thief? Skin so pale it glows in the dark? Not to worry, there is a magical rune for that. If I ever set up a shop selling them, I had my sales pitch all worked out.

"Doesn't this remind you of that time we searched the slave ship, looking for Nanny?" I smiled, remembering. "It was so much fun messing with those goblin mercenaries."

"Yeah. You almost started a fight. If you want to take on Moore's soldiers instead, I'm game."

"No. I want to watch you work." I regretted saying it as soon as the words fell out of my mouth. My face went flush as I tried not to look at him then.

I had been watching the way he moved with lethal grace through the underground passage, to the keel of the ship, up and over the side, like a serpent moving at speed but able to kill anything that crossed its path. Maybe that's where he'd gotten his old nickname, The Adder, before he became the distinguished Mister Rose?

Duane was focused and didn't notice my embarrassment. I did not want to lead him on, but now that he'd said what he felt—I'd always known it without wanting to admit it—and the full 'L' word no less, I couldn't help thinking about him. I didn't want to. My heart was broken in a thousand pieces from losing Thane, the First Soul's touch an abyss within me … but thinking about Duane amidst all that changed my perspective. Like lightning in a storm. It illuminated, briefly, a far shore I might one day reach. If I survived.

We scuttled below deck, and it was dark. I saw in the dark well, and Duane managed better than I expected. I supposed I had my Solhan talents, and he had Avian magic lent to him.

"I really wish we'd searched better the first time," I whispered. I'd been in a hurry because of Dawn. Now I took the time to rifle through wooden crates and lockers, recoiling at the reek of sweaty old sailor clothes. "What does the egg even look like?"

"I don't know. Egg-shaped? White?"

"It's got to be big," I reasoned. "At least as large as a human baby."

I didn't think even pirates would have stored a precious egg stolen from their Avian rulers in a stinky locker, so I made for the captain's cabin. That was more difficult, as it required crossing the deck.

The grizzled veteran who had blocked our way was not the only soldier on guard. Another was in the crows' nest and two more at the top of the gangplank. I thought about trying my sleep trick again, but I wouldn't get close enough to them without the one in the crow's nest seeing.

I was peering through the hatching on one of the cargo doors, assessing the best route, when Duane said, "Look at this."

He led me back to the main cargo hold and to a small section where cages were stacked. They were full of pigeons.

"Aguragas's messenger birds," I said. "He uses them—"

"—I know what he uses them for," Duane interrupted. "I make a habit of intercepting every single one that passes over Kingdom skies. My people do anyway, and I get a daily report."

"So, the mysterious life of a master spy is really all paperwork?"

"More than I'd like. I think they are a distraction, really. The messages are all nonsense, even worse than code. I think he's just keeping me busy."

"Sounds like Gas: 'Look over here at this thing while I stab you in the back'."

"Pigeons mean these pirates worked for him."

"Where do you suppose all the bodies went?" I asked. The ones I'd put to sleep should be awake, and Duane had left even more dead.

"My people secured them before the troops got here. We can question the survivors later if we need."

"The few who survived."

"Look who's talking, troll-slayer. Anyway, the dead bodies were sent to the priests. Cremation."

"That doesn't release the souls, you know. It just creates a lot of angry ghosts."

"You see them?"

"If I want to." There's lots of things I preferred not to see and was really quite expert at ignoring. Things like ghosts, my own feelings, and Duane.

"What have we here?" Duane shifted a few of the cages aside to reveal barrels coated in black wax.

"Wax makes it waterproof," I noted. I helped him roll one out where we could get to it. He used a dagger to slice through the seal and pry the lid up.

"That is no way to take care of a blade," I told him. "Did Morgan instill no respect for weapons in you?"

"Morgan wouldn't teach me. I sometimes got to watch Viktor and you train, but usually he shut me out completely, saying he couldn't pass Solhan secrets onto street scum."

"Morgan would never say something like that."

"I paraphrase. He said, 'the unworthy', which translates to the same."

"Sorry. I just assumed you learned your skill from him. You're good."

"Viktor taught me. Aguragas … others. Why limit yourself to one discipline?"

"Yet, none of them told you how to care for steel?" I swiped the dagger from his grip before he could stop me and used my belt sash to wipe it down.

It was iron and rusty. I tested the edge. "Dull too. Really?"

"That's my utility knife. I do take care of the ones I fight with."

"I hope so. But you never know when you'll need it for more. I've used everything from twisted scraps of metal to nails as a weapon when I've had to. Sharpen it when you get a chance, please?" I held it out to him.

"What's this, Eva?"

"Your 'utility knife'."

He took it and secreted it away among his myriad other weaponry. "No, I mean why this conversation?"

"You prefer I don't speak?"

"You're usually a woman of few words, and usually cutting ones."

"You don't talk much yourself."

"So, why are we now?"

"I..." I didn't want to tell him about the lightning in the storm, or that I felt terrible about not being able to give him what he wanted, or make him think I pitied him for holding out his heart only for me to stomp on it. "I ... let's just look inside already. The mystery is killing me."

I prized open the lid on the barrel and cursed, "By the Devourer."

"What is it?"

"Something not good." I pulled out a rifle and held it out for him to see.

Duane looked at it askance. "Is that a blunderbuss? It has a funny, skinny barrel."

"It's worse." I showed him a bandolier of brass bullets. "A lot worse."

"I've never seen these things before."

"You don't want to. This is really bad. Really, really bad."

"Like the Devourer will destroy the world kind of bad?"

"Ok, not that bad, but rifles like this are not something we want in Highcrowne." There looked to be about ten in the barrel we'd opened and there were at least a dozen barrels stacked behind the pigeon cages. "There's enough here to arm everyone in Gas's base down by the river. Something tells me this is not all of them. If there's more ... these are far easier to use than a blunderbuss, with greater range and accuracy. Each of these bullets means instant death to whoever they hit. I think Gas is planning for war."

"Maybe this is meant for his takeover of Darrub?"

"Rifles come from Darrub. It's where they're built. I've seen the factories. I suppose the Dead God didn't do a good enough job of killing all the humans off, so now they can start killing one another."

"Or elves," Duane said.

"Or Avians." A rifle shot from a tower had the range to reach an Avian in flight as it descended towards the Assembly.

"This is not good," Duane said, finally getting it. "Gas's rhetoric has convinced a lot of people that the elves won't allow free elections and that after General Moore steps down, they won't allow another human Crown. If he gives some of these to an angry mob, they can cause untold damage."

"I don't think Gas will wait until the elections next year. That may have been his original plan, probably why this vessel passed over the Central City, dropping a shipment past the defenses to be hidden away until needed, but I think his plan may change."

"Why? What did you do, Eva?"

"I made up a story to get him to help look for the Avian egg—without harming it. He's to give it to me. But … if he has a revolution in the works, he may speed up his timetable now that he thinks the egg will help Ulric to resurrect a new race of Avian gods."

"What?"

"I should never have said it. The story got away from me. I really should shut my mouth sometimes and write this stuff down where it can't cause any harm, just like Mister Gardens and his Elf Butler detective novels."

"Gas thinks Ulric is a threat now?"

"Yes. One he may want to eliminate, just in case." Sorry Uncle. "I gave him a ticking clock. If we can't find the egg, orb, whatever I told him, then Gas will aim to kill all the Avians and Ulric even before the elves. Anyone he thinks has the power to restore the dead."

"Like you?"

"Yes. Sorry."

"You said that before."

"I know. And it's still not enough." Sorry for damn lies and everything true left unsaid.

"I'm sorrier. There's someone we need to speak to." He grabbed my wrist as quickly as I'd grabbed his dagger before and dragged me onto the deck.

11   SWITCHING SIDES

There were even more troops topside, a full squad kitted out in polished armor and crisp, red tabards bearing the image of a golden crown, but Duane didn't bother hiding from them this time.

"General," Duane said. "You finally showed."

"Seldom does someone think he can summon a Crown," General Moore said. He'd blended in with all the other soldiers, no different from them at first glance, but I knew his face. He was always a severe one, but his expression now was peeved to say the least.

"Did my man avoid punishment?" Duane asked.

"For slipping into my private practice yard and putting a dagger to my throat before saying 'the Shadow King commands your presence at the air dock'? Yes, your spy got away."

"Definitely deserves a raise then."

"If one of Duane's people got to you so easily, you need to protect yourself better," I pointed out.

"Mister Rose doesn't want me dead, nor does Aguragas. Not yet. I have no enemies here, so I have nothing to fear."

"A beloved man of the people?"

"Something like that." He noticed the rifle Duane still carried in his other hand. "Let's talk someplace else."

The general—I couldn't help thinking of him by that title, although he had served as the human Crown for years—led the way inside the captain's cabin.

Just the place I'd wanted to search. I wasted no time opening chests and drawers, ransacking closets, and stomping on the floorboards looking for hidden compartments. The troll captain had been a big man, and it was a big cabin with lots of places to search.

"A little help?" I said, looking at Duane. He and the general stood across the map table from one another, so quiet and focused you'd have thought they were in the middle of a chess game.

"You don't need me," Duane said. Was there too much resentment in his tone? Had he given something away? The general raised an eyebrow, a slight twitch of a smile turning up one lip, before he turned expressionless again.

Duane didn't like being on the backfoot, so he struck. Not with his knives, dull or otherwise, but with words. They were even sharper, which was why he was always so quiet, honing them to deadly points: "These rifles were meant for you, General. That's why this ship was above the Central City. Aguragas works for you."

"He wants me to think he does," Moore said. "I don't trust him."

"Then you should never have accepted his offer." I couldn't help butting in. "Gas can be irresistible, but there is always a price too heavy to pay. Let me guess, you knew he had these weapons and preferred your soldiers had them too, just in case Gas turned the mob against you, but more importantly for when Hilja and the elves turned on you—which they will inevitably do."

"Aguragas has been my staunchest supporter since coming to Highcrowne," the general explained, "providing supplies during the war and as we rebuilt. He helped me claim the human Crown. I accepted his 'offer' long ago, and the bill when it comes due, will be my death. I know that. But these weapons change things. I wanted to see how many he could supply, and there seems to be no end. I can no longer pretend to play by his rules. He may want revolution and a

Highcrowne-bred human army to fulfill his dreams of empire ... I want war, simple and clear."

"Darrub," I guessed. "You want the source of these weapons, and you want to claim it before Gas can. All his machinations and plots tumble down if you launch a full-fledged army against a nation still leaderless and in disarray. I spent years there. I know about the violent and ineffectual warlords, the old hatreds that set one village against another. It will be easier to destroy them than unite them as Gas hopes."

"Is that why you stole the Avian egg?" Duane asked. "To force the Avians to back your call to war?" He was using my old trick for questioning suspects. Make them feel so guilty, even when innocent, that they'll turn on somebody, give up some secret, just to wriggle free of your accusation.

General Moore was too good, too certain, to feel guilt. That's why I hadn't tried it on him.

"I may well have used the egg," he said, "if I had known about it. The fact none of us did, not even Queen Hilja, worries me."

"The Avians worry Gas too," I noted, not admitting I had added fuel to the fire. "Enough that he may do something rash against them. If he's your staunchest ally, then you must have a spy in his ranks. Is there someone who can reveal exactly what he's planning?"

"I may not want to stop him."

I moved before Duane could do anything. I knew his loyalties lay with Calka, and I knew he was still off balance from earlier, that I had left him too exposed to play this game safely. He would give his devotion away with a glare, a stray word, a stiffening of his muscles, so I whipped General Moore around to face me. Made him focus on me.

"The Avians, and my uncle, are the only ones keeping this world safe from the real threats out there." No need to get into the details of all the big scary monsters in the dark, like plant aliens, Unmentionables, and rampaging gods. "If anything happens to them, these rifles are meaningless. Has everyone forgotten how Lili and the Dead God nearly ended the world? Are humans so short lived and short sighted?"

"You admit you are not human." The general's tone was emotionless, and I had no idea what he meant by those words.

"That a problem?"

"No. It means I can trust you more than Aguragas. Our politics are beneath you. The elves' too I see. And the dwarves once served Solhans, so they must be like children to you. You are more like the Avians than any of us."

"I wish I were so wise. I wish you were."

"I am not a man ruled by my emotions," the general said, confirming what I'd already guessed. He was the most passionate of orators, able to sway armies or crowds of citizens, but that was all show, and he had greater control over himself than any person I had ever met.

"That's not the same as wisdom." I wasn't sure I could trust someone without desire or hate.

"Close enough. It stems from experience, anyway. This is what happens to you when everything you really care about dies. It gives you a clearer perspective."

"I've lost people," I said. I wouldn't speak for Duane, but he'd lost even more. Maybe that's why he usually seemed so calm?

"Not everything. There are still people near you whom you love." I couldn't help glancing at Duane nor frowning at the knowing twinkle I'd put in the general's eye. "All that aside, I believe what you say about the Avians. That makes my decision easier. I will keep the Avians on my side and alive, wherever this leads. I don't suppose you know how to convince them to vote for war?"

"Help us find the egg, protect them, and they will listen. I led them to war once before, so it can be done."

The general nodded. "Very well. I will introduce you to my spy in Aguragas's ranks. Actually, you already know her quite well."

***

"Kali?" I said, surprised to see her in the place General Moore had told us to wait.

Part of me had hoped it was Bell he was alluding to, that her fury was all an act. Nope. She did hate me.

"What are you doing here? Both of you?" Kali asked, just as surprised. Kali probably still hated me too. Unless she was upset about Duane being there? She'd always taken Bell's side against him.

He did tend to complicate things, but Duane wouldn't let me go alone. Moore had warned him that the informant wouldn't show if the Shadow King's minions were watching, so he'd sent them away, and it was just the two of us who had walked into the mausoleum beneath the temple district—and we could just as easily have walked into a trap if the general had been so inclined to eliminate us. I didn't think I'd made his hit list, but Duane? Seemed most people in Highcrowne, Kali included, would breathe easier if he was dead. Good thing Moore was a man of honor and had set up this rendezvous in good faith.

Duane ignored Kali and her anger and hung near the entrance, acting as lookout.

"General Moore sent us," I said.

"You're working for Danny now?"

"Since when does anyone call the general 'Danny'?" I asked, but I didn't want to get side-tracked, so I quickly added, "No, we're not working for him but with him, temporarily. He now understands why the Avians are good allies to have, and we in turn can ensure they support his efforts better in future. Our mutual worry is that Aguragas will go off the rails and try to kill them all, and my uncle."

"Your uncle set slave marks for the elves during the war. He deserves to die."

"For a great many things, but there are bigger bad guys to worry about and he's needed for now. Since you apparently work for the general, I mean 'Danny', then can you please tell me what Gas is doing with all those rifles? Is he looking for the Avian orb as I asked, or plotting something else? ... and how is Bell?"

"If I'd known this would be an interrogation, I wouldn't have come. Tell me you plan to stop the guns at least, save humans from Aguragas's plans?"

"Yes, of course."

"That's all I needed to hear. Danny—the general—got my family safely out of Lallaloka, for which I owe him, but they're in Darrub now, working in one of those factories, filling bullets, and I don't want them there."

"I thought you hated your mother, your family. That they sold you into slavery?"

"My mother had no choice, my brothers and sisters were starving, and I do hate her. It's my three sisters and four brothers I'm talking about saving. They don't deserve to slave in Darrub factories making weapons that will kill more of our people—and they are slaves, as all poorly paid workers are—neither do they deserve to be collateral damage when someone decides to attack those factories. I help Danny, he helps me again by getting them all to Highcrowne."

"Right now, 'helping Danny' means helping me. What's Gas up to?" I asked again.

"He stirred up the hive after you spoke to him. Everyone is hunting something and none of us knows what we're looking for. 'Magical orb' was all we were told and that we were to keep our eyes and ears open, but I think Aguragas knows only one group who could possibly have it, and so he's focused his efforts there. He's gone to Faellion."

"The elven capital? Which elves does he suspect, in particular?"

"Someone he's been 'working with' for a while."

"Not 'for'?"

"Aguragas works for no one but Aguragas. No, he's got his fingers everywhere just like you, Shadow King."

Duane had been quiet, hiding well, but now that Kali had brought him out of the shadows, he admitted, "I think I know who Gas went to see."

"I don't have time to chase him to Faellion," I said.

"You don't have to," Duane said. "I know someone we can speak to here. Thank you, Kali."

"I don't want your thanks."

"How is Bell?" I said, trying to diffuse the fight before it started. We all cared about Bell in different ways, worried for her. Whether she was worthy of such concern...? I didn't think she was irredeemable, even if she deserved punishment at least as severe as Gypsum's, but it was hard to give up on some people completely.

"You saw her," Kali said, sadness in her voice. "Angrier than ever."

"When we were business partners, she was always so excited, a dreamer. Will that Bell ever come back to us?"

"She was always angry," Duane and Kali said at the same time, and there was a sudden, grudging comradery at that shared knowledge.

"She wanted to shake the world to its foundations from the day she joined my crew," Duane said. "Why do you think she liked to play with bombs? She never told me where the anger came from, and I never asked. We were all angry then for our own reasons."

"Something from when she was a kid," Kali said. "Not my story to tell, but it was horrific. I should have been relieved when I was freed, my slave mark removed, but Bell got angry enough for the both of us, and soon I felt guilty not being mad about it too. It all got worse when you," now her anger at Duane resurfaced, "and your uncle," that was aimed at me," started branding people for the elves, children even."

"You do know that was to save their lives?" I reminded her. "Those people all came back."

"It was still horrible for them to go through that, for us to feel so powerless. That's how Aguragas recruited Bell. I followed along because I love her. I still love her ... but what they're doing here in Highcrowne. The rifles and war Gas is stirring up in Darrub and everywhere else. I don't want people to get hurt just because I was hurt. Or Bell was hurt. It doesn't give us the right to keep it going. It's wrong. That's why I started helping Danny. Why I swear that, if you don't help him make things better in this world, then I will hunt you down."

"Lots of people are hunting me," I said. "But I'd hate for you to be one of them. I want peace. I want your family safe, everyone safe. Now, tell me everything."

This was my best chance to learn all I could about Gas's operation. There were some things my informants knew and some they didn't (and in case you were wondering, I had other informants besides bogles believe it or not). A fuller picture was always a good thing.

When Kali finished, I thanked her and said a fond farewell. Even she and Duane were a bit friendlier than before. The Shadow King's coffer of secrets was brimming over and so was mine.

Only when we were long past the temple district, surrounded by Duane's well-hidden followers once again, and headed for the barracks—where Duane said we'd find our next subject for questioning—did I admit out loud what I really thought.

"General Moore loves war more than peace," I said. "It's his favorite weapon, and I don't think he truly knows any others. People will get hurt, whether Kali sees it or not."

"And you don't really care," Duane said.

"What? Of course I care."

"Let me rephrase. You don't care enough to stop the general, do you?"

"He wants to take out those factories, which is good. Tactics … I don't want anyone but the bad guys to die. There has got to be a better way, but you're right in that I don't care right now. There are more urgent things to worry about."

"Good to know I can still read you."

"Was that some kind of morality test?"

"Truth test, since you're so fond of them of late. I'm glad I can still tell when you're lying or not." There was a knowing smile on his face I didn't like one bit.

"What else do you think I'm lying about?"

"You…" He stopped and canted his head, listening. "Keep your sword out of this and just go along."

"Go along with what?"

He didn't explain, he just vanished, slipping into some random house we were walking by. Only then did I hear the jackboots, at least half a dozen parade-ready

EEPs marched up to me. 'Go along' he'd said. That was not my style.

"Lay one hand on me," I told the leader, who happened to be Uanal's son, what's-his-name, "and you'll be picking it up off the ground and trying to attach it to your risen corpse."

He kept his distance. "She wants to see you."

"How am I supposed to get any investigation work done when you keep wanting to chat every five seconds?" I asked Hilja.

I had allowed the EEPs to precede me to the elven palace, clearing the street ahead of me, but in no way had I let them surround me or appear to have me under guard.

I was a bit annoyed that they knew where to find me. I suspected the person who had been scrying my location earlier was either Hilja or one of her pet mages. It explained why EEPs were always on my case.

"Something has changed," she said. I'd noticed right away that Hilja was less perky than usual, her golden skin a shade paler, and while she was lounging on a comfortable settee, she didn't look that comfortable. She moved her silk sash aside, revealing a long gash in her dress, the edges soaked in blood. "I was attacked."

The aforementioned pet mages had healed the wound, but she'd obviously lost some blood before they got to her, and it had been so recent she hadn't bothered changing clothes.

"I have an alibi," I said first thing.

"I know you do, but chatting to old friends in mausoleums is not a good use of your time. What am I paying you for? I was nearly assassinated!"

"First of all, you're not paying me."

"I'm not? I thought someone had arranged that?" She scowled and one of her ever-present courtiers blanched, dashing off.

"Second, don't you have EEPs to protect you from assassination? I thought that was their main job?"

"Obviously, they are not perfect. They chased off the perpetrator, who had thrown the dagger from concealment, but failed to catch them." More scowling on Hilja's part made the EEPs who had escorted me and the dozen other ones already in the room look sheepish.

"Third," I continued, "you already have the most famous detective in the Three Kingdoms working for you, so I don't even know why you want or need my help." I looked at Mister Gardens, the famous Elf Butler, who was one of Hilja's hangers-on, but he assiduously ignored my gaze, pretending he had no idea what I was talking about.

"I like multiple options," Hilja said.

"Fourth—"

"—Stop there. I see you can go at this all day. The real reason I want you to look into this is because you are not an elf. And while I should say I trust all of my people without question … I don't really. You see?" She showed me the bloody dress again. "Now, are you going to solve this?"

"I'm already working for the Avians without pay…" before I could finish, the courtier from earlier returned, huffing and puffing, and laid a small but ornate treasure chest at my feet. I'm not so low class that I rifled through it, but I did tip the lid up with my foot and was impressed by what I saw.

Hilja looked smug. "Now that I have your full attention, hear me when I say that an assassin who can get this close to me in my own palace without dying for the opportunity is one who will try again, and soon. The audacity. I am not leaving this spot or sleeping until I see the perpetrator's head on a pike."

"Will any head do?" Uanal's son asked, looking at one of the most sheepish EEPs, probably the one who had been closest to Hilja at the time of the attack.

"No scapegoats. Now, hurry up, Eva. Go."

I sighed. "Where were they hiding? And show me the dagger."

I not only got to see the scene of the crime, but I was also given a reenactment, with the courtier who had carried the treasure chest playing the part of Hilja. He was very dramatic, and I couldn't help but clap.

"Preposterous. That was not how the event transpired, my thespian sycophant," Mister Gardens said drolly.

"You were there?" I think those may have been the first words I'd ever spoken to my detective hero. Or maybe I had gushed embarrassingly when we first met that time years ago? I couldn't recall, but I did know I was struggling to keep my cool, waiting for his sagacious response.

See, I knew big words too.

"Perhaps I was the one who threw the stiletto?" he said, goading me.

"First of all, a stiletto could not have accurately crossed the distance from that hidden alcove behind the pillar to reach Queen Hilja at the base of the stairs, not and cut deep enough to penetrate her layers of fabric and whalebone corset to leave a wound like that. That's not even considering the magical protections she must have. I want to see this extraordinary dagger." I was so proud of myself for getting all of that out as coldly and efficiently as the Elf Butler himself would have. There were a few times I almost tripped over my tongue, but I felt I'd achieved the equivalent of an award-winning acrobatic feat.

"Come with me," he said without a trace of admiration.

I followed Mister Gardens into a locked anteroom to which he had the key. The dagger, edge still laced with Hilja's blood, lay on a marble plinth, illuminated by the skylight above like some work of art. The displaced marble bust of a long dead elven monarch sat on the ground nearby.

The weapon was curved slightly at the tip and at the handle. It was bronze, which was odd, the handle inlaid with ebony and finely cut rubies, the blade embossed with grapevines and as dull as a letter opener.

"That is the culprit?"

"Found beside the queen and coated in her blood."

"Darrubian. Your mages ran a trace on it, I presume?"

"Of course. Only Queen Hilja, no other residue of lifeforce."

"So, either something dead held that or someone who could conceal their essence. What about fingerprints?"

"What?"

Finally. I had him. "A new avenue of investigation in some of the human lands. I'm surprised you haven't heard of it." I buffed my fingernails.

"A human tool? They have no magic to speak of."

"Human warlocks held off the Dead God's hordes for two decades. They are not to be scoffed at."

"Held off is an overstatement. Harried the god's slow and implacable advance is more accurate."

"Whatever. It's science, not magic. Let me take the dagger for further analysis."

"You can bring your analysis here."

It was best not to touch the weapon too much anyway, so I didn't argue. "Who else has handled that thing besides you?"

"Lieutenant Uanal found it."

"I'll need to dust both of you as soon as I return, so don't disappear on me."

"Dust?"

I was loving having the upper hand too much and did not bother to explain.

I and the EEP escort Hilja assigned me, because she was afraid I would run off and ignore her case again, made our way to see Doctor Ghunnan, as he was sure to have the necessary materials.

All this walking around was so inefficient. I needed a portable speaking tube like they used on the great airships to communicate between bridge and engine room. Instead, I used the next best thing. I whistled a certain tune, and one of my invisible bogle informants alighted on my shoulder, my escort none the wiser.

"Look for Duane," I whispered. "Bitten Belly calls him 'rat meat man'. Ask if he knows anything about elf-magic penetrating daggers." Elf magic wasn't my forte. It was all about living things and my talents tended toward the dead.

"Pen-a-tr...?" The word was beyond my bogle friend.

"Just fetch Duane."

I was halfway across the Central City gardens when I spotted the goblin. Although there were more goblins around these days, the doctor was distinctive with his mechanical legs, flyaway hair, and huge spectacles. I veered over to where he waited in a line of people staring at a massive brass apparatus of steaming boilers, gauges, and tubes.

"What is this contraption?" I asked him. "And why is everyone so keen to view it?"

"Miss Thorne, how lovely to run into you again. This..."

"Triple strength, giant, ten sugar ant, leech milk kaffe!" A dwarf I recognized shouted angrily.

"Oh, that's mine," Doctor Ghunnan said, stepping forward and claiming the massive stein of kaffe.

Despite the leech milk odor wafting from the pewter mug, I was drawn to the rich scent of kaffe. Karolyne had introduced them to the city years ago, and I'd introduced sugar ant sweetener to her customers.

"I'll have one too." I pushed myself to the front of the line, waving the Avian glass fragment around like a badge. "Official business." It had some sort of power of authority because no one complained until I reached the counter.

"What do you want?" the dwarf running the kaffe cart barked.

"Reginald. Glad to see you are as grumpy as ever. Is this all yours?" He didn't wear an emancipationist red armband anymore, but I knew he was the independent type and as soon as reforms swept Highcrowne, he would have been first in line to apply for a writ of freedom from his mother.

Dwarven society was a fierce matriarchy, with mothers controlling their sons' wealth and lives, but shortly after humans were granted Citizenship, dwarves had been offered the ability to claim their freedom also. Most dwarves I'd known loved their mothers, but Reginald wasn't one of them, so I was certain he'd jumped at the chance.

"Why, yes, this is my establishment, and I won't be serving the likes of you."

"I thought we were friends?"

"Forced indenture made our paths cross, but I am uncrossing all of that. Now get to the back of the line. No one cuts, not even old 'friends'."

I went back to the goblin, who offered me a sip of his kaffe instead.

"His rules are notorious, Miss Thorne. He once banned King Harley himself for a month when he tried to force his way to the front of the queue. A terrible punishment, for Sir Reginald serves the best kaffe in all the civilized lands. I daresay no one in the Empire has anything better."

"Sir Reginald?"

"King Harley knighted him as a means of re-entering his good graces."

I almost tried the doctor's leech-juice version but stopped myself. Leech milk was terrible, and if the kaffe was fantastic enough to compensate, then I definitely didn't need a new addiction. Better to stay focused.

"Well, bring your kaffe along. I need you to help me dust for fingerprints."

"Fingerprints? My, what has happened? Did my truth serum fail to get the answers you seek?"

"It gave me answers I didn't want, not the ones I needed. I'm doing this the old-fashioned way. After I solve a few other cases in between. I'll explain on the way."

The doctor stopped by his workshop in the Assembly palace. Historians had a whole wing, and the goblin had established himself as the preeminent authority, claiming not only a large office but a series of labs and workshops with craftsmen and scientists conducting a lot more than historical research.

"What is going on here?" I asked before spotting someone else I knew. "Katherine?"

"Miss Thorne, it's been too long." The goblin's former student was wearing a lab coat and tinkering with a series of condensers and alembics that looked to be distilling something green and glowing. While resembling Avian goo, it had a paler, yellowish sheen to it.

"Are you working for Doctor Ghunnan again?" I wanted to add, 'even after he betrayed you and left you to die on a mountainside eaten by werewolves', but there was no need to bring that up if it wasn't bothering her still.

"No. I am a doctor myself now with my own lines of enquiry."

"Yes," Doctor Ghunnan said distastefully. "She insists on employing 'magical' means combined with the chemical, a new alchemical method, to recreate the Avian fluid. I cannot convince her to see sense. Now, this way."

I waved bye to Katherine and then helped the doctor gather the fingerprinting supplies required. They were stashed in a cupboard at the back of a small room devoted to forensic techniques with more humans in lab coats working on examining hairs and blood traces on glass slides under microscopes.

"The CSI team," he said.

"CSI?"

"Counter-Secrets Identification. They will uncover the truth, no matter how many centuries of fruitless and boring analysis work is required to get the guilty to confess because they just can't bear to have their criminal achievements forgotten by history."

"Sounds ... dull."

"Oh, it is."

Duane was suddenly beside me, taking the heavy box out of my hands. "Your messenger said I'd find you here."

It was annoying when he managed to sneak up on me. "Done running away from EEPs?"

"I wouldn't be doing my job very well if I allowed them to detain me too. So, you want to know how a dagger penetrated her defenses?"

"What do you know?"

"Whose defenses?" the doctor asked curiously.

I was pretty sure Hilja didn't want me telling the whole city about the assassination attempt or how close it had come. That sort of information worried the masses and opened leaders up to more attacks when others realized how close someone else had come.

"Not here," I told them both. There were far too many curious people in the labs, ears twitching as we passed by.

Only when we were near the steps of the elven palace and I made my EEP escort stand in a semicircle around us, cordoning off any passerby, did I say, "Hilja was paranoid. I saw all the wards and protections she carries. No way would a dagger thrown at her penetrate all of that without some powerful magic behind it. But whose?"

"Queen Hilja?" the goblin's hairy eyebrows went up.

"Magic is not my area," Duane said. "But I appreciate the excuse."

"Excuse for what? To see you again? Please."

"Was an attempt made on her life?" The goblin was slowly catching up. "Are we to dust the crime scene? How thrilling!"

"You know all about Avian magic," I told Duane. "And a lot more about elvish magic than I do. I want you to examine it too."

Soon we were looking at the Darrubian dagger, Mister Gardens watching us all carefully, scoffing at my inability to achieve anything on my own. "I believe the queen hired you, not a whole team. How disappointed she will be when she sees the great Eva Thorne so easily stumped."

I didn't respond to the goad and, instead, had the goblin take his fingerprints to shut him up. Lieutenant Unal was brought in next, with more fingerprints collected on white cards of paper, which the doctor carefully labelled.

Meanwhile, Duane and I stared at the knife. Just looking at it made my head spin with questions.

"Darrubian automatically makes me think Gas," I said. "But why would he be so obvious? And why now?"

"Because he doesn't care that we know it's him? He's made no secret of his ambitions and desire to end the Crowns."

"I think it's meant to make us suspect him, but Darrub has magic too, and I don't sense any of it on that blade. No evidence of anything Avian either, unless you see something I don't?"

"Nope."

"Then how did it get past Hilja's shielding? Maybe it's anti-magic?" The werewolves had an ability to negate magic around them. Could the dagger contain a werewolf claw or something similar?

"I suppose you have to test it," Duane said.

"After I dust it."

I had talked up the fingerprinting method so much, I didn't let the goblin handle that part. I gathered the prints from the knife myself and found only one clear set, a match for Lieutenant Uanal. Another set was smeared. Even if I found the person, I'd never be able to match the prints when they were of such poor quality.

The dagger had no anti-magic effects either because when I threw it at Mister Gardens it bounced right off his invisible shielding.

Lieutenant Uanal drew his sword at that, so I quickly said, "Just testing a theory."

The elf butler hadn't twitched, but he smiled when he handed the blade back.

"Well, this leaves us exactly nowhere," I mumbled to Duane, trying to ignore Mister Gardens' growing look of triumph.

I had one thing left I could try. I reached out with what remained of my soul sense.

12 SOMETIMES THERE IS SOMETHING IN THE DARK

My power had diminished in the Dead God's absence, but it grew again whenever I made use of the connection forged with the First Soul. That was a dangerous connection. I knew using it would have consequences, but once you've taken shortcuts, it is so difficult to go back to the long route. I needed to find Hilja's attacker, and more importantly, I needed to find the Avian egg. With a powerful enough soul sense, I would know who was responsible as soon as I laid eyes on them. I'd wasted too much time already, so temptation got the better of me.

"What are you doing?" Duane knew something was wrong. Green light emanated from my hands, becoming electricity that danced between my fingers and along my arms.

I didn't answer. There was no need for words because I felt all the fears and worries, his concern, and knew he did not comprehend the true danger, so why explain?

I felt Mister Garden's sharp soul, like his mind, honed and cutting, the ambition hidden behind a legacy of service, the desire for power over others he fought by hiding his true abilities with modesty. He was smarter than me, but also just as uncertain about who he should be, good or evil, and did such distinctions matter to anyone but ourselves? He loved Hilja, was filled with wonder by the Avians, and he was not guilty of anything. Not lately.

Lieutenant Tiebald Uanal, however, had something slippery wriggling inside him. Not shame or regret, more a conflict between duties. One to his Queen and the other to his clan.

I saw through his eyes, him holding the Darrubian dagger. It was clean, but he wiped it against Hilja's bloody dress and dropped it on the floor beside her before clapping a hand over her wound to save her. It was a memory snatched through my connection to his soul. But if that dagger had not wounded her, what had?

"Duane?" I asked. "Who were you taking me to see at the barracks?"

"Lord Marshall Uanal."

"Because his house is the one Aguragas suspects in Faellion?"

"Yes."

"Mister Gardens, do you have the authority to arrest Lieutenant Uanal?"

Tiebald had been waiting for me to say it, and he drew his sword.

Being attacked when I was connected to the First Soul and the powers of the Dead God was not good. Not good for anyone near me.

"Stay back," I warned Duane, as green fire spilled from my fingers. Like molten metal, the magic sizzled against the floor and shattered the mosaic.

The goblin glanced up from packing away the fingerprint kit and said, "I hate these hallucinations."

He had seen me in action during the war, and while he protested the very existence of magic, hoping to explain what I did in more logical terms, he knew destruction ensued when I was like this, and so he dove for cover behind an ornate column, dragging Mister Gardens with him.

Duane too knew what I could do, but he foolishly stayed near, saying, "Stop this, Eva. It's overkill for an EEP."

'Kill.' That is what the First Soul whispered over and over into my mind.

'Devour,' my Dead God-given power urged. Not helping.

Tiebald struck, going for the mage as any good soldier should, but Duane blocked with a dagger and pushed him back.

I reached out with power and felt the lieutenant's soul jerk loose from his body. He crumpled, his ghost like a warm column of golden light rising from his corpse. Like honey, sweet and alluring, I wanted to consume his soul, strip it of memory, free it to enter the Void and join with the Dead God rather than linger here as too many ghosts did.

'They do not need the Dead God anymore', the First Soul told me. 'They only need you to release them, to kill them all. A new god of my own creation. Taste, consume, and let us be one....'

I intended to fight. I would put the genie back in its bottle, tell the First Soul to go to hell. I did not want its offer of power. I did not want it inside my head. I intended to say those things, but pain shot through my skull, and all went dark.

I woke not knowing who I was exactly. Was I a young soldier torn by conflicting duties? An old detective somehow still surprised by life? A god? A killer? Or was I the darkness? The lump of ice in my chest, eternally hungry?

"Eva."

That was my name. I recognized the voice, felt warmth push back the cold as I remembered laughing beside him as we warmed our hands over a barrel fire on the street.

Gem-like eyes of green, peridot, gazed into mine, and I suddenly wondered if he had some non-human blood which gave him extraordinary eyes like that. His burnished skin was pure Darrub, actually a border region now extinct. His black hair raven as a Solhan's.

"Duane," I said, recognizing him before I fully recognized myself.

"I'm here."

"Do I need to tell Uanal I killed his son and ate his ghost?"

Duane smiled. "No. I stopped you just in time. He wasn't dead long."

Tiebald did look shaken and sick, though, the doctor making it worse with leeches. I'd killed him, and I might have killed everyone if Duane hadn't stopped me.

"I presume you're the one who gave me this headache?" I felt the lump on my head and came away with blood.

"Best you rest a bit too. You didn't go down easily. I've sent for Ulric. He can help, and maybe tell us what happened."

"I know what happened, and I don't need him. I'm fine." I stood, swaying, but managed to keep my feet underneath me.

"You ... it didn't look like you were the one running the show. The look in your eyes before—they weren't your eyes."

"That's not important now. I'm fine, and I know Uanal junior was involved. He planted the Darrub dagger. So Uanal senior is who I want to speak to next. After this one tells me the rest."

I stood over the EEP lieutenant, trying not to pass out, and told the doctor, "Get those leeches off him, save them for your kaffe, whatever, but give us a moment."

"It is difficult on the body when someone's heart stops, even for a short time. The lieutenant needs to recuperate."

"He can, in a cell. Not the prison where they have Gypsum, with only elves to watch him. I don't trust his fellow EEPs. Give me a torture room to get him talking. Will you help?"

"I will," Mister Gardens said. "I have access to King Fharen's dungeon here in the palace. Hilja left it relatively unused."

I was going to use it.

Tiebald Uanal ignored my questions, as I suspected he would, and I did not dare use the power of the First Soul again to see through his eyes. I protested that I was fine, but I was not. Far from it. A residue of fury coated my insides, a deep desire to end everything and anything that stood in my way. Even Duane if he dared stop me again.

I think that menacing dark evil vibe was clear to all because no one, not even the professor, said a peep as Duane dragged the EEP down to the dungeon, Mister Gardens clearing the way like a dwarfish snowplow through the streets. None of Hilja's courtiers, guards or other EEPs, even upon seeing one of their commanding officers dragged around like a rag doll, dared say a word when Mister Gardens cast his baleful gaze upon them. They ran when they saw my look close behind.

Duane fastened Tiebald to the rack. He was not squeamish about this kind of thing and seemed to assess the table full of surgical implements and other torture devices with appreciation for the thoroughness and inventiveness of the selection. Duane usually made do with whatever he had at hand while roughing up his enemies in dark alleys, I recalled.

It was me who turned squeamish. The wooden rack reminded me of when Conrad had been tortured in Fharen's other palace, in Faellion. I'd been the one strapped to the rack then, Conrad in a cage and broken beyond belief. I was not like Fharen.

"Let him go," I said, just as Duane was testing the weight of something that looked like a corkscrew with serrated teeth.

"I thought you needed more answers?"

"I saw enough to know you didn't want Hilja dead, did you Tiebald? You helped save her."

"She is my queen."

"You sought to blame Darrub. Was it Aguragas you wanted to point the finger at, or did you want to aim the elvish armies in the same direction as General Moore's? Towards the rifle factories?"

"We must stop the humans from turning against us, here and abroad, so why not make use of the attempt on Queen Hilja's life?"

"But you had the dagger already. You knew someone would try to kill her, and not in the vague, paranoid way Hilja knew herself. You knew it would happen then and there. How?"

Quiet.

I didn't want to set Duane loose on him for fear it would awaken the darkness inside me again.

"I think I know a better way to get answers from you. Shame. Let's take him to daddy and see what the Lord Marshall has to say for his son's behavior."

"Do not fear the queen's wrath or the Lord Marshall's," Mister Gardens said. "The queen would sanction torture in this instance, and so would his father."

"If he weren't involved too," I said. "Tiebald here was torn between his duty as an EEP and his duty as a son of House Uanal. Aguragas did not bother questioning the Marshall, nor Tiebald; he went straight to the elders in Faellion. That means neither Tiebald nor his father know the full story, but I bet daddy knows enough to help me stop them. If he cares for his son enough to spare him the kind of pain Hilja would sanction. To spare him scars he will never forget."

Conrad had been so shattered he never recovered. The ability my connection to the Dead God had granted me is what made me consume Conrad's soul— I was why he died, but it was being tortured and broken that really killed him before that. What made him lose the will to live. Uanal would not want that for his son, not if he was anything like the meticulous, law-abiding mage guardsman I'd once known. The same one who owed me, whether he wanted to admit it or not.

Change of scenery. Duane wasn't about to drag the lieutenant around anymore, Mister Gardens went off to report to Hilja, and the goblin professor lost all interest and returned to his research, leaving me to scowl and berate a few minor palace guardsmen, mostly dwarves—who were strong enough because of their disguised werewolf nature and eager enough because of their own distaste for elves—to haul Tiebald out of the palace and across the Central City to the barracks. Duane did follow along for giggles.

A flash of Avian glass got me in to see the Lord Marshall, even though everyone claimed he was 'busy'. When I saw the piles of reports on his desk, nothing like Duane's or Gas's spotless versions, the mess of a map with tacks and small figures to represent guard dispositions around the city, and the disgruntled merchants and citizenry lined up outside his door and angry to be sent away by 'the Avian's emissary' I realized it was no pretext. He had been busy. He sank into his chair when he saw Tiebald trussed up, arms hanging over a pole, ankles and wrists chained. The final straw.

"You failed," he said, and the hollowness in his voice meant he expected his own punishment to be coming swift and soon.

"No. Your son almost framed Darrub for the attempt on Hilja's life. He just had the bad luck of having me called onto the case."

"And Mister Gardens," Duane pointed out.

"The Elf Butler? The' Kingdoms' greatest detective'? He did nothing," I exclaimed. Duane knew how to push my buttons, and the way he smiled, I knew he did it just for his own amusement. No one else got the joke.

"You've come for me now," Marshall Uanal said. "That's fine. I'm the one who gave the order. Untie Tiebald, let him go. He is loyal."

"And to whom are you loyal, Uanal? What is your first name anyway?" I'd never gotten it. I supposed we weren't the greatest of old friends, more like old rivals.

"Stanley."

I recalled a different elf detective with that same name whom I didn't like very much, so I decided to just think of him as Uanal Senior.

"Okay, Uanal, here's what's going to happen. You will get your son to tell me where the real weapon is that wounded Hilja, and you will tell me who in Faellion ordered you to participate in this traitorous attack on your queen. After that, I will hand you over to Hilja to deal with as she sees fit, while I get on with what I'm supposed to be doing."

"And Tiebald?"

"He saved Hilja when he could have let her bleed out, so she may be lenient on him."

"I want him to have a better chance than that. I will send him to Faellion, and once he's on the airship, then I talk."

"Alright," Duane said.

I didn't think it was up to him, but I didn't need my soul sense to read him. I knew he had a double cross planned, probably one of his caravan guardsmen who could toss Tiebald to the authorities at the next port.

"Yes," I agreed. "Tiebald is small fish, and if Hilja wants to hunt him in Faellion she's welcome to. As long as he gives me the real weapon first."

Uanal unlocked a desk drawer and pulled out something heavy wrapped in plain cloth. "He returned it to me when the mages were tending the queen. I am the one who threw it, who knew how to penetrate her magical protections, and to wound without killing her. I have all the answers you need, so let him go. Now."

13 Confessions and Temptations

My Shadow King shadow was nowhere to be found when I stood on the air dock with Marshall Uanal. Duane was probably off organizing his double cross, but that was fine. I could maintain a better look of innocence if I didn't know anything.

The eagerly anti-elf, dwarven guards reluctantly let Tiebald go, Uanal Junior rubbing his bruised wrists and scowling at them from the deck of the passenger ship. He tossed his EEP beret over the side and blended into the crowd fighting to store luggage and find berths.

When the ship was out of sight, rising into the pink clouds of sunset, I told the Marshall, "Time for your confession."

I had the weapon, still wrapped in cloth. No need to dust it for prints or use my dangerous soul sense, because for once the bad guy was going to reveal his evil plans without me being tied up and ready for sacrifice. This was a first and exactly what I'd always dreamed the detective life would be like.

I should have known it was too perfect to be true.

"Miss Thorne," he began, "despite my continued utter distaste for you and your villainous family of gangsters and necromancers, I find myself strangely compelled to put on the record that I am loyal to Queen Hilja."

"Then why did you throw a knife at her?"

"I am above all loyal to the Three Kingdoms and its people, all of them. Also know that my family is an old and powerful one, and there are members in a position to change things in Faellion if certain circumstances are met, and they asked me … No. Ordered me to change circumstances in their favor. Only…"

"You thought your personal code, your own judgment greater than ours."

None of the dwarven guards' mouths had moved, and while I was used to words in my head that only I could hear, it seemed they'd heard it too, which made all of us a little uneasy. No one had spoken, or I should say 'No-Thing'.

A crate of Jollup nets moved without any Jollups or anything else living touching them. The nets, made of copper wires that could conduct electricity used to stun the flying jellyfish-like creatures, spilled out onto the dock and rearranged themselves into an apparition without defined arms or legs, just the hint of a head and a mouth where the wire mesh opened and closed with the next words spoken: "Your family will suffer for your disobedience, Marshall."

"Who – what are you?" Uanal asked, a tremor in his voice. He was a powerful mage as well as an experienced guardsman and so must sense the strangeness of the invisible creature.

It was not some camouflaged bogle or cloaked sorcerer, but an absence. There was not even a soul, I knew, for this was a Voidwalker, a sentient manifestation of the primordial nothingness from which all matter and energy arose.

And an old friend.

"No-Thing? What are you doing here?" I asked. "Oh yes, I remember you like to hang out at the docks and have vicarious and actual adventures in far flung locations. What brings you back to Highcrowne?"

"Do not interfere, Eva, for I am acting with the sanction of our entire membership."

"Since when do I not interfere in things?"

"True. Return to your barracks, Marshall, and I will deal with you later. We demand privacy."

"No," I countered, "I demand you leave my prisoner here, allow me to solve this case for Hilja, and get on with my life."

"I will provide all the answers you need, real answers that not even the Marshall possesses. Secrets which cannot be mentioned with so many witnesses."

"Unmentionable secrets. Got it. Ok, Uanal, it's your very lucky day. Go back to your office, under dwarfish guard, and solve crimes for disgruntled merchants until I decide what to do with you. You will suffer consequences, so don't think for one second this reprieve will last for long."

Uanal's brow furrowed, clearly still disliking being under my power and even more perplexed by No-Thing. He looked ready to argue, probably wanting to know what was really happening himself, who was manipulating his life and the lives of his family and for what. I knew how he felt, but I also knew he was going to be out of luck.

"Take him," I told the dwarven guardsmen. "If anyone questions why you're frog marching the Lord Marshall around, tell them you're acting on my authority. Actually..."

I didn't know how the Avian glass badge I'd been given worked, how just flashing it seemed to demonstrate my authority when it looked like something from the trash, but I suspected it was some magic that worked directly on the mind. And for some reason I knew it could do more. I pressed it against the upper arm of each guard and said, "I deputize you. Now, don't let Marshall Uanal run off."

"Ma'am!" the dwarves saluted, beaming with pride.

"I would not be so low class as to 'run off'," Uanal protested. "And I have a right to stay and learn what all of this is about."

"Believe me, there are some things you don't want to know, because knowing them means some very powerful people will think you know too much and are better off dead. Now get out of here while you still can." I didn't have to argue further because my new deputies happily hauled him away.

"Come with me," No-Thing said. He scooted like a giant copper slug into a nearby alley.

There were goblin and human dockworkers about, staring open mouthed at the sight, but as soon as we passed, they shook their heads and got back to hauling cargo or swabbing decks. Either Highcrowne natives were immune to being overly shocked by the strange and bizarre, or No-Thing could cast some sort of forgetting spell on them. Such a spell would be useful to know. I had a long list of people I'd like to forget about me, and things I'd like to forget myself.

The slow clop of hooves caught my attention, and I saw a scrawny horse making its way toward us. Closer examination revealed it was too tall and emaciated to be a regular horse, twice as tall and twice as thin, and its head was more bulbous, its dark, liquid eyes facing more forward. I knew this Unmentionable too.

"More than one of you is cause for worry," I noted. "It has been a long time...?"

"Tikaban is my name."

"There are more of us nearby," No-Thing said. "But you know how most prefer the night."

"An Unmentionable convention in Highcrowne, an Avian egg stolen, an elf queen nearly assassinated ... I'm really starting to worry. Why are you trying to destroy my city? My home? Just as I return to it?" I felt a sudden fierce protectiveness, a desire to fight them, however I could, to protect this place and all those I loved here. "You don't get to play games with my town."

"You do not excel at games, my dear. Far too direct for that," the horse guy, Tikaban, said in his slow, plodding cadence which took supreme patience from me not to hurry along. "This is a four-dimensional game played over eons, with millions of pieces each trying to exert their will, just like you."

"No one's will is quite like mine, and not every piece in the game is the same," I warned. "Sometimes one of those pieces will reach up and slap you in the face. So, get over yourself and just tell me why you had Uanal attack Hilja."

Tikaban sighed. "It is not the full picture, but you do know how she has changed?"

"More like the common elf, she told me, meaning...? You think she will reinstitute slavery?"

"More. She has the brilliance and will to forge an elven empire, one never seen on this world before, and for that she must die."

"I shudder at the thought, but why one empire over another? What about Gas's human empire? Or a new dwarven vision for the future? Why not...?"

"It is the Solhan empire that is destined to be reborn."

"No. That's an even worse idea than elves, and says who anyway? I thought Unmentionables shaped this world according to their desires, their whims, so who says it is 'destiny'?"

I wasn't even sure if there were enough Solhans left to count as a small city let alone an empire. They'd been even more decimated by the unchecked aggression of the Dead God on Lili's chain. My mother had wanted everyone dead and beneath her heel. There were some Solhans scattered across the world, on Faellion islands, deep in human jungles, or fled across the ice fields of the north. But who would lead them?

"Wait a minute," I clued in. "Fharen talked of something similar, and the person whispering in his ear then was—"

"—Ilsa," No-Thing confirmed. "Yes, she and you are among the last heirs of Solheim, descended of the

Keeper and the high priestess, leader of the Nine, and the last remnant of the ancient imperial bloodline.

'Among' the last heirs. I didn't think he meant Little Viktor. He knew about Dawn. My poor child.

All I had wanted was Thane, a part of my love for him, to continue, but Dawn would bear the consequences, whether from the likes of Hilja or the Unmentionables, all wanting to use her.

"Ilsa has swayed you somehow," I said.

"She has joined our number."

Ilsa an Unmentionable? No thought terrified me more. She was pure evil, capricious from birth, and lacked wisdom to temper her desires. All she desired was power, but now that she was a vampire, blood had probably made the list too.

"She's as bad as Harbinger," I said.

"She claimed Harbinger's power," No-Thing explained. "A mere fledging, she managed to hunt down his brides one by one, all his surviving spawn, and absorbed their blood into hers. She surprised even us with her ferocity and cunning. And when she found us and demanded Harbinger's old position be hers as well, some of us acquiesced. She is not as powerful as Olyvandra, despite her stolen power, but Olyvandra is still imprisoned. Unless she can claim leadership, most will obey Ilsa's decrees. She calls for us to slay Hilja and undermine the elves before they become a threat to her plans. We need someone to temper your sister. We need you, Eva."

"Me? An Unmentionable?" I shivered at that thought almost as much as hearing Ilsa was among them already. "I'm not a joiner," I said automatically.

But what if I was the only one who could stop Ilsa and whatever else she had planned? No, there had to be another way.

"What if I free Olyve? Tell me where she's imprisoned and how to do it."

"I cannot, for I do not know. Harbinger saw to her punishment and so perhaps only Ilsa knows where she is."

All roads were leading to my sister. Damn her.

"And where do the Avians fit in? Did my sister decree their species was to end too? Did she steal the egg?" With Harbinger's power she'd be able to fly, move as mist, even, steal anything she wanted. Kill anything she wanted. Surprising she hadn't managed to reach Hilja herself. Maybe her power was not yet as great as Harbinger's?

"The Avians do not concern her. I do not know who has the egg," Tikaban said.

"Something Unmentionables do not know about? How lax of you."

"You cannot dismiss this offer so casually, Eva. Join us," No-Thing insisted. "Help us."

"You only want me because you know I've reconnected to the First Soul. For all I know, it's what Ilsa wants too. That's why she sent you and friendly, horse guy here to convince me."

"We are not her allies," No-Thing insisted. "I am your ally, Eva. Your friend. Yes, she and the others want the First Soul, and that is how we convinced them to allow us to make this offer. But Ilsa fears you too, and she will kill you to take it first chance she gets. That's why we will protect you and do all we can to free Olyve."

"The First Soul is borrowed power," I warned. "I will not have it for long."

I intended to perform the ritual soon, to save Dawn and myself. The First Soul was changing us. Because of it, a part of me understood Ilsa, understood how tempting it was to rule, to not be the one at the bottom of the heap struggling to survive but the one on top crushing all foes beneath our heels.

Us. I was thinking of joining Ilsa, and that's what decided me. I needed to stop her before the First Soul convinced me she was right. I needed to release Olyvandra. I could not trust myself to use the First Soul's power. I had to give it up, but once I was powerless, I needed a dragon godmother to protect Dawn. If someone like Ilsa ran the Unmentionables, we would never be safe.

"Alright," I told Tikaban and the pile of copper net that was No-Thing. "I'll join. How do I sign up? Do I get a club ring or anything?"

It was only for now, I told myself. I knew I would regret it, but I would regret not doing it more.

14 THE HALLS OF POWER

Pieces were falling into place, disparate comments and observations. Ilsa had been visiting Gypsum, accessing her knowledge of me. My old friend had spied on me for years while working for the Dead God, and while my sister had been ignoring me, Gypsum had been analyzing me. She understood my weaknesses better than anyone.

All the whispers of Hilja's ineffectualness against the rise of democracy, her lack of an heir, fed through Uanal's clan and others all stemmed from Ilsa. She was planting the seeds for someone to replace the Elf Queen.

Hilja and Duane had already known about Dawn, so Ilsa must have too. She knew there was an heir to both the elf crown and Solheim in one young, moldable person. Ilsa could rule a new Solhan empire as an immortal vampire, but Dawn would be a convenient stepping stone before she was eliminated too. She didn't need Hilja, stubborn Hilja, if she could crown Dawn.

That meant Ilsa needed me to control Dawn—or me dead. She probably intended to see how my club initiation went. Would I join with her, or oppose her? And could she get control of the First Soul either way? I needed her information on Olyvandra, so we both needed time to assess one another and learn secrets none of our spies could glean for us. That meant she wouldn't kill me at first sight. Good.

I went home and kissed Dawn's sleeping brow. I reinforced all my protections, adjusted my commands for Nanny. She was already wary of Ilsa, and I learned she had visited sometime before I arrived. An invitation had been made, and so I made sure to specifically rescind it. My wards would likely have kept her out still, but better to be safe. I also left commands with my most loyal informants to make sure Nanny was safe, that the house was protected and supplied. I was preparing it for a siege, and it was under siege until I had dealt with my sister.

Last, I went to Duane and asked for his protection also.

"You don't have to ask," he said.

We were in his office again, and so I pushed his chair and rug aside and opened the trapdoor to Viktor's secret chamber.

Duane went rigid. He must never have gone down there. Good. He was right to fear the Devourer.

He didn't ask what I was doing, and he wisely waited above as I went down. There was the photo of Emily, the offerings of entrails on the altar now mummified with age. I put my hand on the statue.

The symbol of the Devourer was not a mouth but an eye, opened wide, its pupil a hollow, painted black around the edges. I stared into that empty space and felt my connection to it, to the Dead God, to Thane … the trinity of them connected by the First Soul.

"May you devour the First Soul, Great Devourer," I prayed, "May you free Thane, free me and Dawn, of its burden. May your ancient hunt for it finally end as you swallow its darkness with your own. Set us free."

I was not the praying type, but for this, my greatest wish, I was willing to try anything. I pressed fingers to head, lips, and heart and then scrambled up the stairs to seal the door before fear overwhelmed me. There was something creepy about that shrine my brother had built. The Devourer was there, listening.

"What's going on, Eva?" Duane asked. I don't think I'd ever seen him truly frightened before, not even when we set off for Solheim, and so it took me a moment to recognize what his expression and that tremor in his voice meant.

"Ilsa," I said. That was usually enough for him to glean I was not in a good place.

"She's not dead?"

"She is and isn't. I have to go away for a little while to deal with her."

"Alone?"

"It's the only way." When he looked ready to argue, his preposterous vow to protect me goading him on, I quickly added, "But I will need you soon enough. I intend a jailbreak—for which I think you're eminently suited. I just need to find the jail first."

"I'm in."

"Thank you." I never said those words, so his fear spiked even more as I hurried out the door.

I knew his spies were watching me, but not even they or Hilja's scrying mages would be able to track me for long.

I climbed steps to the cliffs near the air dock and felt the portal before No-Thing opened it. It was a blur, a bubble of refracted light, and I stepped through. This must be the portal No-Thing took whenever he wanted to catch a ride on an airship. A Voidwalker like him travelled through void portals even more easily than the goblin doctor with his scientific equipment could manage.

"Quickly," I told No-Thing, who was invisible but had to be nearby to have opened the door for me. Void portals were dangerous for me. It was easier for the

First Soul to reach me in this plane, and I felt its cold lump inside me growing stronger.

No-Thing didn't waste time with words but tossed me out a moment later into a forest where one of the moons hung full in the sky, making everything bright as midday to my Solhan night vision. I didn't recognize the area. It was not the pine wilderness near Highcrowne nor the jungles of Faellion. It was all oaks and moss-covered stones. Perhaps a valley near the Solhan border of Archon? That explained why it was night here.

"I would have thought Ilsa the type to take our mother's throne. Why are we not in Solheim?" I asked.

No-Thing had not yet inhabited a body, but he stirred hanging moss, giving it a mouth so I had a place to focus my gaze. "She found something here she wants you to see. Know that her ears are keener than yours."

Meaning she could hear everything we were saying. I guessed as much, so I stayed quiet. It was hard to have anything nice to say when contemplating my sister.

No-Thing moved branches aside for me, leading me along a dirt path not made by travelers but by rivulets formed during heavy rains. The forest was damp but not quite a swamp, the air warmer than Highcrowne's but with a chill.

That iciness could be my sister. I sensed the death of her before I entered the ruin.

There was a decayed hut in the clearing, a hermit's abode long abandoned, but the pillars and broken arches surrounding it were what caught my eye. They were Solhan in design, made of dark stone and devoid of writing. Ancient.

"Ilsa," I said by way of acknowledgement when her ghostly white form appeared from the low hanging mist. She and I both wore a lot of black, but she was paler because of that whole undead vampire thing. Her lips looked redder than mine, probably stained with someone's blood.

"Eva. You have decided to join me?"

"Yes. Better to be an Unmentionable than playing catch up with their schemes. I hear you want Solheim back. I assume this ruin explains something you desperately want your big sister to know?"

"How interesting your take on things, how delusional. I think I have always admired your ability to live in a dream world, one where you thought you could defy our uncle, ignore your Solhan nature, and be ordinary, be like some silly detective in one of your books. Has reality hit yet?"

"Like a landslide."

"Good. It's a start. You are right in that I wanted to share this place with you. Who else but my twin would understand?" She beckoned for me to follow her deeper into the ruins.

Traces of silver sparkled on a broken wall, bright blue with moonlight, where ivy and vines and been torn away to reveal a mural. Older than words, it used pictographs, combinations of jagged lines indicating rivers, triangular mountains, circles for the celestial objects...

"I've seen this language before," I said. I'd learned to read it. I'd had to when searching for a way to reverse what the First Soul was doing to Dawn. I'd seen something similar in the Avian refuge. "It's Solhan?"

"The language of our forebears. And this, this is where they first dwelled, before Solheim, before they became lost to mysticism. Here is where they forged an empire, and here is where you first see the name Thorne."

I saw it on the mural, literal thorns encircling a figure with its arms outstretched, all inlaid with that silverish material. Silver would have corroded over the millennia, so it was something rarer, and when I touched it, I understood. I tasted metal on my tongue, smelled blood and green growing things that soaked up the remains of battle. This place was connected to me. The pictographs were more than words or art, they were preserved ancestral memory, summoning visions of the past for those with the right bloodline to read them.

"Our ancestors were the ones who forged this empire, Eva, and we can forge it again." Ilsa said. "Mother was not of the Thorne line, she did not understand, wanting only death or souls to control, wanting only an end to all things. We can have more. We can be a beginning. We can feed on life."

"Talking like a vampire there."

"I have never been more aware of life since my death. I now comprehend the importance of it, and the Solhan line must continue. In you—and Dawn. The name of Thorne should not be writ only on these ruins. It deserves monuments to our glory. I will build us an empire that will outlast all others. I will build it for you."

"How magnanimous. And let me guess, you want only the First Soul in exchange? An empire for me, and godhood for you?"

"Why not? What is stopping us?"

What indeed?

Was that the First Soul talking or me? Sometimes being a Solhan made it hard to tell.

"Do you even know how to use it to achieve godhood?" I asked.

"Do you?"

"No. But I suspect it means losing yourself. Trickster lost his sanity, and when I touch it, I feel it stealing my humanity."

"You are not human, so why does that matter?"

"I guess I mean love. It steals my capacity to love anything but power. What do you think it would steal from you, dear sister, since you already lack that? Is it worth the risk?"

"Of course it is."

"Let's see." I stepped closer to her, and she smelled like the grave. Little fangs peeked from beneath her lips as she scented my life. Was she always so hungry? I knew it was dangerous to call on the First Soul, especially with no Duane to stop me. I hoped No-Thing would know what to do. He lurked, invisible somewhere, the lack of him as palatable as the vacancy inside Ilsa.

The First Soul did not reach for her, sensing the same lack. What did she have that it could possibly want?

I tried to remember my hatred for her, all the slights and evil words and acts from our lifetime together, but I was growing empty too. Such passion was hard to summon. Thane too was gone, a million miles away across the Void, Dawn locked in slumber in dreamlands I could never reach, and as I thought of them all, I felt numb. Where was this life Ilsa wanted to relish, to rekindle?

I glanced at the forest around me and only when the green light of the second moon flashed on the silver lines of the mural did I feel something. Green eyes. Someone who needed me. Life where I was death.

The First Soul suddenly awoke inside me, and its shadow crept out of mine, reaching for the moonlight, touching tendrils to the mural of my ancestors. It brushed by Ilsa and recoiled, but I would not allow it to be so choosy. I forced it to strike. Like an adder, it cut into her bloodless flesh, and as it penetrated, I dug into her soul, into her memories.

Where is Olyve? I demanded to know.

I saw golden scales glint, firelight through a membrane of flesh, heard the flap of wings, the rattle of ensorcelled chains echoing in a vast chamber, and felt heat like nothing I could imagine enduring. Only a dragon like Olyvandra could survive it. She was in a volcano, floating on a life raft of cooled stone, an eggshell thick crust on the surface of the magma. The air was unbreathable, burning, stinking, and I had no idea how to reach her through the clouds of steam.

As the question arose in me, the answer was forthcoming in Ilsa's memory. I saw her mist form hovering, but it was not her then—it was Harbinger, her maker. His memory.

Harbinger laughed as Olyvandra groggily awoke. All the Unmentionables had cast their judgment and deemed her betrayer. It had taken their combined might to subdue her, if only temporarily. She seemed surprised to discover where she was and tried to bite the stony elementals whose feet merged with the molten crust, who tightened the chains binding her. Her teeth glanced off them, and they yanked harder on the bindings, which ran through hoops anchored high up on the walls of the caldera. She chewed on the chains, and then on her own flesh, trying to break free.

"It is useless," Harbinger told her. "We have made your skin impervious, your chains as well. Nothing can free you. The elementals will bring just enough meat to keep you from starving. You will remain here forever, suffering. I am forbidden to kill one of our own, else I would offer you that release. I am sorry."

"You are not," Olyve said.

"No."

I didn't care to watch Harbinger gloat, so I dug into his memory, seeking the location of the volcano, what he knew of the elementals, of the enchantment on the chains....

"Stop," Ilsa said, pulling away from the shadowy touch of the First Soul. It was only too obliging to release her. She was tasteless, unappealing.

"I'm sorry," I lied, backing way up, all the way back to the spot where I'd first entered the glade. "It does things like that, steal memories. Harbinger's are a treasure trove. Perhaps that is what you can sacrifice to it in exchange for godhood?"

She stood assessing, and I knew she knew.

Time to run.

"Home please, No-Thing." I said before Ilsa could countermand the order. The Voidwalker was ready and too fast, even for a vampire. We were gone before she was halfway through saying 'grab her' and No-Thing couldn't actually grab anything, not unless he animated a material form, so it really was a stupid demand. He opened the portal, I stepped through, and then we were back on the air dock in Highcrowne.

"How long will it take her to get here?" I asked.

"Archon is a day's flight by dragon," he said. "And she has no dragon."

"Not even a chained one soon." I smiled.

"She does have Harbinger's ability to move quickly at night," he warned. "So do what you must, soon. I cannot defy our edict, cannot help you free Olyvandra, but I will take Tikaban and join them. He can begin a slow, very slow, debate as to how best to deal with you since you spurned our offer of membership."

Joining the Unmentionables would have meant protection from them, but also needing to follow their rules. I needed to break a few first if I was going to set my dragon godmother free.

"Thank you, No-Thing. And good luck."

"To you as well."

The absence that was him was gone, and I hurried to start phase two of the plan.

15 JAILBREAK

When I filled Duane in, roughly, on what was happening, he wrongly assumed I needed his help to free Olyve.

"No, not even you could steal something from inside a volcano. It's going to take a couple of damsels to rescue this dragon damsel in distress. One of them a royal dwarf with a powerful werewolf bloodline and the anti-magic ability that goes along with it."

"Gypsum?"

"Yes."

"Northcliff Prison is beneath my abilities."

"Easy then, so stop complaining and let's go. I should mention it is now guarded entirely by EEPs who work for Hilja, I think. Could be Marshall Uanal's people? Whomever is after Gas. So, not your ordinary prison guards."

"Get Hilja to release her then."

"She'd never, no matter how much explaining I did. I'm going off mission again. Very off, but in a way, not. It's all linked."

"If you say so."

I was glad someone understood: Just accept the crazy. It's easier that way.

I figured we'd be on the run from Crown authority once we freed Gypsum, the most notorious traitor in living memory, so I thought I'd get phase three of the plan underway before phase two was complete. That meant a visit to the history wing of the palace and Doctor Ghunnan.

Duane snickered at the tapestries we walked by.

"What is so funny?" I asked, offence clearly taken.

"You in a dress. I have seen you wear one from time to time, but I'm pretty sure not during a battle with werewolves."

"Actually, I was wearing one then. It got ripped something terrible."

"That bad?" He indicated one panel where a werewolf claw had created a very stylish tear from ankle to hip.

"Worse."

"Wow. Wish I'd been there."

I walked faster as heat rose in my cheeks. Best to get past the embarrassing 'history' portion of this tour and straight to the labs.

A small explosion and puff of smoke sent some assistants evacuating into the halls and put Duane on edge—if he'd been a cat his claws would have been sunk into the ceiling—but massive ventilation fans hooked up to steam generators quickly sucked out the noxious fumes and everyone went back to work. I found the goblin doctor inside wearing a gas mask and completely unwilling to abandon what he'd been doing for even a moment.

"What is that?" I asked.

The goblin held a pair of silver spectacles with blue lenses. Something like that would have been great to keep the sun out of my eyes when I was in Darrub and might actually enhance my imposing glare if I peeked over the top of them.

He removed the gas mask so he could answer. "It allows one to see different spectra, different wavelengths of light. Let me demonstrate."

He put them on me, and I liked them even more as the room was now a cool blue. He touched a small lever on the side, and suddenly all the people were shades of orange, yellow and red.

"That's heat vision," he explained.

"I need to retrieve something from a volcano, which I already know is hot."

Another touch of the lever, and the people were black but the magical objects—some Avian-goo powered devices, Duane's bracelets and hidden knives, plus my whole outfit—were silver and purple, the more powerful the object the more purple.

"Oh. What's this setting?" I asked.

"I have yet to work out a consistent pattern, but the Avian liquid shows strongly in this wavelength, while my radiant solution does not, so I am keen to identify the cause."

"Magic."

He waved away my explanation. "A blanket term for the currently unknown, hardly useful."

"Can I keep these?"

"No." He took them and put them back on the table.

Duane picked up a few of the spikey metal jacks. "Sticky bombs. I love these. Without Bell around to make me more…"

The goblin snatched those out of his hands too and carefully set them back in the cushioned box they'd been stored in. "These are more than sticky bombs. They contain a small insect, preserved in amber, that when ignited with a chemical reaction triggered on impact, releases an exponentially larger burst of energy, equivalent to a case of dynamite."

"And they're just sitting there?" The goblin was worse than Bell. At least she kept her explosives in the fridge where only a house guest could run across them, and she had very few of those. Here, anyone could pick them up—and I meant Duane who stealthily pocketed several when the goblin's back was turned.

I shuddered at sight of a small blunderbuss with a crank on one side. "I hate those things."

"That one stuns with a stored electric charge and is not fatal unless the victim has a heart condition. I recommend always asking before stunning someone if possible."

"I'll do that." He let me add that one to my traveling backpack, although I didn't really want it.

Duane took a grapnel gun and hid it somewhere in his mysteriously roomy jacket. Elvish magic pockets I suspected.

"That one?" I indicated a stylus with a sharp metal point.

"A self-inking pen." He demonstrated by scribbling on a notepad.

"I know that, but is it special, like the glasses?"

"No. It writes."

"Do you have anything that can help me?"

He showed me a pair of metal boots with springs and a backpack with large, brass cylinders. "Vaulting boots or a jetpack. Which do you prefer?"

"Great for some petty thievery, maybe even not so petty," I said, "but rescuing a dragon from a volcano?"

I shouldn't have mentioned the dragon. He didn't believe in them anymore than magic—wyverns, yes, dragons, no. One was a mindless animal, the other an immortal and mystic beast.

"I can see why you want 'magic' lenses if you are seeking a 'magic' dragon." He made a funny gesture with his fingers whenever he mentioned 'magic'.

"Are you pretending to have claws or something?"

"Those are air quotes to emphasize my disdain for your superstitious thinking. I admire so much about you, Miss Thorne, but just when I think it is possible to educate you, you disappoint me so."

"The feeling is mutual. Nevertheless, you are my best hope. So, let's say I need to rescue a very large wyvern chained inside a volcano, with only a thin crust of hardened magma separating it and me from unimaginable heat and poisonous vapors … how would I do that?"

"Very well. If I am your 'best hope'," he did those funny claw fingers again, "then come with me."

He led us to a huge storeroom where a shiny, brass globe with round, riveted windows hung from chains on the ceiling. It was large enough to hold a handful of people, but as far as I could see it had no wings or other means of propulsion.

"How is that going to help?"

"It is a heat resistant submersible specifically designed for exploring the underworld, the depths where immense pressures and magma threaten life. I've been dying to toss it into a volcano."

"But we need to get out of a volcano."

"There's a winch, which we can attach to an airship to lower ourselves down and then back up again." He had a scale model he used to demonstrate.

"I can supply the airship," Duane said. I knew he meant the pirate's one we'd stolen. He may own others but no use letting that one go to waste.

"It's a plan then," I said, taking a moment to play with the miniature retractable winch in the doctor's toy model. "You get all this ready, and we'll find you at the air dock in an hour."

"That soon? I had hoped to test it under more controlled circumstances with a student 'volunteer'."

"A cranky vampire is trying to beat the sunrise and will be here soon, plus I expect most of the Highcrowne city watch once we secure our package." That was my signal to Duane. "Let's go."

"I do love a good secret mission and all the better with a ticking clock," the doctor said, rubbing his hands gleefully.

I snatched the magic spectacles on my way out.

A short time later, I was flashing my Avian glass badge at the Northcliff prison guards again. When they insisted on me waiting for the warden—delayed by who knows what? A sumptuous elven lunch bought with bribes?—I looked over my new spectacles at them and said, "No. I need to see her now."

The glare and the glass got me inside the front door at least. Once there, I clapped them both on the shoulders, saying, "That wasn't so hard." And they crumpled into a snoring heap of EEPs.

No one was immune to the Dead God's power, which my sleep charm relied on. Elves thought they had been immune to the Risen plague when the god made war on the world under Lili of Solheim's command, but He was merely prioritizing his favorite worshippers first—Solhans and humans. Elves and dwarves had different if similar deities, gods of Rebirth or the Undermountain respectively, but just because they didn't believe in the Dead God didn't mean He didn't believe in them. He was a Primal.

I did the same to the warden and the few other guards I passed on my way to the tower. "Sweet dreams," I told them as they fell.

By the time I breathlessly reached the top of the staircase, I was wishing I could have had Duane's part in the plan, but he would have killed his way inside. At least now Hilja would be less cross with me when she found out about all this.

Getting through the door to the cell meant using a guard's key, easy, but Gypsum's bindings would be another matter.

"Eva?" Gypsum eyed the key and the crumpled guard outside. "What are you doing? This is not part of the elves' plan, is it?"

"Nope. My plan. And you know how crazy those get." I pulled out twin pairs of iron and silver bolt cutters. Getting the timing right and ensuring I used both simultaneously would be tricky, but it was the only way to cut through ensorcelled manacles.

"You're giving me back my powers? Why?" Gypsum seemed more trepidatious than I was.

"I need your help, and you're going to give it without question. You have a lot to make up for, and this is only the start."

"You're willing to trust me again?"

"Not yet, not ever most likely, but this is your one opportunity to try and make things right. Don't blow it."

She sagged, and I hadn't realized how rigid she'd been before, how ready to hear the worst, like I'd decided the tower was too good for her and execution would be better.

"Thank you. I will help. Without question." She held out her wrists, and I tried to be ambidextrous as I cut into the first one. The bolt cutters couldn't manage in one go, so it was a slow and frustrating process.

Finally, she was free, and through the magic detection setting on my glasses, I watched veins of purple course through her body, into her muscles, making her stronger. Then the magic vanished. The anti-magic nature of werewolves was so intriguing, I wished Doctor Ghunnan would study that in his labs, but he had to believe in magic first to understand what could nullify it.

"We need to get out the window," I told her.

She transformed her hands into werewolf paws, complete with dagger-long claws, which sliced into the stones around the window and pulled the rubble down at our feet.

I whistled, and a rope ladder appeared, hanging from the dirigible outside. Duane waved us up.

The ladder was for me. Gypsum leaped, her werewolf strength shooting lines of magical purple into her legs as I watched through my glasses. Ok, I should probably take them off, but it was fun. I'd been able to sense magic before, see it in a way, but not like this.

The dirigible was on the move before I was halfway up the ladder. I held on tight as Duane cranked up the engines, and soon we were hovering above Doctor Ghunnan and a gaggle of assistants. They were preparing the winch and submersible, which had been transported to the docks in a large wooden crate.

As the dirigible sunk into its berth, I leapt to stand beside the goblin before I could get crushed. Duane had been practicing his landings, obviously, but wood still screeched against wood.

"Quickly now," the goblin ordered. As soon as the gangplank was down, they were hauling things aboard, the sound of drills loud in the predawn as they secured the winch and a series of guide rails for the submersible to the ship's deck. There was an industrial automaton as well.

"I don't like those things," I told Doctor Ghunnan, meaning I didn't want it.

"I need it." He broached no further argument, and there wasn't time anyway. There was a siren from the direction of the prison.

The swarm of 'history department' workers finished quickly, and dispersed just as quickly, leaving only the doctor behind.

A blur, which had to be Gypsum in werewolf form, cast off the lines, pulled in the gangplank, and then vanished into the captain's cabin before the goblin's eyes could fully focus on her.

"Is that...?" he began. He shook his head. He didn't want to know. He's seen werewolves in action before and never stopped insisting they were mere hallucination.

I joined Duane at the helm just as a golden ball of light appeared on the horizon. "It's morning," I said, relieved. "We beat Ilsa."

"And the Watch." He indicated the guards just now reaching the air dock far below.

"We'll have to face them all eventually."

"Why not keep sailing, forever, never touching ground again?" Wind blew through his hair and his green eyes shone.

I had not seen such joy on his face since ... ever. A glimpse here and there when we played as children, but he'd already lost everything then, already had a ball of sorrow inside that no amount of twinkle in the eye could mask. For once, with no minions surrounding him, no Highcrowne to survive or wrest into submission, he looked happy. The expression suited him.

"You know why. Dawn. Everything I do is for her." I meant it. I didn't even really care so much if the First Soul claimed me, or if I joined Thane at Death's side, but she deserved to be free of all of that, as free and joyful as Duane in that moment.

"I know." The sorrow settled inside him again, and I regretted saying anything.

"Maybe it's enough to know this is possible? Someday," I added.

A twinkle returned, a half-smile, and I felt myself copying him, unable to resist as a lightning strike of possibility filled me, warmed me, pushing the dark away.

"Now, where is this volcano?" he asked.

16 OUT OF THE FRYING PAN....

I had stolen memories, stolen from Ilsa who had stolen them from Harbinger, so my attempts to navigate were frustrated by sketchy information, and both Duane and the goblin doctor grew frustrated as I shifted our heading once again.

"I know it's in this region," I mumbled, studying the topographical charts. Airship navigation was new to me. Give me land or sea, the infiniteness of sky was just too much.

Harbinger had flown to the volcano, but his shadowy mist form navigated with a feel for magnetism and gravity, not sight or compass. I recalled what the view from the rim of the volcano had looked like when he resumed his more human form, and there had been a chain of sharp peaks all around. While I had steered us to the correct mountain range, it was dotted with too many possible volcanoes. This was a primordial region where eruptions happened regularly, plumes streamed from several summits, and layers of ash covered slopes of volcanic rock as far as you could see.

"If there was a lava pool," the goblin said, "it would generate plumes of steam or other gases, and lenticular clouds might form above it."

"That narrows it down to about ten volcanoes." Duane indicated the expanse before us.

"I didn't see any other plumes in the memory, so it must be one of the volcanoes on the edge with no view of the others," I reasoned.

"And was it a dome volcano or a caldera with a new cone of lava forming inside?" the goblin asked.

"What's the difference?"

He sighed, as he always did when explaining things to me and other simpletons. "Orange lava might be visible from a distance if it was a dome with an active vent, while the ancient caldera structure would hide the glowing vent inside itself."

"Then it's a caldera," I said, more certain. "The lava wasn't visible until you climbed way down inside."

"So, we are looking for a flat summit, with gas plumes, no visible lava, and on the edge of the volcanic range," the goblin summarized. "This one."

He pointed to a wider, flatter spot on the topographical map, surrounded by high peaks on one side. Looked as good a place to start as any. I gave Duane the new heading, and we turned toward a section of the range that looked more normal, except for a single, misty plume and a strange, circular cloud that hung over it like a giant dirigible balloon.

When we were in the shadow of the massive cloud, the caldera below was dark except for glowing circles of lava covered in black islands of rock.

"I think this is it." It felt right.

My soul sense detected something familiar. Olyve? Or simple danger? It was hard to be certain, as Olyvandra had always filled me with a deep sense of dread, of barely contained evil in a charming form. While Harbinger and other Unmentionables had given reign to their darker impulses, Olyve had fought hers, even though she might well be the darkest of all. That's why I admired her. And needed her. Not just to protect Dawn, but for her guidance.

"Ready the submersible," I told the doctor. "I'll scout ahead."

I went to put on a harness and saw Duane already donning one. "I'll scout," he said.

"I need you to steer this ship and keep it steady."

"I've anchored it to the caldera."

"I know you're an accomplished thief, a cat burglar extraordinaire," I said, "and under normal circumstances, it would make sense for you to go first, but if my hungry dragon godmother is down there, she's going to think you're just lunch on a string."

"Good point." He took off the harness and held it out to me. "Here, if you're certain she won't eat you."

"I'm never certain of that, but I have a better chance."

A few minutes later I was being lowered into the jaws of death, possibly literally. I had on the doctor's gas mask which protected me from invisible noxious fumes but not from being blinded by the visible clouds of steam fogging up my goggles.

A thick underwater diving outfit, also borrowed from the doctor, shielded me from the heat at this height, although it wouldn't work well lower down, which was what the submersible was for. I'd seen Gypsum and the doctor's industrial automaton moving it into position above, readying it for when I confirmed this was the right place.

I couldn't see a thing and wiped the round window set in the brass helmet with my gloves for the dozenth time. I tugged the rope once, sending a vibration up that signaled Duane to lower me further. He was frustratingly slow at it, but after a few more tugs, I was past the plume that had obscured my view and caught sight of huge chains anchored to the cavern walls. This was the place.

Dark shapes swung from giant link to giant link along the chain, like monkeys swinging branch to branch. Were they guardian elementals? Gypsum's problem, not mine, as she'd be coming down next in werewolf form to carry out her part in the plan.

Eyes glowed as one of the dark figures turned toward me. Suddenly, it launched itself, kicking off from the caldera wall, and came flying at me. I saw white fangs, reaching claws. A vampire.

I yanked twice on the rope, the signal to go back up, but there was no time, and the vampire hit me, sending me swinging wildly. It clung to me, claws digging into the leather padding along my shoulders. Face to face with the creature, I saw it was not Ilsa, but some red-eyed, blood-hungry fledgling.

I was being pulled up, but it was slow going, the pendulum motion and extra weight making it tougher for Duane, but then I moved faster, and I suspected werewolf muscles had joined in on the rescue effort.

The vampire was so bloodthirsty it was stupid, trying to bite through my face shield. Glass cracked, and my derision turned to worry. Then terror. It let go of one shoulder and slashed the rope with its claws, sending us plummeting.

We were at one extreme of the pendulum when the rope broke, so I didn't fall straight down, but hit the wall first before bouncing and falling in a rain of dislodged rocks. I reached out and caught the link of a chain, the force nearly dislocating my shoulder, but I held on. My charms and pockets with tied cords of battle magic were all inaccessible inside my suit, even the handheld electric blunderbuss was in my belt pouch, so I had nothing to fight with except my most dangerous powers—those lent to me by the Dead God via the First Soul.

Claws penetrated my leathers, and blood leaked from my shoulder. I felt the hand holding me up slipping, sweat filling my thick glove. Teeth kept snapping at my faceplate, like some piranha or enraged shark.

So, I summoned necromancy: a green glow that began in my palms then turned into claws of my own. I tried to contain the power to my free arm, bending my elbow and digging my power into the vampire's side. I could shred the creature, but there were more of them. I intended to use it instead.

Vampires were dead things, their souls fused for all eternity to their body, fed by blood, by the lifeforce stolen from others. Unless their soul was as powerful as Harbinger's or Ilsa's, I could command a vampire as easily as Ilsa had once commanded the souls of dead mice, turning their bodies into puppets.

I made the vampire pull me up onto the giant chain. My command was soundless, soul to soul. Once sitting, it was easier to hold on, but my relief was short lived. More hungry, vampire fledglings scurried over as they scented my blood.

The vampire under my control turned and fought the next to come for me, but there were too many, at least a dozen swinging across to me on the chain or scurrying over it like spiders. That's when something larger and hairier came hurtling down the side of the caldera. Werewolf claws dug into the stone, then there was a blur of glowing eyes and snarling fangs, growls and hisses, blood flying, as Gypsum tore her way to my side.

Her muzzle was covered in blood, chest heaving, but I sensed her enjoyment. Not only was she finally free of her tower prison after so many years, she was free of everything, if only for a moment. It was similar to the joy Duane had shown, only a bit madder and more brutal.

She picked me up like I was a child and threw me, and I worried she had gone completely feral, except her aim was true, and I landed in the open hatch of the submersible, which had been lowered parallel to us.

I lay on the floor in a jumble, arms and legs caught on seat backs and instrument panels, but Duane helped me up, and the goblin unscrewed the ungainly helmet, so I could remove the suit.

"If both of you are here, and Gypsum's out there, who's controlling this thing? Who's going to pull us up again?"

"The automaton," The goblin said.

"Just great." I didn't trust those things.

I saw through the submersible viewing window that Gypsum had finished butchering the few remaining vampires and clung to the stone wall, ready to sever the first chain. She looked back at me, and I gave her the signal to go ahead—a Conrad-like salute.

Gypsum's anti-magic claws cut through the ensorcelled chain like a flame through cobwebs. As it fell into the reddish glow far below, the shredded bodies of our defeated attackers fell with it.

"Vampires in a volcano?" Duane wondered.

"Maybe Harbinger left them as an added layer of protection? Explains why they were so hungry."

I worried about my own explanation, though. Ilsa had supposedly hunted down all his offspring. Were these hers? Had she been here herself?

Was she here now?

Gypsum made her way around the walls of the caldera, cutting the other chains, and then jumped onto the top of the submersible. By the time she climbed in, she had resumed her genteel dwarf form and took a seat.

I'd need her to break any other bindings Olyvandra might have, but our only insulated suit was ripped. She wouldn't be able to climb around outside once we were further down, her werewolf fur sure to be singed, so I took to fixing it as best I could, trying to sew shut the tears with wire and tools in the goblin's toolbox.

"Your stitching has always been atrocious," Gypsum said, taking over the repair from me.

The submersible slowly sunk deeper into the caldera, the red-orange light of lava brightening yet darkening the world in contrast around us. The goblin looked giddy with exploratory excitement.

My dread just grew.

There was no way Ilsa could be waiting deeper inside the volcano, I told myself. There was no sunlight here, but she was vulnerable to fire. I was just paranoid.

Although ... it would be just like her to have headed straight here rather than trying to catch me in Highcrowne. It's what I would have done, and as much as I hated to admit it, we had the same brain, the same everything—hers was just bent on evil by her own design, while evil tended to lure me in against my will.

There was a thump on the roof, and the submersible swayed.

Not waiting down below, then. Ilsa came from above.

She tore open the top of the submersible like peeling an orange, and her too perfect face smiled evilly down at me.

"Now, now, sister. You left in the middle of our conversation. As I'm sure you've guessed, we would have eventually gotten to the part where I revealed I have no need of you, only of Dawn. She too is connected to the First Soul, and oh so much easier to manipulate."

"You're wrong there."

"I can't let you free Olyvandra. That would ruin everything. Sorry about this." Her face disappeared from view.

Gypsum turned into mist, part of her transition to werewolf, but before she could regain her deadly form, the submersible jerked. I heard the twang, twang, twang of metal cords snapping, and then our tether gave way completely.

A giddy feeling of weightlessness filled me as we fell into the lava field below.

Blackened stone crust crunched on impact. Through the viewing window, I saw red-orange cracks shoot out from the spot where we'd landed, ripping open oozing veins of lava.

There, not far away, was Olyvandra, floating on a crust of hardened stone, asleep. Or dead.

She was a massive golden dragon in her natural form. She had many forms. A shapeshifter. If not magically imprisoned, she could have become a bird and flown away. I first met her as a girl with golden eyes. Her eyes now were closed, wagon-sized head tucked into her massive body like a cat, tail coiled over her snout. Severed chains still weighed down her arms and legs, attached to her by manacles. She didn't seem to notice how close to freedom she was.

It was too dangerous to walk over the rivers of lava our crash had opened up, so I told Gypsum, "Can you get to her in mist form? Try materializing just a claw or something to finish cutting her free?"

"It doesn't work that way," Gypsum said, "but I'll try something." She was a ball of mist again and floated out the hole in the roof Ilsa had made.

"Nice to see how focused you can remain on your goal," Duane said, "but personally, I always like to know my escape plan."

"That's why I have Doctor Ghunnan with us." I turned to the goblin. "Can you open a portal, get us out of here somehow?"

"Portals are not to be found everywhere, my dear. They do not just appear 'magically' when needed. I will, however, survey our supplies and see if it's possible to craft some sort of balloon to lift us to safety. Perhaps the range of the ejection seats can be increased?" He began digging through hidden compartments and tearing open seat mechanisms while mumbling to himself, "Why did I not remember to bring the jetpack? Oh yes, those previous test flights that went awry, losing an entire cohort of test students...."

"How long can this submersible last?" I interrupted him to ask.

"Based on the rate we are sinking, and the fact I cannot seal that hole your strangely strong sister tore in the roof ... not long."

"Sinking?" It was then I noticed the viewing window was a little lower than before.

Duane was taking his own inventory of items in pockets, Avian bracelets….

"Anything?" I asked him.

"The same issue the doctor has. Range. I could make it to a wall, possibly climb up, but there's only one suit."

"Go without us."

"You know I can't. Besides, there's Ilsa out there, and I think you, dark evil necromancer that you are, are the only one capable of stopping her. You take the suit, take these." He handed me one of the Avian bracelets that reduced weight and some climbing hooks and the grapnel from his pockets. "Climb out of here and stop her. Then come back and rescue us."

"I can't scale walls like you can."

"Of course not," he smiled roguishly. "But do you really want to rely on the doctor here?"

The goblin was pulling stuffing from the seats and was half buried in a small mountain of fluff, still muttering.

"You're right. Better to have a few backup plans."

As I was suiting up, I saw Gypsum had made her way across the lava field. Olyvandra was farther away than I realized—she was just so big she had seemed closer. Gypsum appeared in werewolf form, a blur of tearing claws that shredded manacles on arms, legs, ripped hooks from wings, and finally the ensorcelled collar from Olyve's neck.

The dragon still did not stir. She must be starved, in some sort of hibernation.

Gypsum was a werewolf for only a moment, and returned to mist form, hurrying back towards us.

I was all geared up by the time she got back. Werewolves healed when they transformed, so I was surprised to see the burns all over her body and the sweat pouring off her. She lay in a half-dismantled seat, gasping.

"What went wrong?" I had the hatch of the helmet open so I could speak.

"Those chains. When they fell into the lava. There's..." she gasped for air and fanned herself, sweat pouring off her. Duane and the goblin too were sweating now, while the suit protected me from the heat pouring through the tear in the roof.

"There's what?" I prompted.

"Silver gas. From the melted chains. I've breathed it in. It's keeping me from completely healing."

She also wouldn't be able to fight until it cleared her system. There wouldn't be time for her to recover, not with everyone sinking. I had to get going.

"Boost me up," I told Duane, and he took my foot, lifting me up, so I could use the hatch. I was too bulky in the suit to wriggle through the hole Ilsa had made.

The Avian bracelet was already activated, so I weighed no more than a feather, and when I kicked off, I went flying. It would have been fun if I weren't afraid of heights, but like all my fears, there had never been time to indulge them, not when things needed doing.

Ilsa. I spotted her high above, dangling from the severed submersible cable by one arm, calmly observing us like a hawk watching mice scurry away from its talons.

I wasn't scurrying, I was headed right for her, but the boost Duane had given me only allowed me to fly so far. I felt gravity begin to pull, and so I aimed the goblin's grapnel gun. The recoil pushed me back, and I hadn't compensated for it, so instead of hooking on the cable above her, which I'd been aiming for, it dug into her shoulder. She tried to pull the metal hook out of her flesh, but it was already retracting, and I went shooting toward her. I had the climbing hooks ready, and a moment later we were face to face, her arms caught by the hooks.

Her vampire strength was incredible, but I was so light, her thrashing amounted to nothing, like trying to dislodge a piece of thistle clinging to you. She wasn't getting rid of me easily.

"You stay away from, Dawn," I told her, trying to catch her gaze with mine. She was a powerful vampire, not as easily controlled as her scions, so I needed to make a strong connection with her soul. If it would even work. I hadn't been able to control Harbinger, but I'd faced him before I had the First Soul or came into full possession of the Dead God's power. Back when I'd fought that side of myself.

She avoided my gaze, pulling at the hooks, but Duane's tools were the best, these ones infused with elven magic so they wouldn't dislodge from a wall or cliff before the climber wanted them to. She couldn't budge them. She stopped trying and reached for my faceplate, poised to tear it open and then my face soon after, but like all villains, she just had to share her diabolical plans. Who else but your mortal enemy can truly appreciate your efforts after all?

"Once you are dead, sister, your protections die with you. I will be able to enter Viktor's house and compel Dawn to obey me, to accept me as her mother. With her under my power, I can finally claim all that should be mine."

"Ilsa, listen. I decided long ago not to kill you, to cross that line. There will be no going back for me then. Don't make me."

"You can't stop me." Her fingers pressed into the brass helmet, and the glass cracked from the pressure.

I saw her beautiful face through the cracks and realized how ugly she was, had always been. How cruel she had treated everyone around her, and I couldn't help thinking about what I had done to Nanny. How I had Marked and used her because I could not trust her. How I kept everyone who might truly care about me at arm's length, afraid I would inevitably hurt them. Only Thane had been safe, unkillable, unshakable in his love for me because he was without judgment. I would never be that 'dark evil necromancer' to him, the femme fatale, the murdering Solhan harlot ... all that others saw. What matter such things to the Dead God Himself?

And because of the defenses, the barriers I had created, there was no one who dared to tell me I was already becoming like her. Ilsa had her reasons for power, to fight and kill and use, and I had mine.

As the glass fractured even more, a shard fell out of my faceplate, and her pale eyes stared into me. Into emptiness. Darkness. The soul of a vampire was locked inside a dead shell, impossible for Death to extract, so they could go on living until that shell was destroyed by fire or cracked by sunlight. I could pull the soul from her if I wanted. I could shred it, devour it. I could be more frightening than even she could imagine.

I did not want that. I had never wanted to be a monster. I had so much power I had never wanted, yet the only thing I could truly control was me. My choices.

I had left my Ashur on the dirigible above, but Duane had given me his utility knife along with all the other tools, and I pulled it from my belt, ignoring her slowly crushing grip—she just had to drag my murder out as long as possible, villain that she was—and I cut into the arm she was using to hold onto the severed cable.

The utility knife was rust tinged iron and as painful to a vampire as silver was to a werewolf, but I sensed some extra enchantment on it. None of Duane's weapons were ordinary weapons. She screamed, but I kept cutting until she released my helmet. She tried to pull the knife out of my hand, but her strength failed her when she touched the metal, weakened her. The arm I was cutting was so weak it suddenly gave way— and we were both falling.

The lava would kill me, insulated suit or no, and Dawn would be vulnerable, but at least Ilsa would die too. Uncle would find a way to sever the connection to the First Soul. He would save his niece. Nanny would be free too, and I knew she would care for her. Everyone would be better off without the two of us, Lili's dread daughters, sisters in sin, mucking up the world.

We did not have far to fall, but it seemed an eternity. I would see Thane soon, I told myself. It would all be over soon.

Trust Avians to have plans of their own.

Kerrik hooked my helmet with his talons, Ilsa's weight suddenly pulling at him, but he carried a magical band in his beak and dropped it over her head like a well-played game of ring toss. We were now both light enough, but he didn't pull us up. He brought us to the submersible, which was now a third of the way covered in stone-encrusted magma. I thought his feathers would burst into flame, but there was some sort of magical shield around him that glowed blue the nearer he came to the heat. The shield grew larger, surrounding the entire submersible.

We were on the roof, and I peered in to see Duane, Gypsum and Doctor Ghunnan all gasping and sweating. Kerrik's beak was next to my helmet. "There are too many. I don't have any more bands."

Duane took off one of his bracelets and put it on Gypsum's wrist. "Take her. The goblin has ejection seats."

"Just a few ... more ... adjustments," he said, as he picked up his tools again. The Avian shield was cooling the interior enough for him to function again.

I reached an arm down for Gypsum when I felt claws dig into my back. Ilsa.

She backhanded Kerrik, and the Avian fell over, tumbling onto the lava field. She rolled me over and stood, smiling down at me. "You're next. Goodbye, at last."

She readied herself for a kick that, with the bracelet making me so light, would send me hurtling into the orange lava vent nearby.

She made a surprised sound when what looked like several, thick, golden pythons coiled around her torso, pinning her arms to her sides and lifting her into the air. It wasn't snakes but scaly talons—Olyvandra had Ilsa in her grip, and her wagon-sized mouth came close enough that breath from her nostrils stirred Ilsa's hair like a windstorm.

"I smell Harbinger's power on you, little one. For once, it is easy to tell one sister from the other." Then she looked at me. "Eva. Don't tell me you're the one come to my rescue?"

"What can I say? I missed you. And ..." I had to admit how self-serving I'd been, "I needed you."

"That is no surprise."

Kerrik was back, swaying, but his shield was intact as he alighted next to me. "Olyvandra, we need you as well. Come back and claim your rightful place as leader."

"I betrayed the Unmentionables. You all passed judgement on me."

"Rules that were written can be re-written by the powerful. There are many of us who want you back. We will support you if you seek to wrest control for yourself."

So Kerrik too had his own reasons for coming.

"I'm hungry," Olyve said. I remembered how grumpy she got when she had low blood sugar. She had been imprisoned for years, and if a herd of sheep or goats was nearby, I'm sure she would swallow them all in one bite if she could. "Let me think on it." She beat her wings, nearly sending us both flying until we clutched the railings around the submersibles' hatch. Then she grabbed hold of the whole submersible in her other talon.

As we rose into the air, I looked down to see frightened elementals emerging from the lava field, their orange eyes set in black stone faces awed as we disappeared into the clouds.

The goblin had climbed out with us to see what was happening. "That is the largest wyvern I've ever seen," he remarked when he realized Olyve was carrying us to safety.

"Lucky for us. We don't need your ejection seats after all."

"They were nearly ready." He waved and smiled down at the elementals, who were bowing and prostrating themselves, before we disappeared from their view. "I must return once repairs are made to study these natives. Fascinating their adaptations to such a hostile environment. I suspect they have met few if any outsiders, and I wonder what they must think of us in our unidentified flying object?"

The submersible left scorch marks on the deck of the dirigible when Olyvandra deposited us there. She had shifted her talon to cover Ilsa's face as well, and I could barely make out my sister's muffled curses and threats. Olyve couldn't land, not without breaking the airship, and she couldn't take human form without releasing Ilsa, so she stayed airborne, Kerrik flying beside her, waiting.

"Why did you come for me?" she asked. She knew my motives could not be unselfish.

"I needed you to stop Ilsa, which I think you grasped right away." I smiled at my pun, seeing Ilsa squirming and fighting against the dragon's grip. "I also need you to watch out for my daughter. Her name is Dawn. Will you do that? Look out for her as you looked out for me? Actually, doing a better job than you did with me would be nice. That's my price for your freedom."

I knew I should have charged my fee before letting her go, but there'd been no chance. I hoped she had some form of personal honor that would compel her to meet my demands.

"Very well," Olyve said. "I shall pay your price, but why must she be protected? Does she not have you?"

"I am finally going to get rid of the First Soul. That's been the point of all this—why I came back to Highcrowne, why I'm running around doing errands for Avians—but when I do get rid of that cursed god artifact, the power it lends me will be gone. What's more, the Dead God will take it even farther away from this world, where it can't touch us anymore, where the Devourer can have it. The farther He goes, the weaker my connection to Him too. The weaker the magic He lends me will be. When this is done, I will be like any other Solhan necromancer. Nothing special. Dawn is special and needs special protection."

"You will always be special, no matter what you believe," Olyve said. "I hope to see you again, Eva."

"What will you do with Ilsa?"

"What should I do?"

"You Unmentionables have a code. You broke it before to help me. Don't break it again. I can't always be coming to your rescue."

"Very well. I will find some place to imprison her, just as Harbinger imprisoned me."

She flew away, and I felt relief. I wasn't sure if it was from knowing Ilsa was no longer a threat, or knowing that Olyvandra would spare her. We both had second chances.

I hoped it wasn't a big mistake.

Duane took back the utility dagger he'd lent me but let me keep the Avian band after showing me how to deactivate its weightless effect.

"How did Kerrik find us here?" I asked.

He pointed to another of his many bracelets. "I called for help. I told you—I always like having a getaway plan. I was expecting Roosal, though."

"Are you and he friends?"

"Of a sort. I can't afford friends."

"I didn't think I could either, but I was wrong. I was so very wrong about so many things lately."

"Like what?" he asked, cautiously.

"Like love." I looked away from his green eyes, afraid of what judgements he would pass whether he meant to or not.

I wanted to drop the defenses, but I wasn't as ready as I wanted to be, so I hurriedly added, "Love motivates like nothing in this world. It can make you elated or despondent, and it can drive you to make grand gestures, risk death—and it can make you crazy. What if the theft of Calka's egg was not motivated by politics or fear—but by love? Isn't that the oldest and most dangerous motive of all? We should go back to Highcrowne."

17   ...Into the Fire

I was at the helm, steering the airship towards the lowering sun. Even with fair winds it was slow going, as the volcano fields had been far off the main air streams. We would be lucky to make it back before dawn, especially as the coming dark made the gas in our balloon denser, dropping our altitude. The goblin was adjusting the burners to raise us back up before reactivating main thrust. The wheel I held regulated fine jets that ensured we maintained our heading and did not get turned around in the process.

Duane stood next to me, whispering a few words of guidance. "A little more to the left. Feel that shudder? That's the edge of a trade wind. We want to catch it, but slowly, else it will put us in a spin."

"Don't you mean more to Port, not left?"

"You want to use nautical terms?"

I had learned them when I'd stolen a pirate's riverboat. I couldn't help remembering, but there was less sadness when I did. Now I saw the parallels: that ship and its wheel with Thane beside me, this ship and its wheel with Duane.

"We are on the quarterdeck atop the stern castle, are we not, Captain Rose? So let me know when I can turn Starboard once more."

"Snob." He smiled. "I've been taking airship lessons, not language lessons. Keep left, okay?"

"Aye-aye. I mean ... okay." I smiled but focused when I felt another shudder. Airship sailing was very different from a riverboat. There was a lot more vertical and horizontal to deal with, not just currents, airstreams, whatever. Although, there were no rocks to worry about, which was a huge plus.

The goblin was a master at most things, so it was no surprise when he soon had us at elevation and soaring along the trade wind. We tied off the helm, but Duane lingered nearby, finding an alcove to sink into and watch as the stars came out.

He'd always been like that, going quiet, needing time to himself. I used to think he liked to hide from the world to better hide his thievery, but I learned it was how he calmed himself, regained his strength. I didn't comment, only left him to it as I sought out Gypsum.

I sank down onto the deck beside her. I processed my world with a very active internal monologue, but sometimes I needed to make it more external.

"You haven't said much since we rescued Olyvandra," I noted.

"I'm kind of hoping I blend into the deck. I'm the same brown, my prison dress just as stained as the sailcloth around us. Now, if I could just slow my heartrate and breathe as shallowly as Mister Rose over there, I'd be invisible."

"Or you could go mist form and actually be invisible. Or just turn wolf and escape some other way. That is what this is all about, right? You don't want to go back to the tower."

"There's a big hole in it now. I think they'll have to lock me up someplace else. And yes, part of me wants to leap out, maybe close to a snow-capped peak so there's not too much pain and damage done before my werewolf power heals me. I'd make my way overland, feeding off wild game, hunting and feeling more like my true self than I've ever known. I'd have some sort of self-realization, an epiphany, and know just what to say to my husbands and children when I get back to Gernwold. I'd make them forgive me, hold me. I'd be home."

"But?"

"But it's all just a waking dream. Delusion. I'm enough of a cold-hearted politico to understand the world does not work that way. Epiphanies come when the hangman's noose is around your neck, when it's too late, and no amount of contriteness will stay the executioner's blade."

"I don't know. I'm pretty good at epiphanies and talking my way out of deadly situations. There's always hope. Besides, no one in Highcrowne wants to execute you. Not anymore. They've forgotten all that."

"Not all. And they still want to see me punished."

"You mean you feel you deserve punishment."

"Yes."

"Then go back to prison. Show them how good you've become, how reformed. Maybe they'll let you out on good behavior in another dozen years or so."

"Whose side are you on, Eva?"

"No sides. I'm playing devil's advocate. I want you to realize what you want."

"You don't want to see me punished?"

"I did. I really did. Ilsa too. Duane, Ulric ... myself. We've all done terrible things, and when I get on my soapbox, I'll be the first to admit I should be in chains too. I'll rail against injustice, against slavery, against EEP bigotry and the subjugation of humans, of dwarves. I'll risk my life to change things, to save as many as I can ... and I have. But I can always do more. There is never, ever enough done. I learned from Death, from taking souls, feeding on them..." I remembered the troll, Conrad... "I learned that it's not about punishment in the end. It's about innocence. Finding innocence. Washing the blood away to reveal who you truly are underneath before the world and your mistakes got hold of you. Sometimes there is no innocence to be found. I doubt Ilsa has a shred. That is its own punishment—never being able to wash off the blood, never feeling clean. Do you think you can ever be clean?"

"I hope so."

"Then do whatever you need to do to get there. That's what matters."

She nodded then lay back on the deck, looking up at the stars. That was my cue to shut up and leave her alone too. She'd be thinking about what I said, deciding her own fate. I had enough faith my old friend was in there somewhere that she'd choose well.

That speech had been as much for me as her of course, as I worked out my feelings about Ilsa. About how I'd nearly condemned both of us to the lava. I'd been all too willing to punish the guilty.

Duane had been listening in too. He did that.

"What about you, Eva?" he asked from the dark. "Would dying have made you clean?"

How had he known? I thought he'd been melting in the submersible not watching my battle with Ilsa.

"I don't know. At least it would have stopped me from getting even more blood on my hands."

Light blossomed on the ridge of mountains ahead. It was far from dawn, and after the light came a delayed roar of sound.

"That was a bomb," Doctor Ghunnan said coming up to us.

Duane stood. "That was Highcrowne."

We made the best speed we could, but it was still near dawn when we arrived. I didn't like the smoky orange glow that grew larger as we drew near. Fires burned all around the city, houses, shops, but the most terrifying sight was what had happened to the mountain. One side was sheared off, an avalanche, which had taken out a portion of the Central City. There were no fires there, just darkness smothered by stone.

It looked worse than after the war.

"Dawn." She was my one thought. There was so much destruction, so much to worry about, too much. Focus on making sure she's safe.

The air dock was on fire.

"Land in the river," Duane said.

My knuckles were white as I turned the wheel. The gorge was narrow and deep, the river not wide, but I didn't hesitate to risk it. The goblin furiously darted about venting the balloon so that we descended gently. The airship sunk into water and floated, just as if it had always been meant to sail seas instead of skies. Duane dropped anchor, and Gypsum climbed the rigging, pulling and tugging and tying off sheets of balloon until everything was stored safely and there was no risk of us being pulled downstream.

I fumbled with a dingy and cursed at the bolted down straps. I needed a tool. Airships were built with several as life rafts in case of water landings, but what good were they if you couldn't use them?

"I can get you there faster," Gypsum said. "I assume your daughter is with Nanny?"

"Yes. Please."

Gypsum became mist then a beast of fang and claw. She wrapped furry arms around me and then we were moving so fast the world became a blur. Water splashed us as she dived for the shore, plants tore at my clothes, but soon we were on the streets.

I was holding my breath from fear but could still smell the smoke. The crack of bullets slicing through air terrified me. Aguragas's rifles. Were they being wielded by General Moore's soldiers or the Upside Down Party's insurgents?

The boom of blunderbuss and canon replied. I heard arrows and ballistae whistle through the air.

Then we were past the gates where fighting was fiercest and in my neighborhood. The bazaar was empty. Some shops barren and closed, others deserted with wares left behind. Gyspum sped through wending ways and left me in the deserted shipping office. She couldn't go any further.

"My wards," I told her. "Go and see what's happening out there. Help whoever you can."

She nodded, an angry growl bubbling in her throat. She was gone in a blink, and I hurried up the staircase.

My protections remained in place. I sensed no one had crossed uninvited, but I wasn't sure if my wards kept out bombs and debris. I knew the Lyssian one protected from fire, and I hoped that included war.

The lights were off inside, but I saw well in the dark. I was in Dawn's room in no time, and exhaled only when I saw her lying there, sleeping peacefully. Nanny sat beside her in a rocking chair.

"Are you both alright?" I asked.

"Yes, mistress. She wakes from time to time to eat what I could give her, to take her toilet and bath, but it's like she is sleepwalking. She won't speak to me."

"That's how the enchantment works. Thank you for taking care of her." Like I had left her any choice.

I sighed and took hold of Nanny's arm. I focused my will, and she squirmed and then screamed as I removed the mark of compulsion from her. Her soul was freed.

"That's how Kali once felt," Nanny observed. "When she was a slave, her will was gone, her world muffled and not her own. I never understood before."

"Forgive me."

"You are a Thorne, Eva. Never ask for forgiveness."

"I'm trying to be who I want to be, and so yes, I do need to ask. I am so sorry. Please stay here and take care of her and yourself. The house should be protected. I need to go out there and stop whatever is happening."

"Do what you must do. I'll be here. This is my home and Dawn's too."

"Where's Little Viktor?"

"At school in the Central City."

Oh no.

I took off running and pulled the blade of my Ashur as soon as I was on the street.

I'd only sensed and glimpsed the chaos when Gypsum carried me, but now there was time for it to sink in. The top of the mountain was gone, the Avian sanctuary. It had to be Aguragas.

Was this all my fault?

Blaming myself was what I usually did, easier to pile on the self-hatred as I was used to it, but my gut told me this was too big to be some knee jerk reaction to the tale I'd spun. This had taken years of planning. It was always his goal to take out Highcrowne from the top down.

The cracking, popping sounds of more bullets echoed off stone houses and cobblestones. I made my way toward the fighting because it was also the quickest route to the Central City.

I saw General Moore's soldiers first, wearing the white of the City Watch. Elves and dwarves were among them, some in uniform, some civilians. Most had crossbows, except for the General's men, who were firing bullets with deafening speed. They were shooting at a barricade, splintering wood barrels and planks but not reaching the humans on the other side. I was watching from a side alley, so I could see behind the barricade.

There were several of Gas's followers, the cool hatred in their eyes a dead giveaway as they ordered around the civilians with them. They moved them where they wanted, put guns in their hands and told them where to stand. Some were killed but some got off a few shots before fear made them sink down again.

No way would I allow them to make war here in Highcrowne.

"Hey!" I shouted.

Startled glances my way, guns turning toward me, I whipped out a vial from my belt pouch and hurled it at their barricade. Purple smoke billowed, choking and suffocating them until they slumped to the ground. Elves aimed arrows my way, and I shook my head, moving the purple cloud to engulf them as well. I sent it ahead of me, clearing a path, as I took the weapons from Gas's troops and tossed them to where the general's soldiers slept.

I made a more direct line for the Central City then, weaving my purple cloud around here and there to knock out fighting wherever I found it. I only had the one vial, which I'd stole in Archon and could not recreate. I'd been saving it for when I truly needed it for something, and today felt like that day.

Duane found me as I reached the Smiths' district. He'd avoided my cloud of magic and came up beside me with a small army of his own. I glimpsed only a few of them as most were hiding in doorways, shimmying up walls to balconies, and there were more snipers hidden that I never saw until an arrow flew impossibly far to hit someone a block away.

"You got here fast," I observed.

"I'm not a werewolf, but I have my ways. My people have filled me in."

"Aguragas."

"You had your doubts? It was foolish of the elves to try and play the long game with him. They are ancient and patient, but he is not. They should have destroyed him here when they had the chance."

"I'm not arguing." Although I knew Highcrowne was only the start for Gas. Had his trip to Faellion been just to get out of the line of fire here? Or was Illul next on his list? I wished he'd started there with freed slaves. I would have had sympathy for the cause, but not now.

Vikky was in the Central City.

Duane must have known where I was headed because he didn't ask. He just followed, fanning out his people to deal with rebels who surged forward in the vacuum of space my purple haze created. The cloud was thinning, knocking people out slower, leaving many to rise quickly after it passed. Too soon, it was time for the sword.

I hesitated at sight of a woman loading a rifle. She pointed it at me, and I knew that expression, the fear and disgust. Despite the goblin's revisionist history and Crown-erected statues and propaganda, hatred of Solhans ran deep in humans. She pulled the trigger and missed, and I still didn't move.

"Eva," Duane warned. He had seen how bad her aim was, just as I had, but he had no compunctions about stopping her permanently. I stepped forward before she could reload and hit her over the head with the sheath of my Ashur. I pulled the rifle strap off her shoulder and tossed it to him.

"You can kill more with this."

"Not my style." He passed it to one of his people who vanished.

A thunder of stomping boots warned me of approaching soldiers, too coordinated to be rebels. I waved my Avian rock about, flashing it like a badge, and however it worked, I found guards and soldiers rallying behind me, leaving Duane's people free to range further afield.

I knew where Viktor's school was, thanks to bogles, although I had never been there before. It was elvish and expensive and untouched. I saw teachers and students through windows, huddled behind their walls and defenses. EEPs as well as city watch already had it protected, so all I did was reach out with a tendril of soul sense. Vikky was safe, excited more than scared, and so when Duane made to go in after him, I grabbed his arm.

"Viktor will want to fight for his city—and I don't know on which side. He wants democracy. Leave him where he's safe."

Duane pulled away and took a step forward before he stopped. He knew I was right. He nodded then turned his gaze to the shattered mountain above us. The Avians were his family too.

There were hills of broken rock and rubble in our way. I found Gypsum and other dwarven werewolves digging out survivors. The dwarf and elven palaces had been covered. My soul sense told me both dead and living were to be found, Hilja among them.

I told Gypsum, "You can smell Hilja, can't you?"

There was a growl of acknowledgement.

"Free her and she'll owe you."

"That's not why I'm helping."

I wanted to help too, but this would take days, and no one else could help the Avians but us. Duane had his climbing hooks out, scaling the rock face. It was unstable, and he dodged mini avalanches as he slowly made his way up.

"Stupid brave," I whispered. The history wing was close to the human palace and untouched, so I hurried inside and fetched the doctor's jetpack.

"I wouldn't use that thing," Katherine warned. "At least not without this."

She affixed a valve to one of the hose lines, before strapping me in.

"You improved it?" I asked.

"Professor Ghunnan is brilliant but not at everything. Especially listening. I worked on this in secret."

"Do you have anything to help dig out survivors?"

"My colleagues do and they're working on it. I thought I'd do something about the fighting."

"Be careful out there, Katherine."

"Always. And good luck to you, Miss Thorne."

"Eva."

"And its Doctor Suttner now, not Katherine."

"Doctor."

I lugged the heavy pack outside and flipped the switches she'd shown me. "Whoa!"

I was airborne, rising steadily, but Duane was mad, moving at speed, and I barely beat him to the top. I had an issue turning the thing off at the right height and position to land without breaking something, which took most of my time, so I was quite happy when I touched ground. I stripped off the atrocious gadget and took a few breaths to still my heartbeat before sending down a rope to help Duane up the last stretch.

I wanted to be there when he saw it. He assessed things quickly, the ash and rubble, the lack of anything recognizable. "It's not that bad," I said to calm him.

"Not bad?" he said, incredulous.

"I sense no dead here."

I didn't know if the Avians had flown away or were all hiding in the chamber that I had difficulty reading. It was the room where they manufactured the green goo. I'd never been able to get an accurate sense of that place. It was too strange—magical and raw and powerful and alien—but such a place would have powerful protections. They would be safe there.

"I know where to look. Come on." I led him to the chamber. There was a broken obelisk, the one for wisdom. Fortunately, the marker for air and warmth was still intact, which was why we weren't struggling at this altitude.

I began digging my way towards the goo chamber, tossing rocks aside. Duane dug in with his bare hands at first, prying stones up with his utility dagger, as frenzied as he'd been climbing up the mountain. I cast about and found broken planks and nest material and made shovels. I wished I had a digging spell and decided I would include one when I restocked my vials and cords, but then I remembered something that would work.

"Stand back," I told Duane. When he was clear, I activated the wooden rune I had. It turned sand into water—very useful when crossing the desert—and I hoped it worked on dirt and stone also. It did, and soon we'd washed away the obstacles, leaving the door clear.

"I've never been in there," Duane said. "It was forbidden."

"And you didn't see a locked door as temptation?"

"Usually, I do. Not this one. I'm careful when it comes to magic."

"Then I'll go first." I reached out to touch the engravings in the stone, and they flared with green light.

18 FORBIDDEN

"I didn't do that," I swore. Uncontrolled or barely controlled green magic was usually my doing, but this was the acid green glow of the Avian goo. It outlined the runes on the door, and as it did, I noticed traces of ancient Solhan I'd been learning to read mixed with the Avian. It reminded me of the silver etchings Ilsa had shown me, but this was not linked to our bloodline. This was something else, and I knew I should not touch.

The door rumbled and rolled to the side, revealing a green-lit chamber. Calka stood there, covered in dust and weary.

"You're not Kerrik," she said.

"He's with Olyvandra. What happened? Where are the others?"

Roosal raised his winged arm. "I'm here. Naren is deeper inside. We can't get to him."

I saw the rubble then. I thought the whole chamber was protected, intact, but walls and ceiling had caved in but for a pocket before the door where Calka and Roosal stood.

"I have this." I indicated the water rune, and they let me try.

"We were afraid to cause even more destruction," Calka explained. "There is too much of the Celon, the volatile green fluid, inside. Your Darrub magic is different. It may work."

She noticed Duane then, the cold blankness of his expression, how he stood still as a stone pillar. Calka wrapped him in a feathered, motherly embrace, and I recalled when she'd first hugged me like that. She always knew just what you needed. I could see why Duane had adopted her, if not why she had adopted him back.

"I will hunt Aguragas to the ends of the world," Duane swore to her.

"No. You won't. You will protect Highcrowne as I have requested. It will be even more important when we go."

"Go?" he spluttered.

I nearly dropped the rune. The Avians were leaving? Our one protection against the nasties of the world? It was like a bomb had gone off all over again.

"It is no longer right for us to be here. The weapon they used was launched from an airship at range. We were unprepared, our protections lowered as I travelled to the Assembly. They knew our patterns and how to strike. And we had grown complacent. It is time for us to gain altitude, distance."

"They'll have won if they drive you off. Highcrowne needs your guidance," Duane argued.

"We are a wedge between the younger races now, not the bond we set out to be. There comes a time when children must be allowed to grow up."

I had removed most of the rubble blocking the way to the next chamber, my boots squelching in water and mud now, so I spared a moment to interrupt. "The children are not growing up—they're just fighting more. You should have seen people in the city. The hate."

"They know they are not free. Lies would not work so well to sway them without a touch of truth behind them."

"Freedom to shoot at each other and blow up our home?" Duane guffawed. "Give me tyranny."

"You don't mean that," Calka said. "They are merely misled by Aguragas. They need a better leader."

Duane shook his head. "Not this again."

"What again?" I was still butting in, but the next door was visible, and I couldn't pry into their conversation as much as I wanted. Naren could be hurt. And I needed to talk to him. He was where I'd been headed before this chaos began.

"Help me," I said, struggling to open the door to the next chamber. I could melt it like the rubble, but it was laced with those lines of ancient script and felt—dangerous.

"That is the sacred Chamber of Celon," Calka said. "Only Naren as high priest is permitted entrance."

"And Naren is stuck inside, probably unconscious. We need to get in."

Calka shook her head. Was she really willing to risk one quarter of their remaining species like this?

Duane pulled one of the bejeweled bracelets from Calka's scaly ankle, his thief's fingers deft at undoing the metal hasp and getting it away from her before she could stop him. He placed the bracelet against the door, and the script lit up, glowing with silvery light, before the door rumbled aside.

"How did you know that charm would open the door?" Calka asked, not as angry as I thought she would be.

"Because I remember when Naren gave it to you, when he said he hoped you would find your way to him." Duane bent down and gently refastened the bracelet.

I was closest to the entrance and so I stepped inside first. I wasn't sure if Calka would commit sacrilege, Duane probably, me definitely.

The chamber was black but illuminated with veins of glowing green Avian goo, the Celon they called it. The glow wasn't strong enough to illuminate, so the room could be massive or smaller than the bedroom Nanny let me use. It sounded smaller than I expected, muffled. The goo was throwing off my Solhan night vision, so I activated a light rune, which made as much light as a kerosene lantern at full power. They used kerosene in the uncivilized human South—it was equivalent to a warlock crystal-fueled streetlamp in Highcrowne—and I saw that the cave in had extended here too. Large boulders, slabs of mountain, were piled around what was once a larger chamber. I spotted a patch of cream-colored feathers, and my heart sank.

"Naren," I said.

The small pile of feathers suddenly puffed up and Naren stood. He'd been coiled so tightly into a ball I thought feathers were all that had been left of him, but he was okay.

"You're not hurt?"

"Celon protected me."

"What were you doing? Could you not hear us outside?"

"I had to protect it."

"It. The egg you stole." I'd guessed already, but now he shifted aside to reveal the infant-sized prize he'd been huddled around. The egg was slightly golden, with a rough, sandstone like texture.

"Why?" I demanded. "What is it doing in here? I thought you loved Calka, so how could you do this to her? How could you take it?"

Calka was in the doorway, not daring to cross the threshold, but she clearly awaited Naren's answer. And she did not look happy. Her black magpie eyes and sharp beak looked ready to attack.

"It's precisely because I love Calka that I had to protect it. Here. It's safest with me and Celon. Here I could make it ... mine."

"What do you mean, Naren?" Calka took a step inside, sacrilege committed, but she was being careful as Naren still stood between her and her unborn child.

"Kerrik is strongest, I am wisest, but you chose Roosal, the buffoon, the one who travelled across the Wall with the Dead God's bride, who endangered himself over and over again to help them, all of them. You see what they have done to us? They destroyed our home. They do not deserve our help. And your child deserves to inherit the best of the Avian species, for a queen will remake the next generation in her image. Now that image includes me. The Celon has made me a part of her, the father."

Calka, always so serene and noble, suddenly struck in a blur of black and white feathers. She sent Naren flying against the back wall, and then gently cradled her egg. "My child. What has he done?"

Naren had regained his feet, but the tiny nostrils set in his curved, orange beak bled. The equivalent of a nosebleed I suspected. "I have made her better. Our race better. You will see."

"You will not. We three will go to the Great Peaks, far into our ancestral lands. I'm taking my child with us, and you will never see her Naren, never have a chance to influence her again. I condemn you to this chamber, to your Celon, until I can forgive you. And that day may never come."

"But ... I love you."

"You love only your Celon, your arcane arts. Yes, you made this child possible, and I am grateful for that, but you had no right. Roosal is her father. I chose Roosal because he is brave. He does. He lives. You have lost your way and represent all that has failed us, why our kind is no more. They were all like you and Kerrik—only Roosal was different. He is my love!"

With that, she turned her back on him and marched out carrying her egg. Duane had not dared step inside, and he retreated even further, but Calka called to me, "Eva. Come, before you are shut in too."

"What is the Celon?" I asked Naren quickly. "What is in the next chamber?" I had realized all the veins of glowing goo emanated from a third, deeper chamber, sealed by another stone door etched with archaic writing. Rubble had blocked the way, so there was no way to quickly dash over and investigate.

Doctor Ghunnan would be giddy hearing I'd come even this close to the great secret.

"Celon is all, and none. Eternal and no more," he replied, enigmatically.

"I see Calka's point," I said before hurrying out. Enigmatic, out of touch. Calka had already set the door rolling back into place, so I had to roll to make it out.

"Would you really have sealed me in?" I asked, annoyed. "We had a deal. I help you, you help me."

"What did you accomplish?" she asked. Like all my past clients, she didn't seem to appreciate the value of my services.

"You would never have gone in there without me. You would have thought Naren dead and left him the sanctity of his refuge as a tomb. He would have kept the egg and raised it without you ever knowing. I knew he had it, by the way."

She was too angry to appreciate my sales pitch, but she did say, "I will help you, but only because the First Soul threatens you and your child's life—it threatens all of us. Now, what must I do? Make haste, for I have an overwhelming desire to be gone from this place."

"I need your help with a ritual to free me and Dawn from the First Soul. But first, you have to quell the uprising in this city—or I'll use the First Soul to do it, and then it will dig so deep into me there will be no getting rid of it."

"Very well. I must get my egg to safety, but when I return, I will assist with your ritual. Roosal and Kerrik are powerful enough to bring this city to its knees in my absence."

"Really? I mean, nothing permanent right?" Avians had always seemed so nice, but Calka was not happy now, and who knew what she would order them to do?

"You and the Dead God are fond of sleep, and my kind can achieve something much the same to stop this rebellion. For now. The cause of it all, however, the discontent and inequity, the elven hunger for power and human thirst for revenge…. These things are not so easy to quell."

"I know. I've known nothing else my entire life."

19 RITUAL

The Avians were minus an egg-stealing arcane-expert, but Kerrik and Roosal were still an impressive sight when they rose from the ruins of the mountain and Central City to cast their spell which promised to put an end to the uprising Aguragas and the Upside Down party had instigated. Calka had set off to search for some secret hideout in distant, snow-capped mountains to protect her egg, although she promised to return soon.

Duane worried Kerrik and Roosal were clear targets now, hovering overhead. "One well aimed arrow or rifle…." he said, miming firing at them.

"You don't have magic sight. Here." I handed him the glasses I'd pilfered from the goblin's lab. He put them on and started, seeing the world in a new way.

I could see without them. Magic shimmered around the two Avians. Orbs of it radiating from their bodies and showering down from their wings like sparks from a molten blade on a blacksmith's anvil.

Roosal and Kerrik were Calka's blades, her weapons. Always in the past they had chosen protection for Highcrowne. Now they chose subjugation.

Only I and now Duane with his glasses saw. Well ... maybe other magic wielders and elves too I supposed, but they didn't know what was going to happen.

I had my circle ready—meaning magic circle painted with blood and salt on the flagstones surrounding us. I was a necromancer, so sue me, blood was a vital component of all my best spells. Not any sentient species, I promise. Ok rats. It was rats, thanks to my bogles and Duane's 'rat meat' contacts in the underworld it was easier and more ethical than other blood to obtain.

The point is the magic circle protected us. And by 'us' I meant me, Duane, Gypsum, the goblin and his students, Moore's loyalists, Hilja's EEPs, as well as some of Duane's more trusted associates. It was a big circle.

And by 'protection' I meant that the massive wave of concussive force the Avians suddenly unleashed stunned absolutely everyone not inside it. Or inside my house. That was another super safe place. Ulric's temple too. Oh, and an inner sanctum the Crowns were holed up in. Ok, there were probably a few other powerful magic people who may have had some previously established sanctuaries in place that would protect them also.

The other point then is that (almost) everyone in Highcrowne was knocked out. And they would be for a while.

"Most impressive," the goblin doctor said. "Some sort of sound-based weapon?"

"I didn't hear anything, did you?" I said, not daring to mention magic.

"There are frequencies beyond the range of our hearing, my dear."

No use.

Duane held the glasses out to me.

"You don't want them?" I was surprised.

"I've seen enough." He shook the Avian bracelets he wore and gestured at me—I knew I was stitched head to toe in protective magics, pockets full of less protective and more offensive charms and curses.

"Does it disturb you seeing the world differently?" I asked.

"Nothing disturbs me. And it's not different. The world is as strange and dangerous as it always has been. These glasses don't tell me anything I didn't already know. They just make it harder to see anything more than magic—and there is so much more."

For a moment, I wanted to see the world through his eyes. He had always been the observant one, green eyes in the dark, weighing life and death, when to fight and when to run. I'm not sure I'd ever seen him run, despite the dangers all around. I took back the glasses, his fingers brushing mine, and the way it jolted me, I was certain he must have some non-human talents of his own, something the glasses were blind to.

General Moore's soldiers, city watchmen, and EEPs set about rounding everyone up. They went for known troublemakers first (thus Duane had a lot of his people in my circle as well as hiding in Ulric's temple). This included everyone they saw holding rifles and other Upside Down party weaponry or markings.

The Upside Down hideout outside town was not beyond the range of the Avian's power. I went in with the EEPs to search for Bell, Kali, or, unlikely, Gas. I found no one. They had cleared out long before the fighting started.

When they were done with the real threats, the EEPs took the opportunity to lock up everyone else they could fit in a cell. Hundreds were taken and tossed into prisons that soon overflowed. Part of me wondered if they had wanted an uprising like this, an excuse?

When I saw merchants dragged off, including Reginald, I went up to the highest ranking EEP in sight and flashed my Avian glass badge. She flinched, blue eyes squinting so tight I thought she expected me to jam the badge in her face. The Avians had just felled the entire city, so me wielding an Avian artifact obviously made my point.

"Let him go. He's a Citizen. I wouldn't go so far as to say 'good' but certainly not a criminal. Anymore. Lots of these people are just plain citizens and have done nothing wrong. Hear me?"

"They will be tried," she said, still shrinking away. "The order comes from Queen Hilja herself. We are to hold trials to sort the guilty from the innocent."

"Will they be trials by torture perhaps? Forced confessions?"

"I ... No. Our Queen only seeks an end to this fighting and true peace."

"Which you also get when everyone you dislike is dead. You can stop cowering. Let Reginald go, I vouch for him, and I'll take this up with Queen Hilja directly."

The EEP woman bowed then hurried off, probably seeking some more innocent Citizens to incarcerate— just out of my line of sight.

"I should go," Gypsum said when she found me.

"Yes, get out of town while you can."

"No. I'm going back to Northcliff prison."

"Really?"

Gypsum had done terrible things, deserved punishment, but I never thought she'd admit that to herself. I knew I didn't.

"With everyone being arrested, I should stake my claim on that tower room while I still can, invoke royal privilege if necessary to keep my private accommodation."

"You sound like you're vying for the best hotel in town."

"It does have a good view, especially now we've opened the wall. I'm a werewolf. No one can stop me from being there if I want to be. No chains this time though."

I hugged her. "I'll visit whenever I can."

"Come by any time you want advice on court politics. I get the sense you'll need lots of it."

"No way." I was doing the ritual, finishing the deal with Hilja, then laying as low as possible. I would live the quiet life after all my wandering the world. That was the dream anyway. Gypsum just smiled, knowing full well my life tended to resemble nightmares more.

With 'peace' restored in Highcrowne, at least until everyone woke and started screaming to see their lawyers (there's a profession I should have learned), I took advantage of the quiet to finish preparing the ritual.

The moment of truth had come. Civil unrest, explosions, stolen eggs, plots, and investigations ... all of it had been distraction. The ritual to free us from the First Soul was the only thing that mattered. We were all doomed, not just Dawn and I, if this failed. The First Soul sowed chaos and destruction, and the Devourer would 'cleanse' whatever it had corrupted. We all needed it gone.

Ulric's temple to the Dead God was as useful to me as my uncle's power. The walls were seeped with belief. Worshippers filled the seats and stood in the rows between. They had heard of the miracle, and with the chaos all around—literally piles of rubble from the mountain that nearly smashed them—they had sought sanctuary here, which also protected them from the EEP round up. You can bet any Death worshippers would be on the 'to arrest' list.

Supplicants reached out to Dawn as we carried her past in a palanquin of dark polished oak like an enchanted princess. None dared touch, but like green growing things reaching for the sun, they sensed something in my child, a divine connection beyond the First Soul, that dark passenger she carried: She was Thane's child. The Dead God's.

That's why I knew this was the right place to be. The right place to save her.

Morgan and Duane set down the carrier, and I lifted her out, holding her in my arms as I had when she was an infant. Keeping her asleep was the only way to keep the First Soul from controlling her, from acting against us before we were ready. I could lie to it, hide my plans, but she would be its puppet. She was defenseless. I laid her on the altar beneath the winged and shrouded statue, and there were gasps when the statue brushed a lock of hair from her brow. It raised and readied its scythe before the darkened hollow that was its face gazed at me, questioning.

"Soon." I told Him.

The statue held its new, more dangerous pose.

I laid out the artifacts I'd gathered in Lyss. There was a nickel spearhead, perfectly sharp and preserved despite being eons old, which I placed on Dawn's right side. The electrum coin of palest gold bearing the face of an Avian I wrapped in her left hand, and at her feet I positioned a disc of stone so worn by ages the carvings in it were no longer identifiable. I'd only known it was the right piece due to some magical detective work. Lastly, I cut the heel of my palm, careful to avoid any tendons or causing permanent damage, and smeared my blood across her brow. I kept my hand against her, feeling the dark thread that was the First Soul stretching between us. Blood to blood. Soul to soul.

Calka had returned from the mountains, her egg safely hidden, and she stood next to Ulric at the foot of the altar. As she moved to take her place beside me, a swipe of her wing gently pushed back a line of worshippers who threatened to press too close. Most

Avian magic had come to rely on the Celon, the green goo, but what I needed from her was older, rawer, purer, and so she was naked of any magical artifacts. Instead, she concentrated, murmuring to herself, before pulling loose a black feather and laying it above Dawn's head, her hair the same dark shade.

Calka's feathers could hold tremendous power. She had given me Truthspeaker, which allowed me to reveal the true nature of any being and neutralize illusions. The Avian script writ in gold upon the haft of this feather translated to 'Deathblade.'

My chest felt tight, breath hard to find. It was almost time. Ulric stepped forward, but before he found his place, Duane held out a hand to stop him. "A moment, please."

Ulric looked quizzically at me, but I was just as confused. Then Duane turned so I saw his eyes, and I knew. The next words that came out of his mouth were spoken in Duane's voice—but they were Thane's.

"Eva." The way he said my name always sending shivers down my spine. "Once you are free, We must leave this place. And you can never call Us back. Not again."

"I didn't mean … this world needs the Dead God still."

"And it will have Us when We are done. Be patient. Know that I think of you and Dawn always." He pressed his lips to Dawn's cheek, but when He turned to me, I pulled back from His goodbye kiss. That face, those eyes. They were not Thane's.

"Why are you using Duane's body? Why not Ulric or one of these worshippers? I thought you needed someone who bore the Dead God's mark?" I knew Duane would never give away his freedom like that.

"He let me in just this once, lending me a face you will look kindly upon. To say goodbye."

Thane had always known my deepest soul, but his words in Duane's mouth felt wrong.

"Leave. Get out of him. Please."

"As you wish." Thane was gone.

"Wait." I should have said a proper goodbye. Should have....

I should not have lowered my guard so much, shown such weakness.

The First Soul fought.

It felt like a burning blade had impaled the hand I held to Dawn's forehead. I almost jerked back but stopped, forcing myself to endure the pain. The ritual had begun.

"Ulric," I gasped, urging him to take his position. He hurried forward and laid his hands upon the stone disc, pouring his power into it, awakening long dormant energy.

The disc had once held up the sky, as legend told it. It had the ability to wheel stars, bring an eclipse, or, for my purposes, close off this world to beings from beyond it. Ulric's power was activating it, creating a slowly tightening circle that would leave the First Soul nowhere to go but out.

Dawn spasmed and clutched the nickel spearpoint. Eyes closed, she slashed blindly at me with it, but Calka whispered something soothing, and her murderous swings lost their frantic energy. I disarmed her. The electrum coin in her other hand forced her down like a weight, its density spreading, so she was soon pinned and unable to move any part of her body.

Frustrated, the First Soul readied itself to speak. Would it be sweet temptation or threatening rage?

Its voice burned in my brain, no longer a whisper but a gale, now that we had begun to drag it from hiding: "If I leave you," it said, "you will be powerless to protect her, Eva. What if Ilsa comes back? Or any Unmentionable? Who can protect you? The Avians have abandoned you. When I am gone, the Dead God goes too. His power. My power. You will be nothing. Have nothing."

It had chosen temptation. Little did it understand.

"My mother was willing to sacrifice me for power," I told it. "I am willing to sacrifice power for my daughter. Anything for Dawn. Now!"

I cut with the spearpoint, just as the Dead God's scythe swung, and Calka's feather rose into the air and slashed in the opposite direction. Together, we sliced through the cords tying the First Soul to Dawn and to me. The black cloud, the miasma that was the First

Soul, reached out to fight but it could not stop all three of us, and in one swift strike it was done.

The pain in my chest was terrible, like an organ had been removed. Ulric pushed more power into the disc, tightening the noose. The First Soul was compressed into a thread of darkness, shrinking, sucked through a crack between universes. The worshippers around us fainted as Ulric drained them, adding their power to his as he worked to seal the crack and seal out the First Soul from this world forever.

The Dead God followed it into the Void. I felt Him slip away.

"Eva," Thane whispered, His voice so quiet I barely heard it. "I want you to live."

Then He was gone. The door was shut.

I crumpled, tears pouring out of my eyes in a most un-Solhan-like fashion as I held my daughter.

"Dawn," I said, kissing her. "Wake. Please."

She opened her eyes. Cornflower blue. "Mama?"

I held her so long and so tight that everyone wandered away and left us to our reunion. It felt like this was the first time I had truly met her. The first time both of us were finally free of the darkness. Disentangled.

When I finally let her go, she stood atop the altar on tiptoes. She reached up to touch the now immobile statue of winged Death and said, "Goodbye, Papa."

I was heartbroken again. I had lost Thane before like this. Felt him slip away from me. The ache inside choked me, had never stopped choking me for six long years. The loss had been never ending.

Only now... the ache faded. The tears receded. I was free.

The hollow the First Soul had dug into me was yet to be filled in, and I wasn't sure with what. But something terrible had been taken away, a wound cleaned, left raw, able to heal.

Something else was missing too. With my tether to the First Soul severed, the Dead God was no longer being drawn back to me. He was fleeing as far as He could, and the further away He got the more the power He had given me diminished. I tried to summon green fire, and there was nothing.

I reached deep for rage, remorse, anything to fuel necromancy, but I couldn't find it. I exhaled. I didn't really want to find it. Not yet. One day again I could be more powerful than Ulric, but today I wanted nothing but to be happy, if only for a short while.

"Morgan," I said, bringing Dawn up to him. "This is my daughter. And Dawn, this is the only father I've ever known."

"Grandpa?" Dawn said, and the stoic Morgan turned into a pile of mush as he hugged her.

Ulric was watching, bent over some of his fallen parishioners and checking they were alright. He didn't argue, for he knew he had given up any right to be my adopted father long ago. We were alike in many ways, but I hoped utterly different in all the ways that truly mattered.

I'd refused the godlike power the First Soul offered, lost my connection to the Dead God's soul sight, so that left only me. Eva. I was ordinary. Or maybe extraordinary in the way Duane was?

I left Dawn to be doted on by Morgan, who was already finding sweets and other things to spoil her with, and went looking for Duane. I found him outside on the stoop, like an unbeliever.

His green eyes met mine, and that jolt of electricity, that lightning in the storm was right on top of me. I sat down beside him, keeping quiet until the storm clouds in my mind parted, thinned, and vanished. Nothing but blue skies of possibility.

"We lived again," I finally said.

"Living always makes for a good day. I don't think I was in the same danger you were in, though."

"I don't know. You almost baked in that submersible."

"Sauna time? That was a holiday from my every day."

"So, your dramas are so much more dangerous than mine?"

"To me they are. You should try a week in my shoes."

"No thanks, Shadow King. I presume you're going to join in with the EEPs knocking heads and rounding up Enemies of the State to question?"

"I already know who the bad guys are and most got away. I am going to hunt Aguragas down ... and find Calka and the others and ask them to come home. She left without saying goodbye."

I looked around, realizing he was right. The Avian Queen was gone without fanfare or time for tears.

"We always forget to say goodbye too," I noted. It had been six years, and although I had tended him as he recovered from his wounds in the war, I'd fled as soon as he opened his eyes. No goodbyes.

"And hello." He reached out his hand. I took it. It could have been a handshake between business partners ... except we both relaxed our grips and turned so that our palms met and fingers interlaced. His thumb brushed against mine, and I shivered.

"Hello, Duane."

"And it's never goodbye, Eva. Never."

20 EPILOGUE

It was weeks before the destruction was cleared, even using the combined magic of elves and human warlocks, along with goblin ingenuity and brute dwarven muscle. That's what happens when a mountain falls on you.

I'd done my part and was finally clean after weeks of wielding runes and other magical paraphernalia I'd collected to melt piles of rubble and move dirt aside. Sometimes, it came down to digging with my hands when I found someone. Dwarves especially were hardy and used to cave-ins, while elves sustained themselves on conjured honeydew and frilly things like that as they endured the tedium of being buried. It was the humans I didn't always find alive.

I really hoped Duane caught Aguragas soon. I was itching to go after him myself, but there was something that needed my attention more.

Today was the city's first day of 'returning to normal', and so I thought I'd try the idea out, not entirely sure what was involved. I sat at a miniature table with Dawn and her stuffed animals—not the taxidermy kind Ilsa played with in her youth, but the toys humans were fond of—while Nanny served us tea in tiny cups on saucers.

"There's some for you Gray Owl," Nanny said, filling the cup set before a blob of fabric with feathers embroidered on it. Its huge black eyes were made from glass and seemed to say 'thank you' in return.

"She's not Gray Owl," Dawn corrected. "That's the newborn Avian Queen, or so Uncle Duane tells me."

The owl toy shifted, looking more Avian for a moment as Dawn cast a glamour over it. The illusion faded quickly, she was unpracticed, but there was potential. What would her magic turn out to be in future? She was part elf and part Thorne, a new and strange mixture.

There was a knock downstairs. While I'd freed Nanny to come and go as she pleased, I still had protections in place against everyone else, so I said, "I'll see who it is."

I opened the door to find a real queen on my doorstep.

"Hilja."

"Eva." She moved to come in but seemed startled when she couldn't.

I noticed there were no EEPs with her, just the Elf Butler, Mister Gardens. The two of them wore nondescript cloaks, apparently trying to blend in with the little people.

"What do you want? Finally bringing the second half of the payment you owe me for completing the job?" I folded my arms.

"Excuse me? You did not find the people trying to kill me."

"I found Marshall Uanal, full confession."

"An underling."

"You didn't hire me to take out a rival house in Faellion. I was to find and stop whoever was trying to kill you. Did that. Aguragas was behind it all through Faellion underlings." I didn't mention Ilsa. She was my problem.

"Aguragas is still free."

"Not for long. Besides, there's no reason for him to kill you anymore. He only wanted to destabilize Highcrowne before he attacked, and in the end, he skipped that step and went right for the explosives."

"Was that your doing?"

I feared it was, and so I didn't say anything. My silence was duly noted.

"Well, I'm certainly not here to pay you, or take back what's already given."

I had the first bit of treasure hidden well, so she would not be getting that back anyway.

"Then let's finish our bargain," I said. What I really wanted more than gold was for Hilja and her EEPs to stay away from Dawn. I hadn't forgotten Gypsum's advice, though.

"I'm not going to discuss this out here on the street," Hilja insisted.

"Come in," I said. "Both of you."

Mister Gardens and I shared assessing looks as I took his cloak and hung it beside Hilja's. I directed them to the parlor and shut the door.

"I'm afraid there's no tea. Nanny is serving more important guests upstairs."

Hilja was never one for niceties, anyway, not when you were alone with the real her. Her public persona was very gracious and entertaining, and too sickly sweet, which made me glad we weren't in public. Instead, she went right for the jugular.

"Dawn will be my heir and you will continue to work for me against more threats like Aguragas. If you intend to dwell here in Highcrowne, then you will obey your Queen."

"Nope."

"So, you're leaving?"

"Just so your EEPs can harass us everywhere we go, and so my daughter never gets a chance to be a child? Nope to that also."

"You cannot win here, Eva."

"I can. Because, yes, Dawn will be your heir, and I will work for you—on a generous retainer—to protect you from those who want you both dead."

"How is that different from what I said?"

"I will not obey you without question, Hilja. I'm not a monarchist, and you may see me at a democracy rally now and then."

She gritted her teeth. "Lovely. And hypocritical. I thought you wanted Dawn to be a Crown?"

"I didn't say that. I said I'd let her be your heir—and that means teaching her to survive court politics. She needs skills I can't give her." I still hoped there was a way of extracting Dawn from all politics and whatever future others wanted for her, but until I found it, I needed to train her, protect her, in every way imaginable.

"Then, she will live with me?"

"No. A secret heir. Safer that way. I'll bring her along to the palace whenever I'm working with you, give her lots of opportunity to observe and learn."

"Not good enough. Mister Gardens here will stay with you. I'm making him her butler. He can teach Dawn night and day, and she will need a bodyguard despite whatever spells you have placed on your home. She will need to go out, and he will be there, watching over her."

I already had lots of people watching over Dawn, like all of Duane's networks and my own informants, not to mention Morgan.

"No, thank you. Besides, Nanny rules here, and he wouldn't survive the day. No offense, Mister Gardens, but you are no match for a Solhan necromancer like her."

"You might be surprised."

"Eva, darling," Hilja said, bending forward and taking my hands. She'd turned on the sweet. Good sign I was making progress. "We both want Dawn to be safe. Why refuse?"

She was right. I was just being stubborn. "Fine. He stays. Now, you go."

"I want to meet her first."

I brought two extra cushions from the couch with me and set them at the table as I told Dawn, "We have more guests for tea."

Mister Gardens stayed standing in the doorway looking butlery, and Nanny narrowed her eyes at him, while Hilja breezed in all smiles and taffeta and sat down on her knees next to Dawn.

"It is so good to finally meet you. You are so beautiful."

Dawn was too clever, even at six, for flattery and frowned. "Who are you?"

Hilja and she looked each other in the eyes for a long moment, assessing. Some understanding passed between them, and they both relaxed. Hilja's smile became genuine. "I'm your sister. I've always wanted a sister."

"Me too."

Dawn poured her a cup of tea and one for Mister Gardens. "Sit down," she ordered, and he obeyed. Only when everyone had taken a sip, pinkies out, did she smile a satisfied smile.

That one was going to be trouble. More trouble than me, I suspected.

Until Next Time...

Did you enjoy this book? Please take a moment to leave a review. What you say will determine whether someone else takes the plunge into Eva's world, so please ask them to dive headfirst. Thank you!

Join our mailing list at lorelclayton.com to get a free Eva Thorne novella, short stories, and other book deals.

ABOUT THE AUTHORS

Lorel and Clayton were teen sweethearts, brought together by a fierce love of books (and hormones). Despite being married for 35 years, they are still madly in love and still writing. As writing partners, they meld logic, creativity, and genres. Fantasy, science-fiction, mystery, horror, steampunk, thrillers, the classics ...

they read them all, and if they can mix them, they will!

Still reading? Want to know more?

Lorel has a PhD in molecular biology and Once Upon a Time did cancer research before turning to the dark side (aka marketing), but she uses her powers for good, helping to raise funds for charity. She loves books, movies and animals, and would gladly spend all day with a cat on her lap and the wind in her hair (Conan reference there), while tapping out a story on her keyboard. Or maybe a movie script. With coffee of course. And lots of chocolate!

Clayton is a classically trained artist who learned digital painting, mostly because there's a hyperactive thirteen-year-old boy running around the house (their gorgeous son, in case you were wondering if that's normal). Clayton is severely dyslexic but loves books and storytelling. He adds vast imagination and a discerning ear for effective prose to their creative collaboration, not to mention the book cover art.

Born and raised in the western United States, they traveled to Sydney, Australia in 1997 and never left, finding the sunshine and beaches of "Oz" too irresistible. Look them up if ever you're Down Under.

Connect with Lorel Clayton

Website: www.lorelclayton.com
BookBub: bookbub.com/authors/lorel-clayton
Instagram: www.instagram.com/lorelclayton
Facebook: www.facebook.com/AuthorLorelClayton
Goodreads: www.goodreads.com/lorel_clayton